"There's no reason to assume that this is a murder," Jed insisted, trying to salvage their vacation.

"There is every reason to assume it's a murder," she argued, stealing herself for a second look at the body and the area. "Jed, don't move!"

"What?" He looked around anxiously.

"Look, we've been making tracks in the snow. We've probably destroyed valuable evidence." She looked at the crisscrossing lines from multiple ski tracks.

"I think it's a little late to worry about that. And we have to keep the animals away."

Susan sighed. He had a point. The ravens were flying around, and every once in a while a coyote peeked out of the forest. "It erupts every hour, so there's probably another coming sometime soon. Let's just hope that help arrives before then."

AN OLD FAITHFUL MURDER

VALERIE WOLZIEN

FAWCETT GOLD MEDAL • NEW YORK

A Fawcett Gold Medal Book
Published by Ballantine Books
Copyright © 1992 by Valerie Wolzien

Library of Congress Catalog Card Number: 91-93157

ISBN 0-449-14744-4

Manufactured in the United States of America

First Edition: May 1992

For Pat and Eldred

Yellowstone National Park was established by an act of Congress on March 1, 1872. It is the largest geyser area in the world, studied by scientists, protected by park rangers. Here trumpeter swans still fly across pristine lakes and rivers. Here deer and antelope still play, and buffalo roam right down the middle of paved highways.

Over two million tourists visit the area each year. The boardwalks, built through geyser basins and hot springs, are surrounded by high rails to keep the tourists away from boiling water and dangerous steam. Bulletins are published and signs are posted warning of bear attacks and the dangers of seemingly harmless bison and elk. And, in the winter, ski trails are patrolled and fires are kept burning in a system of warming huts so that hikers and skiers don't succumb to the below-zero temperatures that last for weeks on end. But even the most well-prepared ranger can't be blamed for not anticipating murder. . . .

ONE

" 'MANY EXPERIENCED SKIERS TALK LOUDLY, SING songs, or shake tin cans filled with rocks.' "

"We won't have to worry about surprising bears with Chad along." This announcement was made by the older sister of the boy who had been reading from the park bulletin. "He has a perpetual-motion mouth. He never shuts up."

Her fourteen-year-old brother scowled at her. He was sitting at her side in a vehicle carrying ten tourists and their driver the fifty miles from the south entrance of Yellowstone National Park to their hotel. Snow Lodge, a group of dormitories and cabins surrounding a main lodge, was located near Old Faithful Geyser, and they traveled to it over a road carved from packed snow. Their elegantly named snowcoach rocked from side to side, bouncing passengers in their seats. Luggage and half a dozen pairs of skis were piled on the rear and top of the half-moon-shaped vehicle, and Chad, who had been quoting from the official park brochure, looked up at the ceiling as a particularly sharp turn caused some shifting. But his sister was still (he would have said always) talking.

"No one told me there were bears around here." She frowned at the sheet of paper she had taken from her brother.

A very pretty girl sitting directly across from the feuding siblings spoke up. "Me either. Besides, I thought bears hibernated in the winter. If I had known there was danger of bear attack, I'd never have agreed to come on this trip. I'm too old for family vacations anyway," she announced, flipping her long ponytail over one shoulder.

1

"It says here—" Chad grabbed the paper back from his sister and shook the half dozen sheets of newsprint "—that bears can be dangerous in the winter—that they come out of their caves to search for food. This is printed by Yellowstone National Park. I didn't make all this up, you know."

The driver of their vehicle glanced back at his feuding passengers and decided to interrupt. "You people probably won't have to worry about bear this time of year. It's been real cold since December, and most of 'em are still tucked away in their dens. But there are other dangers for you—if you're all skiers—mainly hypothermia. The weather here in Yellowstone will kill you faster than any bear."

"Then why did the National Park Service include bear warnings in the information they handed out?" Chad asked.

"They keep expenses down by publishing only one brochure for the entire winter season. And the grizzlies do start leaving their dens in a few weeks —at the end of February. Come back then and you'll have to worry about bears—real hungry bears." He took off his hat and scratched his straight, sandy hair as he spoke. "I guess it's time to introduce myself. My name is Dillon Jones, and I've been living and working in the park for four and a half years. I'm a fishing guide in the summer, and I've been driving these things in the winter for the last two years—"

"These 'things,' as you call them . . . Do they ever slide off the road?" Chrissy, Chad's sister, interrupted to ask.

"Nope. There hasn't been an accident in a snowcoach that I know about. They were designed and built to transport schoolchildren in northern Canada—they may look silly with those skis on the front, the tracks over the rear wheels, and their coat of bright yellow paint, but they're safe, I can tell you that. Now, these snowmobiles that you see all over the roads are a different story." He waved out the window as a trio of those vehicles skidded by. "Course, down in Jackson, they'll rent a snowmobile to any idiot who wants one— and most idiots do."

Eight people in his audience either chuckled or smiled appreciatively. The remaining two passengers, an attractive young couple in their mid-twenties, didn't look up from their Penguin paperbacks: *A Tale of Two Cities* for him and *The Bostonians* for her.

"We'll be stopping in a few minutes for a short lookout, so maybe it's time we all introduced ourselves. I told you that my name is Dillon. And you're . . . ?" he prompted the woman sitting next to him.

"Joyce Ericksen. And my husband, Carlton, is sitting behind me—"

"And I'm Heather and this is my brother, C.J.," the teenage girl who had worried about bears spoke up before her mother could introduce the whole family.

The back of the snowcoach contained seats in a horseshoe-shaped arch around an open aisle, and the two readers were next in line. The young man looked up first.

"I'm Jon," he said seriously.

"And I'm Beth." She pushed her glasses farther up on her nose and smiled at the group before returning to her book.

The Henshaws, Chad and Chrissy's parents, were seated along the wall of the coach directly behind the driver. The mother, a brunette in her mid-forties with the tired smile of someone who had spent four days getting ready for the family vacation, spoke up. "I'm Susan, and this is my husband, Jed. And the kids can introduce themselves."

"I'm Chrissy," said the girl, "and I guess everyone's already heard from Chad." She grinned at him. He didn't return her smile.

"The place where we're stopping has a nice trail down to a real pretty waterfall." Dillon forestalled any more squabbling by explaining his plans to the group. "The water is still running, but ice has been piling up at the bottom of the falls since November. It's really something to see."

"Is that the only stop we'll be making?" Joyce Ericksen asked, looking at her children's feet. They were both wearing running shoes. "I didn't know we were going to be sightseeing on the way to the lodge."

"Actually, this is the shortest stop we're going to make," Dillon answered. "We'll be at West Thumb for quite some time. Time enough, in fact, for everyone to walk down to the geysers that line Yellowstone Lake there. If we're lucky, you might get a chance to see your first buffalo—they hang around the hot springs to take advantage of the warmth,'' he added, pulling hard on the steering wheel and guiding the cumbersome vehicle over to the side of the road. He opened the front door for his passengers to exit, and they all filed out into four feet of snow.

Susan Henshaw, tugging her knit hat over her brown curls, was one of the last to exit, stepping directly from the snow-coach into a snowbank.

"We could use some skis right now," Jon commented. "Are you all right?"

"Fine, thanks," Susan lied, feeling the snow in her hiking boots melting against her already cold ankles.

· Beth smiled again and followed Jon down a path through the drifts, anoraks billowing out behind them, nylon gaiters protecting their legs and feet from the high snow.

Susan turned to her husband. "They look like they were born on skis. Are we going to be the only beginners up here?"

"When I called, they told me that there are two beginning ski classes each day, so I doubt it," he reassured her before following their children down the trail.

"Don't worry. Neither of my kids have skied before, and my husband and I have only gone cross-country once or twice."

Susan turned and found Joyce Ericksen by her side. The two women leaned back against the snowcoach and squinted into the bright sunlight. "That's good to hear. This will be the first time for everyone in my family."

"Your kids will pick it up easily," Dillon said, joining the women. "Don't worry. Yellowstone in the winter is fabulous. Everyone has a good time here," he promised, and hurried off to follow his group.

"What he didn't say is that old folks like us won't learn quite as easily as our children do," Susan said.

"And that we're going to be miserable each night . . ." Joyce picked up the theme.

"And stiff every morning," Susan chimed in. They smiled at each other.

"Is this your first time here?" Susan asked, now that they felt more comfortable with each other.

"In the winter. We camped one summer when the kids were little. But we've been living out of the country until recently. We just moved to Los Angeles a few months ago. What about you?"

"We've never seen this in the winter either. We did come here twice in the summer—although Chad was just three years old the first time and doesn't remember it."

"I'm getting chilly," Susan added. "Do you think anyone would mind if we waited inside?"

"I can't imagine why," Joyce said, opening the door and climbing on board.

Susan followed quickly. "Oh, look," she said, moving aside the Henry James novel so her coat wouldn't douse it in snow. "They left their books. I'm surprised they didn't take them along to read at the overlook."

"Silly, aren't they? It's an affectation. Jon is completing his doctorate in geology, and he's got this idea of being a Renaissance man, so he's taken to doing serious reading in public places."

"I . . ." Susan didn't know how to begin, she was so embarrassed.

"He's quite a good cross-country skier, though. And so is Beth, I understand."

"I . . . You know them," Susan said, finally able to collect her thoughts. "I didn't mean to—"

"I didn't meet Beth until today, but Jon is my brother-in-law. My husband's brother. And don't be embarrassed. After all, he's doing all this for attention. I suppose we should have explained that we are all related. Except, of course, Beth—unless Jon marries her. In fact, we're on our way to a family reunion. My husband's father arranged it as an anniversary present for his wife. They have five kids, although none of them is exactly a child anymore, and we're all going to spend the week at Snow Lodge." Joyce pulled her hand-knit ski cap off, revealing a long ponytail that was only different from her daughter's in that it was streaked with gray. She used the hat to scrub off the frost that had formed on the windows.

"Wait till you see the whole group of us. We probably appear pretty eccentric to outsiders. Especially since everyone is expected to bring his or her significant other."

"How many . . . ?"

"I'm not sure exactly," Joyce admitted. "In my experience, significant others tend to come and go—becoming more or less significant, I suppose. My husband is the oldest child and the only one who got married, so Heather and C.J. are the only grandchildren in the family. This will probably be an interesting vacation."

Susan got the impression that Joyce wasn't looking forward to this particular family event. She explained her family's plans. "We're meeting friends—a couple we've known for years and their new baby—but they've skied before. All except the baby; he's only three months old," Susan added to explain this deficiency.

"How old are your kids?" Joyce asked.

"Chad is fourteen, and Chrissy is almost seventeen," Susan answered, looking curiously at the other woman, admiring her Nordic good looks and the confidence with which she carried off the straight ponytail, freshly scrubbed face, and hand-knit clothing. It was not, she thought, a style that many carried successfully into middle age. Joyce Ericksen had done so beautifully.

"Here come the kids," Joyce announced, peering through the cleared spot on the window. "It looks like they've paired off. The boys are together, and the girls, too. How lucky they're the same ages. I do hope C.J. has found a friend. He is apt to pester Heather to death when they're the only kids around."

"I know what you mean." Susan leaned forward to look out the window. "Chrissy and Chad are the same way. Oh, look. I hadn't noticed that the girls are wearing identical parkas in different color combinations.''

"Different, but equally bright," Joyce answered, getting up to open the door for their children.

"Mom, Chrissy and Heather are wearing the same parkas—and they bought them on opposite coasts," Chad announced, following C.J. into the vehicle and sitting down next to him.

"Just goes to show . . ." C.J. began.

". . . that bad taste is a national problem," Chad finished for him. Both boys were apparently thrown against the backs of their seats by the force of their laughter.

"Ignore them," Chrissy ordered Heather, appearing in the doorway.

"*Naturellement.* What other way is there to deal with *mes enfants*?"

"You speak French," Chrissy said, awed.

"My family has been living in Paris for the past ten years, so my French is pretty good," Heather agreed modestly.

"Yeah, she can be stupid in two languages instead of just one," C.J. crowed.

"Paris!" Chrissy breathed a lot of envy into the one word.

"But I've only spent one single day in New York City in my whole life. You shop at Bloomingdale's!" Heather reassured Chrissy of her own worth.

"And that certainly stands up well against the Louvre and the Eiffel Tower," Jed Henshaw laughed, climbing into the snowcoach and sitting down between his wife and Jon Ericksen.

"Next stop: West Thumb and our first look at a geyser basin." Dillon put the snowcoach in gear and pulled it back on the road.

"And maybe a vicious buffalo or two." C.J. leered at his sister.

"And everyone knows that buffalo hate neon ski parkas," Chad added.

"Especially ones that are pink and purple," C.J. said.

"Or orange and green," Chad added.

The adults just looked at each other and sighed. Susan wondered if anyone had ever done a study on the ecological impact of dropping a teenager or two into a geyser.

TWO

"DO YOU FEEL COMFORTABLE WITH ALL THIS ROOM switching?" Susan asked her husband as she crammed three pairs of long underwear into one small dresser drawer. "I mean, I don't worry about Chrissy and Heather sharing, but Chad is still young, and we really don't know the Ericksens all that well. . . ."

"What can happen? We'll be right next door. The boys will probably keep us awake all night talking and joking around." Jed pulled a pair of L.L. Bean boots from a duffel bag and looked inside them. "Are these Chad's or mine?"

"Yours. Chad ripped the top binding from one of his," Susan answered, stopping in the middle of folding a sweater to look out the window.

"Is there a moose out there? Or maybe a sexy ski instructor?" Jed joked, joining her.

"It's just so quiet and beautiful. . . . Oh, look, there are skiers—all in a line. They're moving so smoothly. Do you think we'll ever look like that, Jed? When can we take a lesson? What did they tell you at that place?"

" 'That place' is called the ski shack—it's that quaint Nordic building next to the main lodge. Actually, it's a rustic log cabin stuffed to its hand-hewn rafters with technologically designed skis, gear, and clothing made almost entirely from petrochemicals. There's also a supply of herbs, raisins, and whole grains sorted into plastic bags—for eating on the trail, I suppose. Anyway, Carlton Ericksen was there, and he had just signed his family up for the beginners' lesson tomorrow at nine. They added our names to the list. So we should be out nice and early.''

"I wonder if it is just the four of them or if other family members are going to take a lesson, too," Susan mused, carefully folding pearly pink silk glove liners and explaining about the anniversary reunion to Jed.

"I'm glad to hear that." He dumped half a dozen rolls of wool socks on the bed and flipped the now empty duffel bag into the wardrobe.

"Jed, that's messy," Susan protested, removing it and starting to roll it into a ball. "Why are you glad about the reunion?" she asked when she had neatly replaced the duffel.

"If they're with a large group, we won't be together all the time. I was beginning to worry that we might become irrevocably tied to Joyce and Carlton.''

"Don't you like them?''

"Joyce seems all right, but Carlton is rather dull, to be honest.''

"Dull? But you and he walked so slowly around the geysers that the snowcoach had to wait for you!''

"*He* walked slowly—as he told me all about the scientific research that he was doing in Paris.''

"How inter—''

"Don't say it. He's a biologist of some sort. He studies genetic traits in fruit flies—French fruit flies.''

"Flench fluit . . .'' Susan began to giggle and fell onto the bed. Jed joined her, and they spent a few moments together before Susan returned to the matter at hand.

"I think we were lucky to run into them," she insisted. "We'll have more fun if the kids have friends of their own. Besides, we'll be spending a lot of time with Kathleen and Jerry—as soon as we learn to ski and can keep up with them.''

"I hope their new au pair is working out. They won't have much fun on a ski trip if they have to drag the baby along," Jed said.

"It's too cold outside for Bananas," Susan answered, referring to Alexander Brandon Colin Gordon by the only name anyone used when speaking to, or about, the three-month-old. "And Kathleen said this girl came highly recommended by the family she worked for previously." She got up and looked out the window. "Heavens, there's Jon and . . . and I don't remember the name of his girlfriend. They're skiing already. I—"

She was interrupted by loud banging on the door of their room. Jed opened it, and Chad and C.J. stood before him.

"We're going to the ski shack. We'll meet you at dinner. Jon—he's C.J.'s uncle—"

"My uncle," C.J. confirmed.

". . . he said he would give us ski lessons—"

"You don't have—" Jed began.

"He said we could rent the skis and charge them to your room." Chad answered the question he wouldn't allow his father to ask.

"All they need is your room number," C.J. confirmed.

"There's more than an hour of daylight left, and you said we weren't going to eat dinner until six, and I can meet you at the restaurant then—"

"My father said yes." C.J. added the finishing touch to their argument.

"Okay, okay," Jed said, laughing. "But be at the dining room at six P.M. exactly."

"With your hands and face washed," Susan called out.

"Okay. Don't worry." The boys turned and ran down the hall.

"I wonder if he unpacked anything at all."

"You can check on that at dinner," Jed assured her.

"Well, at least I'm done," she said, throwing a long cashmere scarf into a drawer and shoving it shut. "Whew. This clothing is sure bulky." She turned to her husband. "How about a quick walk around the place?"

"You really want to get back into heavy clothing?"

"Why not? We have to go over to the main lodge for

dinner, don't we? And I'd like to see the Visitor's Center—if it's open.''

Jed was already struggling into insulated hiking boots. ''Do you have any idea exactly where the Visitor's Center is?''

''In front of Old Faithful,'' she replied promptly. ''I asked the ranger in the lobby when you were checking in.''

''Ranger? You mean that pretty redhead you were talking with is a park ranger?'' He pulled the laces tight.

''Her name is Marnie Mackay. She did her undergraduate work at Cornell. She has a master's in biology from UCLA, and she completed the program at the police academy in California before joining the Park Service. She was stationed in the Everglades for three years and came to Yellowstone two years ago. And yes, she is a ranger. She can be pretty and a ranger, you know.'' Susan frowned at her husband. ''Aren't you ready yet?''

''How do you get all your stuff on so quickly?'' Susan was wearing dark green ski pants, a black parka, a green and white hat, and white ski gloves. Her scarf was red wool, and her hiking boots had green and red laces. ''And how many stores did you have to visit to assemble that particular outfit?''

She shrugged and opened the door. ''Do you want me to wait for you?''

''I'm ready, I'm ready!''

''It really is beautiful, isn't it?'' Susan asked as the door to their building closed behind them. ''Look how there are ski trails leading all directions.''

''And look who's coming.'' Jed pointed to their daughter, who was walking toward them, Heather by her side.

''You missed it!'' Chrissy called out. ''It was fantastic! All this steam and then ice crystals that made the most incredible noise as they hit the ground—like tiny pieces of shattered glass! It was fantastic! We couldn't believe it, could we, Heather?''

''Fantastic,'' she agreed.

''Missed what?'' Jed asked.

"Oh no," Susan cried, catching on. "Old Faithful! We missed the eruption, didn't we? And it won't go off for another hour or so!"

"No, and it will be dark by then. You and Daddy will just have to wait until morning."

"Did either of you happen to notice the Visitor's Center over there?"

"You can't miss it, Daddy. It's right in front of the geyser. We'll meet you at the restaurant for dinner at six o'clock, okay?" Chrissy added, running off. "We ran into Chad, and he said that's what he and C.J. are going to do."

"Fine," Jed agreed, noticing that his left boot was untied and the lace was gathering a small snowball around it as he walked.

"But where is the geyser?" Susan cried out.

"Back there." Heather turned and pointed. "You can't miss it."

"You don't know my parents," Chrissy explained to her. "They can get lost anyplace. Once we were on the New York Thruway . . ."

But Jed and Susan quickly moved out of hearing range.

"Do you remember when our children thought we were perfect and hung on to every word we uttered?" he asked his wife.

"No. You must be talking about some other family. I think Chad's first words were 'No one else's parents make him do that,' and Chrissy isn't much better." She looked around. "So where is this geyser?"

"Right over there." The answer came from the ski trail behind them. "That is, if it's Old Faithful you're looking for. But I'm afraid you just missed the big show."

"Actually, it's the Visitor's Center that we're trying to find," Jed explained to the two young men, one of whom had answered his question.

"Keep going straight. You can't miss it." And they hurried off.

"What attractive young men. The blond one looked just

like a younger version of Jon. I wonder if he could be another Ericksen?''

''Just how big is this family?'' Jed asked. ''You said that Carlton is the only married son. . . .''

''Or daughter,'' Susan added. ''And I don't think either of those young men are interested in marriage. Not if that affectionate look they exchanged means anything.

''And have you noticed that they weren't on skis either? Almost everyone else is. Look.'' She pointed. ''Even Chad—'' She stopped as her son, picking up a ski pole to wave at them, fell over into a snowbank.

THREE

''HE ABSOLUTELY LOVES THE SNOW. HE GIGGLES AND PATS it, and tries to crawl out of the arms of whoever is holding him so he can get right down into it. And guess what? He's learned to take off his mittens!'' The proud mother stopped bragging long enough to put a piece of prime rib into her mouth.

''And how's your au pair working out?'' Susan asked. The Henshaws and the Gordons were eating dinner together. Susan's enjoyment of the meal was peppered by her amusement at Kathleen Gordon's enthusiasm over her new son. Susan and Kathleen had known each other for almost four years since Kathleen had left the police force and married a widower in Hancock, Connecticut, where they all lived. The two women had solved several murders together before Kathleen got pregnant and presented her husband with a new heir.

"She's wonderful. She loves little Bananas, and he's beginning to recognize her. Wait till you see him giggle. . . ."

"We saw him just last weekend," Jed reminded her.

"But he's changing so fast. You really won't believe him," Kathleen insisted. "You know, he's starting infant swim classes when we get back to Connecticut."

Susan remembered the Kathleen she met years ago, a beautiful woman scornful of suburban wives and their families. Still beautiful, Kathleen had learned that there were some good things to be found in the suburbs. "That will be interesting. . . ."

"Kath is disappointed that we can't get Bananas on skis for a few years," Jerry laughed, reaching across the table and patting his wife's hand. Balding and middle-aged, he was an unlikely man to be paired with this beautiful blonde, but Susan knew it to be a very happy marriage.

"You know, these days children are skiing as soon as they learn to walk. And Bananas is very advanced, so he might be skiing as early as next season," Kathleen answered. She looked around the table. "You're all laughing at me, aren't you?" she asked her grinning friends.

"We're all very happy for you," Susan answered. "And Bananas is lucky, too. Where is he, by the way? We looked around when we came in, but there was no sign of him or his keeper."

"Chloe has him up in her room. She convinced one of the waiters to bring her meals up there. That way she can keep Bananas happy while we eat, and eat dinner herself. I fed him right before we came down."

"You're staying here in the lodge?" Jed asked.

"Yes. We had rooms in the building you're in, but once we arrived, I could see that it was going to be difficult to live if we had to bundle up Bananas every time we went to dinner—we thought he would be with us then. But the people at the desk were very understanding and they moved us when the situation was explained to them."

"Everyone here seems very helpful," Jed agreed.

"And Chloe has a way of making everyone more helpful than they might ordinarily be," Jerry added.

"Did you get Chloe through one of those agencies that specializes in importing au pairs?" Susan asked Kathleen.

"Not exactly. The girl who was supposed to come to us was arranged by an agency in the city," she explained, "but she decided to get married at the last minute. The agency was looking for a replacement when we got a letter from Chloe. She is a cousin of the girl we were expecting, and she wrote offering to come in her place. She has a relative who works for the embassy in Washington, so the visas and everything went through quickly. By the time the agency had found us another girl, we were already expecting Chloe."

"You were lucky."

"We sure were. There's no way we could have taken a trip like this with a baby—unless one of us spent most of the time at the lodge while the other skied. And you know who that would be."

"You're still nursing?" Susan asked.

"Yes, although Bananas is very good about taking a bottle, so I get a break sometimes. But we can't go on any all-day ski trips, I'm afraid."

"I'm wondering if I'll even manage to stand up on skis," Susan said. She knew that Kathleen had been skiing since high school.

"You'll be fine. Cross-country isn't difficult. The scenery around here is fantastic. And it changes all the time. Every eruption of Old Faithful is different—and fascinating."

"I still haven't seen one," Susan admitted. "We're taking our first lesson tomorrow. I really don't know what to wear. Everyone seems to have those funny things around their ankles. I bought ski pants, but no one told me about them."

"They're gaiters, and they will rent them to you with your skis—or you can buy them. I stopped in the ski shack once or twice. Don't worry; they're very organized. No one is going to let you go out on the trails without everything you need.

"This is good, isn't it?" Kathleen added, looking down

at her almost empty plate. "The breakfasts here are wonderful. I've been consuming an awful lot of cholesterol, though. Granola tomorrow, I'm afraid . . . Look who's coming."

Susan turned and saw Bananas Gordon being carried on the hip of a young woman. She had long, crinkled red hair, which the baby was clasping in both hands and stuffing into his bud-shaped mouth. Both of his parents rose to greet him.

"Susan, this is Chloe," Kathleen began the introductions. "Chloe, this is Mrs. Henshaw and her husband. And you should meet Chad and Chrissy—I'm sure they're around somewhere. . . ."

"They're at a table in the back of the room. They are having dinner with some new friends," Jed explained. "You might be interested in meeting them, too—they've been living in your country for the last few years."

"That would be nice, but I can meet them later," Chloe suggested. "I just came down to see if you wanted me to give Bananas his bath now or whether I should wait a while," she explained to Kathleen after greeting everyone.

"Now is fine. Then I can come up and put him to bed in forty-five minutes or so."

"You'll miss the ranger talk," Jerry warned his wife.

"That's okay. I'm exhausted tonight. You can go without me."

"I'll take him back up then," the au pair said, removing the child from his mother's arms. "Don't rush. He's having a good time with his new stuffed moose. The horns are perfect for teething."

Jerry laughed. "They're called antlers. Kathleen wasn't happy buying out most of the toy stores in Connecticut, so now she's trying to collect everything the gift shop here offers for babies."

"Those stuffed animals are adorable," Susan said. "And unusual. I don't think you would have much luck finding a toy coyote on the East Coast."

"I think I'll order dessert," Kathleen said. "But no coffee. Bananas is a little off schedule from the flight out and the time change. He woke up at eleven-thirty last night—just as I was about to fall asleep.''

"It's not easy traveling with an infant," Susan consoled her friend. "But Chloe is a big help, isn't she?''

"Is she really?" Susan was surprised to hear Jerry mutter under his breath.

FOUR

JUST AS THERE'S ONLY ONE RESTAURANT AT SNOW LODGE, there's only one form of public entertainment in the evening. Without television, those who have finished their dinners, grown bored with their books, and aren't standing in the shower or lying on their beds trying to soothe aching muscles have no option but the nightly ranger talk.

Susan and Jed had hurried to the elegant modern auditorium behind the Visitor's Center immediately after their meal, having promised to save seats for their children. Jerry had decided to join his family and make it an early night. No one knew where Chloe had gone. In the partially filled room, conversation hummed around them. Susan was listening to one in particular.

"I suppose it's really necessary to be here? I'd much rather be sitting in front of the fire back at the lodge reading a book or having a brandy.''

"It's necessary. You don't think I'd be here if I had any choice, do you?''

"I don't know how I let Father talk me into this. . . .''

"You shouldn't be surprised, you always do. We both always do. I don't know if it's us or if it's Father. Now, let's just try not to be more miserable than absolutely necessary.

"What is tonight's topic, by the way?"

"Something like 'Predators: Friend or Foe?' "

"Well, that certainly sounds boring."

"This place isn't bad. At least the food is good."

"I can get great food at home. I only wanted to spend my winter vacation someplace where I could get a tan. Was that too much to ask?"

"Don't you think your eavesdropping is a little obvious?"

"Jed! Shhhh! They'll hear you!" Susan leaned down to tie her boot. The two women sitting in front of them had been fascinating her since she first noticed them during dinner over an hour ago. They would have attracted her attention in most places because they were, quite simply, two of the prettiest women she had ever seen. In fact, now that she thought of it, she realized that she didn't know many truly pretty adult women. She knew women who were attractive, unusual, chic, striking, and even a few who were beautiful, but the term *pretty* she would have reserved for children, girls in their teens, and the very few who carried that quality over into their early twenties. But these two sisters—for sisters they must be—were certainly at least thirty, and both maintained a golden blond prettiness unusual even in younger women.

The older of the two was the tallest, and wore her hair in a smooth chignon from which curly tendrils escaped down onto her collar. Her skin was creamy, her eyes blue; she reminded Susan of one of the famous portraits in shampoo ads of the early sixties. The younger had slightly more golden hair cut shoulder length and left to curl naturally; her cheeks were slightly less pink than her lips, and her eyes were the blue of the summer sky. Susan was too cynical to believe this could all be real.

They wore hiking boots. This appeared their only concession to the rigors of the environment. If the exquisitely tailored wool slacks or silk shirts of either hid long underwear, Susan would have been surprised. They both wore delicate gold jewelry, the older woman earrings, two necklaces, and the type of gold and diamond bracelet advertised as a tennis bracelet. The other sister wore diamond and pearl earrings, a headband fashioned from silk spun with gold threads, and a gold Rolex watch. In this group of people dressed for winter sports in jeans, turtlenecks, bulky wools, and an amazing assortment of brightly colored sportswear, they looked as if they had taken a turn at the corner of Park and Fifty-seventh and miraculously ended up in a geyser basin.

She had seen them in the lobby of the lodge as the Henshaws joined the Gordons for dinner, but wasn't sure where they had ended up until they sat down in front of Susan and Jed. Now . . .

"Aunt Charlotte! Aunt Jane! Do you know where my mother is? She said she would meet us here."

Susan heard the distinctive voice of C.J. and realized he was speaking to the women in front of her. More Ericksens! She glanced at Jed and realized he was grinning.

"We're surrounded," he whispered to her. "They're everywhere!"

"Jed!" she hissed back, elbowing his down-covered ribs.

"Here comes that cute redhead. Maybe she's an Ericksen too—she's just disguised as a park ranger."

"Her name is Marnie Mackay," Susan whispered back. "I told you."

"She just says her name is Marnie Mackay," Jed quipped.

"Good evening, folks, my name is Marnie Mackay. I'm a park ranger and I'm going to be giving the interpretive talk tonight. We'll be starting in about ten minutes. We'll just wait that long for the people who are outside right now watching Old Faithful do its thing."

"I'm missing it again," Susan wailed.

Jed patted her shoulder. "Don't worry. We're going to be here for a week. We'll see it more than once."

"Hi, Mom!" Her daughter dropped down in the auditorium seat next to her.

"Chrissy! Where's Chad?"

"Watching Old Faithful, where else? He said it's the third

time he's seen it. Have you seen him on skis? He's going to be sore tonight.''

"I don't seem to be seeing much of anything," Susan said.

"Have you seen Call Me Irv?"

"Who?"

"That's what we call him because that's what he says to everybody. His name is Irving Cockburn—Dr. Irving Cockburn. He's a psychiatrist. And he's short, dumpy, and bald, and he says to everyone, 'Call me Irv'—like it's a big deal that we call him something beside Dr. Cockburn. He was watching Old Faithful go off with Chad and C.J. and Heather and me, and he talked so much about himself that he almost blocked out the sound of the eruption—and that's some explosion to drown out! And he told us how he started his practice working with teenagers and they spent session after session deciding what to call him until they decided to—''

"Call him Irv," Susan finished for her.

"Yes. And C.J. and Chad kept asking why they called it 'practice,' and Call Me Irv didn't get it.''

Susan wondered just how rude her son had been.

"There he is now. That's Call Me Irv.''

Susan followed her gaze to the double doors at the front of the auditorium. Her daughter's description, if unkind, had been accurate: he was short and overweight. Irving Cockburn was a man around forty years old who had, apparently, never learned to dress to show off his good points. His too stiff jeans hung above expensive and, in this weather, slippery cowboy boots with too high heels. His bright parka hung open over an "I SKIED THE BIG ONE AT JACKSON HOLE" T-shirt. A cowboy hat with a feather band topped this attire; it also hid any lack of hair. He looked ridiculous.

"He's from Miami," Chrissy announced.

"I'm not surprised," Susan answered.

"I'm on time," he announced to the crowd at large before turning to Marnie. "I'm not late, right?"

"Watch how he's always trying to get all the attention," Chrissy said. "Heather thinks it's odd that he's a psychiatrist.

She says he's invented a new type of therapy; he talks, and the patient *listens*."

"I didn't mean to be late, but I just had to grab a few minutes and check on waxes at the ski shack—I want to get an early start tomorrow morning, you know. Say—" he leaned closer to Marnie Mackay, but didn't lower his voice "—do those guys at the ski shack really know what they're talking about?"

"Yes. Definitely." She shook her red curls for emphasis. "But sometimes they're great jokers, too." She turned slightly so she was speaking to the audience as well as to Irving Cockburn. "One of the things they like to do is take greenhorn rangers out on their first ski trip. We all learn to ski pretty quickly here in the winter—when there's over ten feet of snow on the ground, you don't have any choice.

"Well, my first ski trip, one of the guys who runs the shack took me up to Solitary Geyser and suggested I ski down. Now, that's something none of you folks should do. That trail is for snowshoes only—it's very steep. Well, of course, I fell immediately, and then I had to scoot down the rest of the way on my butt, pulling my brand-new skis and poles behind me."

Her audience chuckled. Dr. Cockburn blanched. "They suggested I take a trail . . . Let's see, I wrote it down and put it in one of these pockets. . . ." He started pulling handkerchiefs, sun block, and ski goggles from his parka. "You don't think—"

"I'm sure they only play those games on staff. Believe me, Yellowstone can be a dangerous place in the winter. We're all here to keep you safe—not to cause problems.

"Maybe we should start on our talk," she continued, moving to the front of the room. Dr. Cockburn, ignored, noisily sat himself down in the front row, distributing his belongings on both adjoining seats.

"Mother and Father are going to be late," the older sister, the one C.J. had called Aunt Jane, whispered to the other as the lights, responding to a button Marnie had pushed, began to dim.

"When did Father ever miss anything—" Charlotte began, when the rear doors of the auditorium opened to reveal a couple in their sixties. The man was tall, and both his clothing and his build implied that he hunted, fished, climbed, and split logs daily. He wore jeans held up by bright red suspenders over a wool plaid shirt, and heavy hiking boots on his feet. A wool watch cap covered longish gray hair that led to a full beard. His wife, whose dainty shape only accented his largeness, wore similar clothing, minus the suspenders. She, of course, didn't have a beard. She wore tiny gold glasses, and her gray hair was short and fluffy. Of course, she had two pretty adult daughters, Susan thought, she was still pretty herself.

"See, they made it. I told you Father never misses anything," Charlotte whispered to her sister, waving to get her parents' attention.

"Too bad. We'd all be happier if he did," was Jane's enigmatic reply.

FIVE

"I DON'T KNOW ABOUT YOU, BUT I'D LOVE A MUG OF HOT buttered rum before going back to the room."

"I told Chad to hurry, unpack, shower, and get into bed. We should all be up early—and I'm pretty tired tonight," Susan said, letting her husband lead her into the tiny rustic bar next to the dining room.

"It's vacation, hon. Don't worry. He's old enough to start taking care of himself. And you're tired because of the time change—it's almost midnight back home in Connecticut. Remember, we were in a taxi to Kennedy Airport at five-thirty this morning. . . . Two hot buttered rums,'' he said to the young waitress who immediately appeared at their table. She hurried off to get their order, and Jed leaned back in his chair and yawned. "That was an interesting talk. I didn't know how few wolves were left around here."

"Amazing, isn't it?" Susan muttered, not paying much attention, her eyes wandering around the dozen tiny tables and their occupants.

"Chad said that a coyote came up to him when he and C.J. were stopped to fix his ski binding. He said it looked just like a dog—until it opened its mouth. I think they were more than a little surprised to see the length of the fangs. . . ."

"Fangs!" Susan's attention could always be commanded if she thought one of her children was endangered. "Did it snap at him? Did you tell him not to get too close?"

"Evidently it didn't do anything," Jed assured her. "He said it just sat down a few yards away from them and yawned."

"Yawned?"

"Some of the coyotes around here have become beggars—like the bears used to be." The waitress had reappeared with their drinks and some information. "They're getting to be a problem. The naturalists don't like it because it alters the natural environment—coyotes are scavengers, not beggars—and, of course, it's always potentially dangerous when a wild animal gets too close to people. They're asking everyone to report beggars to the rangers."

"We'll have to tell the kids," Susan said, picking up the cinnamon stick protruding from the steaming white ceramic mug and licking it off.

"Anything else?" their waitress asked.

"Not right now, thanks."

"Done any skiing today?" she asked before trotting off to help another tourist.

"No. We just got here."

"Well, have a real nice visit."

"Everyone here is so friendly," Jed commented, sipping his drink and watching the charming girl hurry off.

"Do you think we should get hold of Chad right away?" Susan insisted.

"He's in his room listening to C.J.'s tape deck. No coyotes are going to attack him there, Sue."

"Well, okay." Susan took a sip of the warm liquid and tried to relax.

"What time do you think we should set the alarm for?" Jed asked, after a pause. "We should be at the ski shack at eight-thirty to get our skis. The lesson starts at nine. We'll all want to have a good breakfast first. And knowing our daughter, she'll want to wash and dry her hair. . . . Sue, are you listening to me?"

She wasn't. She was leaning back in the chair with her head resting on the partition that divided the bar from the rest of the room.

"Sue?" Jed realized what was going on. "Hear something interesting?" he asked.

"Shhhh!"

Jed gave up. He knew his wife well after nineteen years of marriage, and if she found something intriguing on the other side of the wall, she would listen to it. It wasn't that she was nosy in an ordinary sense; it was more that she found people fascinating. And since this fascination had helped more people than it hurt and had, in fact, helped one or two of their friends out of serious trouble, he certainly wasn't going to discourage her. He smiled and reached across the table for her hand.

Susan looked up and grinned. "It's the Ericksens again—I'm becoming obsessed with them."

"Which one this time?" he asked, pretty sure that they wouldn't be overheard in the low hum of the full room.

"Jon and Beth—although Beth isn't an Ericksen." She laughed at herself. "See, I even know all their names."

"They're some family."

"Interesting." She agreed with what he didn't say. "Don't

you think it's a little unusual that out of five grown-up children, only one is married?''

"Well, the youngest, the boy that was sitting at the end of table who was wandering around before dinner . . ."

"His name is Darcy—and he's gay. I know." She scraped the bottom of her empty mug with the cinnamon stick.

"How . . . ?"

"Just look at the way he and his friend—I haven't managed to catch his name yet—look at each other."

"His friend's name is Randy," Jed said. "I overheard Darcy talking to his parents. They didn't appeared to be thrilled—to say the least."

"Really!"

"In fact, Mr. Ericksen senior—"

"George," Susan prompted.

"Okay, George. Well, he looked a little like he was going to have a stroke—he turned red and purple, and clutched the glass he was holding so hard that I was surprised it didn't break."

"How did Phyllis take it?"

"Phyllis is the family matriarch, I presume?"

Susan nodded.

"She seemed to be more in control. She held out her hand to Randy with only a slight hesitation. And she smiled— possibly through gritted teeth. In truth, she seemed more interested in how her husband was taking the introduction than anything else."

"That's interesting. . . ." Susan looked off into the distance.

"It's always a little sad when adult children are so influenced by the opinions of their parents," Jed suggested, wondering about the future of his own family.

"True," Susan muttered. She moved closer to her husband. "Do you know what I was listening to when we first ordered? A conversation about whether to tell Dad. About what would happen if they told him—or what would happen if they didn't tell him and he found out."

"What?"

"What?" she repeated his question.

"When—or if—he found out what?" Jed explained patiently.

"Actually, I don't know." She drained her cup. "I missed that part."

"Maybe you should ask them to speak up next time." Jed laughed at the expression on his wife's face.

"I—" But Susan didn't have a chance to defend herself: embarrassingly enough, they were joined by one of the people they had been discussing.

"Mr. and Mrs. Henshaw! I wanted to introduce myself. I'm Phyllis Ericksen, and my daughter-in-law tells me that my grandchildren have become great friends with your children."

Susan and Jed exchanged looks: Had their conversation been overheard? They had the same thought, and both of them blushed. This habit was possibly one of the reasons they had been happily married for so long.

But Phyllis Ericksen gave no indication of having overheard. "May I sit down for a few minutes, or were you just leaving?" She appeared to detect some hesitation in their hospitality.

Jed set to work to make up for any lack on their part. "We were just going to order another hot buttered rum. Why don't you join us? Or—the waitress recommended the mulled wine. . . ."

"That sounds wonderful. If you're sure you were planning on staying."

"Definitely." Susan swallowed a yawn.

"Fabulous." Phyllis Ericksen pulled an empty chair up to the table and sat down. "You know, the change of altitude affects everyone differently. I know it makes some people sleepy, but I find it invigorating. I actually find I need less sleep at higher elevations."

"Do you ski?" Susan asked, as she had asked everyone since arriving in the park.

"Of course. We've been cross-country skiing for years. We used to downhill, too, but George—that's my husband—

took a bad spill about four years ago. The first thing he did after getting out of the hospital was sell all his downhill equipment. He had been complaining about the crowds on the slopes for years. Cross-country is much quieter, much less destructive to the environment, and more civilized."

"So you gave up downhill, too?" Susan asked.

"Of course. And the cross-country trails here are fabulous. We're lucky that the snow is perfect right now."

"You've been in the park for a while?" Jed asked.

"Three days. We did eleven miles yesterday."

"Joyce said that the family was here to celebrate your anniversary. Was it a surprise party?" Susan asked as Jed waved over their waitress and ordered their drinks. She wished she could suggest leaving the rum out of hers; she certainly wasn't finding the altitude invigorating. It was 1:00 A.M. at home; she had spent four and a half hours flying from New York to Wyoming, one hour on a bus, three and a half hours on the snowcoach. She was exhausted. But Phyllis (who asked to be called that: "We believe in informality in our family") was answering her question.

"No, it wasn't a surprise. In fact, I spent hours and hours phoning long distance trying to work out the arrangements. It isn't easy to gather twelve people from all over the country in one place at the same time, I can tell you."

"I'm sure it isn't," Jed agreed.

"Where do you live?" Susan asked politely.

"Just outside Chicago. Joyce and Carlton are living in Los Angeles. They probably told you about their recent move from Paris. They decided it was time to come home. Carlton got a wonderful job offer in California, and I know that they're hoping their children will go to American universities in a few years. My daughters, Jane and Charlotte, live on opposite sides of the continent. Charlotte lives in San Francisco. And it is almost impossible to get Jane to leave her condo in New York City. She has become a true New Yorker."

"And the rest of your family?"

"Jon is finishing up requirements for his doctorate in geology at the University of Colorado in Boulder—and he wants to stay somewhere in the West when he's done. It depends upon job availability, of course. And Darcy, my youngest, is in college in Boston. He's an artist," she added, displaying pride in her youngest's choice of vocation.

"Really! A painter?" Jed asked, distributing the drinks that their waitress had brought.

"Yes. Although he does some design work to pay the bills. He's a very talented silversmith. He started with precious metals as a freshman in high school. So he's had almost six years of experience. He's worked in various galleries in Provincetown—out on Cape Cod—for the last three years. He's saving his money. He hopes to study in Europe this summer."

"How interesting," Jed said as she stopped to drink.

Very, Susan agreed, but she didn't say anything. It wasn't difficult to see which one of her children Phyllis preferred. Darcy was certainly her delight, but had she detected a note of sadness when mentioning his approaching trip to Europe?

"This is excellent. I must tell George about it. He would love it." Phyllis sipped from her glass mug. The deep ruby liquid shimmered in the light of the candle on the table.

Susan felt a chill shimmy up her spine, and suddenly, incongruously, she remembered a feature in a magazine her children had loved in their preschool years.

Each month a full page had been devoted to a black-and-white sketch of a common scene: a classroom full of children, a family on a picnic, a baseball team competing on a summer day. Except that in the classroom, the writing on the blackboard would be upside down and one of the children barefoot, or the scene would show men in the moon staring down upon it instead of a bright sun, or the boy up at bat would be swinging at a cabbage instead of a ball. And the heading at the top of the page, in bold type, would ask a simple question: What's wrong with this picture?

She looked around the bar, its paneled walls, the people in outdoor clothing looking happy and relaxed, healthy people who braved the cold and skied or hiked to find their fun in this beautiful place. She looked at Phyllis and Jed poring over a map of beginner ski trails that Jed had bought at the gift shop in the lobby.

What, she asked herself, was wrong with this picture?

SIX

"I'VE NEVER SEEN ANYTHING SO FUNNY. MOM WAS JUST standing there. There weren't any hills around, no moguls, she wasn't even moving, and then she fell flat on her face!" Chad laughed.

"Chad . . ."

"It's okay, Jed. And Chad did ski over to help me up."

"He had to." Her daughter spoke up. "You were right in the middle of the path. He doesn't ski well enough to break a new trail around you."

"If you ski, you're going to fall," their instructor announced from the head of the trail. "I still fall myself, and I've been doing this for five winters now. But you don't have to worry. The skis you rented are very sturdy—almost unbreakable. Unless you hit a large rock going fifty miles an hour, they'll hold up."

"What about us?" Susan gasped, trying to keep up with the rest of the group.

"You . . ." began Darcy Ericksen, skiing up beside her and stabbing his poles firmly in the snow for balance. "You," he repeated, "are not rented. You are not their problem."

"Actually," their instructor said, overhearing him, "taking care of your skis is taking care of yourself—in an area with temperatures below zero, with twenty feet of snow on the ground, if you lose your skis, you could endanger your own life.''

"Jed!" Susan looked at her husband, fright in her eyes.

"You mean no one checks the trails at the end of each day?" he asked the long-haired youth who was teaching them to ski.

"Only a few of them. Too many trails and not enough rangers. But it is a good idea to let someone know where you're going to be skiing and when you're going to be back.''

"Did you hear that?" Susan checked with her two children. "You are not to go off again unless I know what trail you are going to be on and exactly when you plan to return. Understand?''

"Mother—" Chad began his protest.

"Your mother's right." Their teacher stopped the boy's protest. "We employees do it. The rangers do it. It's just good sense. You have to have a healthy respect for the environment around here—that's how you survive."

"We better tell your mother if we go anywhere. Your father wouldn't send help if we were missing. He'd have a party," Susan heard Randy say to Darcy. She thought he sounded sad.

"My mother won't do anything unless my father lets her," came the angry response.

"Look, come over here where we can talk without being overheard," Randy urged his friend, tugging on his sleeve.

"No, we can talk later. Let's get this lesson over with. Whoever invented skiing—"

"Hey, it's going to be fun," Randy insisted.

"I don't like being cold, I don't like sports, I don't like falling down. Believe me, I'm not going to like skiing.''

"But you do want to see the geysers in the winter, remember? Last night you were even talking about painting the trees covered with frost. And skiing is the best way to get around here. . . .''

"Okay. Okay. Don't nag. I'm trying, aren't I? Even my father would be pleased to see me taking this damn class.

I'm finally joining in the family's motto: Work hard, play hard, don't leave time to think about a damn thing.''

"You're not going to do anything stupid, are you?" Randy asked Darcy.

"Nothing as stupid as you are planning, that's for sure."

"Look . . ." Randy began as their teacher called for the group's attention.

Her children and their friends followed the instructor down the trail, and Susan was obliged to do the same. Jed trailed behind her, and Randy and Darcy brought up the rear, still arguing. The next stage of instruction was snowplowing, or what Susan thought of as going down hills without killing yourself. After the first few attempts, she decided it was impossible to get to the bottom without falling. For the first time in her life, she was thankful for the extra cushioning of fat on her hips. The class herringboned up a small incline and skied back down, forgetting to bend their knees, leaning back instead of forward, flinging poles about in the air over their heads. They stopped only to watch a bison amble out of the woods and across the trail. After an hour of this, their instructor gathered them together and gave them his blessing.

"You're all doing real well. Any questions you have can be answered by anyone at the ski shack between eight A.M. and five P.M.," he announced before leaving them.

"That's it? We graduated?" Susan asked, watching as Darcy and Randy hurried after their instructor.

"I think Chrissy will be visiting the ski shack a lot. I saw the way she was watching our teacher. She thinks he's cute," Chad kidded, stretching out his legs and flying down the slope.

"Where did he learn to do that?" Susan asked.

"In the same lesson you just took, hon. That's the difference between being fourteen and over forty."

"No need to remind me of my age. Every muscle is telling me exactly how old I am—and that I should be in bed."

"Did you notice Heather's uncle Jon? Wasn't he wonderful?" Chrissy breathed, leaving her mother wondering exactly who her new crush was on. Jon and Beth had skied through the group at the beginning of the lesson. Both of them carried large packs on their backs, with small shovels hanging below, and topped with rolled down sleeping bags and ground cloths. "They're practicing carrying their camping equipment," Chrissy continued. "They're going to be sleeping near a geyser basin out in the wilderness later this week. Isn't that exciting? I'd love to do that!"

"Where would you plug in your curlers and blow dryer?" Chad asked sarcastically. He skied off before his sister could reply.

"We could ask to go with them," Heather suggested. "Jon and Beth are really sweet. If we can get all the equipment, I'm sure they would take us."

"Can we ask? Could we go, Mother?" Chrissy asked both questions in the same breath.

"Let's see how well your skiing progresses," Susan temporized. "Jon and Beth appear to be very strong skiers. You'd better practice a lot if you're even thinking of keeping up with them."

"Good idea. Let's go around that practice circle near the lodge," Chrissy urged Heather. "I think your uncle and his friend have been there for a while."

"Beat you there!" C.J. took off, with Chad behind him.

"Be back at the restaurant by one o'clock for lunch," Jed called out to the kids.

"Don't worry! That's when my parents are meeting us, too!" Heather called, legs and poles moving in synchronization.

"I assume one of them is wearing a watch," Jed said to his wife.

She shrugged. "They're resourceful. They'll figure out the time."

"How are you doing? Want to go back to the room and rest before lunch?"

"If I take these skis off, I may never get them on again. Why don't we ski over to the Visitor's Center and see what's on the schedule for tonight?"

"Are we going to be able to move by tonight?" Jed asked, pushing off.

"Good question." Susan followed his lead, moving more rhythmically than she would have thought possible two hours ago. They skied back toward the complex of buildings surrounding Old Faithful, each of them privately impressed with his or her own progress. The midday sun sparkled off the snow, and Susan had to squint to watch the trail ahead. Rounding the corner of a summer cabin, she overshot the path and, propelled by her own momentum, skied through the deep snow and into a lumpy mound directly underneath a sign directing people, presumably only in the summer, toward ice cream cones and cold soda. She felt her right ski strike something under the snow, and fell.

"Damn!" She lifted her head up and noticed that Jed, unaware of her plight, was continuing on. "Damn," she repeated, trying to maneuver her legs so that both skis were on the same side of the invisible impediment. After a few minutes of struggle, she had only succeeded in sinking deeper into the snowbank, her legs still spanning the lump. She plopped her head back into the drift, exhausted.

"It's almost always easier if you take your skis off." The voice came from behind her. "Or are you really hurt? I can get a ranger—they have gurneys if you think you've broken anything." Susan looked up into the face of George Ericksen. Ice covered his beard and one of his eyebrows. He reached down and used his ski pole to unhitch the bindings keeping her skis on her feet. "You're not hurt, are you?"

"No, just stuck. That is, I *was* stuck. There's something here—some fabric or clothing under the snow. I don't seem able to get my skis out from under . . ." She scrambled to her knees and then stood up, sinking down in the snow as she did so. "Damn."

"Look, you're only digging yourself in deeper. You shouldn't be moving around like that. Move back and let me do this." He was beginning to sound angry, and he pulled her skis from the lumpy snow. "This is so disgusting. They're under some sort of garbage some stupid tourist left. Just stay away." George Ericksen scowled again, but Susan couldn't tell whether it was at her for falling or if he took her for a representative of messy tourists everywhere. He turned and held up her equipment. "Now, I'll put your skis on the snow in front of you, and you step up into them one at a time. Slowly . . . very slowly. You're going to have to get that caked snow off the latch if you want it to close properly. . . ." He guided her, step by step, through getting to her feet. Susan felt grateful, foolish, and more than a little childlike.

"Now, where were you going, my dear?"

"The Visitor's Center. I was on my way to—"

"If you were planning to watch Old Faithful, I'm afraid you're going to be late." He took a large gold watch from his pocket and flipped it open. "I'd calculate that it should almost be finished erupting by this time."

"Well, I just wanted to get some information—although it would be nice to see an eruption. . . ." Susan adjusted the straps around her wrists.

"You are doing that all wrong. Let me help you. You haven't been skiing very long, have you?" He twisted the poles and the straps into the proper position.

"I just had my first lesson," Susan admitted, her previous feeling of accomplishment vanishing.

"Well, some people take longer to learn than others do. Just keep working at it and stay on the trail at all times!" And leaving those orders behind, he slid effortlessly on his way, leaving Susan feeling almost as bad as she would have if she had broken a leg.

SEVEN

"YOU'RE DOING FINE NOW. DO YOU WANT TO JOIN THE ranger-led trip this afternoon?" Jed was sitting next to his wife on a bench in front of the wood stove that heated the main room of the Visitor's Center. "It says on the bulletin board that it leaves in fifteen minutes and lasts three hours. Is that too long for you?"

"Of course not!" Susan was indignant at her husband's lack of faith in her skiing abilities, and more than a little chagrined since she knew she was lying about her own endurance. She didn't know if she could ski one more hour, but she was sure that three was impossible. She tried to put a confident smile on her face. "It sounds like fun," she lied.

"Chrissy's going to take the tour, too. Heather is busy with her mother this afternoon. At least that's what she said during lunch."

"What about Chad?"

"He and C.J. are together on a trail to Fern Cascade. It begins right behind the lodge, and they'll meet us at six for dinner. They did just what you told them to, hon. Hey, there's Chrissy!" He waved to their daughter, who was coming in the door.

"Hi. Is this where we meet the ranger? Are you coming, too, Mom? You looked pretty worn-out at lunch." She threw her new gloves onto the bench and bent down to retie her boots. "Isn't this place fabulous? I'm thinking about becoming a park ranger when I grow up. Wouldn't it be wonderful

35

to live in the wilderness, to ski all day, and be one with nature?''

Susan resisted an urge to repeat Chad's question about where her born-again environmentalist was going to plug in her electric appliances, and settled for a noncommittal ''It does sound like an interesting career.''

''Which ranger is guiding our group?''

''I don't have any idea, Chrissy. You could ask the man at the desk over there.''

''That's okay. We'll find out soon enough.''

''Three hours is a long time,'' Susan commented. ''I'm going to visit the ladies' room before we leave.'' She stood up.

''We won't leave without you,'' Jed assured her.

Susan smiled and limped over to the rest room. How was she ever going to convince her legs to put on those skis again and then to actually move? . . . She entered a booth and sat down on the cold seat gratefully. Privacy at last. Here she didn't have to pretend she wasn't in pain. She figured she had five minutes to rest. She leaned her head against the pine wall and closed her eyes. Only to open them almost immediately as voices drifted from the booths on either side of her.

''We have to stop him, you know. He's going to drive poor Darcy crazy.''

''How Mother could ever have let Darcy bring his lover on this trip is beyond me. She must have known Father would react this way. He can hardly stand to eat in restaurants in the city when they come to visit; he claims all the waiters are gay and says it 'puts him off his food.' ''

''He didn't actually say that.'' The voice Susan had tentatively identified as Charlotte's sounded incredulous.

''Of course.'' Jane's voice had changed location and was muffled by running water. ''Why do you think they never visit you in San Francisco?''

''Because of the homosexual population? Oh, Jane, that's just sick.''

"That, my dear, is our father. You don't think he's completely normal, do you?"

"I don't know what to think. I'm just so tired of it all."

The slamming of the door indicated to Susan that it was safe to leave her booth. She washed her hands thoughtfully. The Ericksen family appeared to be ready to explode. Were Chad and Chrissy too close to the chaos that might result? She looked at Chrissy carefully when she rejoined her family. The child looked very happy, standing up when her mother arrived.

"I'm just going to check with the ranger at the desk . . . about where the ski tour is leaving from and all," she explained.

"I think our daughter has a new crush," Jed commented. He nodded to the blond ranger manning the information desk.

Susan followed his glance and smiled. "That explains her sudden interest in nature." She looked at her watch. "It's time for the tour to begin. Jed, I was thinking about something I overheard in the ladies' room. . . ."

Chrissy rushed back to them. "We're in the wrong place. The group is meeting outside. . . . See?" She pointed. "We have to hurry if we don't want to miss them."

"Why don't you run out and tell whoever is in charge that we would appreciate it if they would wait for a minute or two," her father suggested.

"I will. Right away!" She ran out the door.

Jed stood up slowly. "This is going to be a long three hours." He followed his daughter.

Susan tripped behind, her pace and enthusiasm for the afternoon's trip enhanced by a glimpse of the group waiting for the tour's start. Charlotte and Jane were there; maybe she could maneuver close to them.

Fifteen minutes later, she was standing in front of a beautiful tiny hot spring, admiring the color of the water bubbling there. She was sore, tired, and having a wonderful time. Much to Chrissy's disappointment, Marnie Mackay was leading the tour. To Susan's delight, Jane and Charlotte were novice skiers also, and through pace alone, the three of them were going to be spending much of the trip together. She smiled happily and listened to their guide.

". . . Actually, the demarcation between a geyser and a hot spring is very simple. A geyser erupts. Some erupt regularly, predictably, like Old Faithful, and some aren't quite so regular. Hot springs tend to just bubble away. Although there is the case of Solitary Geyser, which we won't see on this trip. Solitary was a hot spring until 1915, when someone decided to make money by draining off the hot water, funneling it into a bathhouse, and offering hot baths for tourists. When the pipe was placed in the spring and the water drained away, the integrity of that particular thermal feature was upset in such a way that it began to erupt—thus becoming a geyser.

"Now, we're going to be crossing some spots of dry pavement along the trail today—the thermal heat keeps some areas snow-cleared for the entire winter. I usually take off my skis and walk—you can do what you please. It probably depends upon whether you own or rent your equipment."

"Not me. I own these things, and I don't give a damn if they get wrecked," Jane said to Charlotte, digging her poles into the ground for emphasis. "I don't care what Father says—I don't care how terribly Mother feels. I am not going to do this ever again after I leave here. In fact, I am going to leave them in the ski rack outside the hotel when I go."

Susan skied up to where Jed and Chrissy stood. She'd decided to end all eavesdropping. These weren't happy people. Getting more involved wouldn't improve her vacation. She concentrated on Marnie Mackay, who was still bubbling forth interesting information.

If surface tension could be called interesting.

"To destroy the surface tension of a hot spring can destroy the integrity of the feature," Marnie explained.

"Do people often thrown things into the . . . uh, the thermal features?" asked a man wearing a bright red parka.

"Not so much now—and, of course, it is totally illegal to do anything of the kind in Yellowstone National Park—but in the past, a lot of things were done which are frowned on today.'' She gave her charges a stern look of warning. ''There were laundries and bathhouses—like the one I mentioned earlier—which took advantage of the steam and boiling water available for free. In fact, Chinaman Spring was named for the man who set up a laundry there in the eighteen eighties.''

''I'll bet all the hot water really got clothes clean,'' someone said.

''Well, I don't know if it did that, but it erupted and ejected the tent and wicker basket of clothing that the man had set up. And surely you've all seen the famous picture of the fisherman boiling his catch in a hot spring right on the bank of Yellowstone Lake. None of that is allowed today. In fact, the health of these thermal features is carefully monitored by the Park Service. If you do happen to be around an eruption of one of the major geysers, we sure would appreciate it if you would take the time to report it to a ranger back at the Visitor's Center.

''Now, watch this next patch along the boardwalk. It might be slippery.''

The lecture stopped as the skiers tracked across ice and water on the wooden boardwalk built around the numerous geysers and bubbling springs. But when they had all traversed it successfully, the questioning continued.

''What about animals?'' Jed asked. ''Don't they ever fall in?''

''They certainly do, especially in the winter when some of them manage to survive by using the steam for warmth. And once in a while one of them gets too close. That's when we end up with something like buffalo stew. The carcass simmers until the meat rots and falls off the bones. It smells something awful. In fact, you can usually smell it before you see it.''

Members of the group made various understanding noises, and Susan, who loved to cook and frequently produced homemade broth, was rather wildly considering the addition of onions, salt, and possibly some summer savory to the mixture.

''But it doesn't last long,'' Marnie continued cheerfully.

"Yellowstone's full of scavengers—coyotes and ravens. There are lots of animals around that are on the lookout for anything of nutritional value."

"Don't fall into a geyser," Jed kidded his wife. "You'd hate being something of nutritional value to a coyote."

"We're coming to a typical pool up here," Marnie continued. "It's a pretty good example of some of the things we've been talking about. It's one of the most beautiful pools in the park, but it has lost some of its vivid coloration because so many people have thrown so much into it over the years. In fact, the bottom of the spring is so littered with debris that less water gets into it than is supposed to. This has caused the water temperature to cool, so there's been an increase in the growth of algae, and that has destroyed some of the bright blue coloration."

Everyone gathered around her on the boardwalk built a few feet above the pool. They chattered and laughed until, one by one, the sight at the edge of the pool shocked them into silence. The last to arrive were Jane and Charlotte Ericksen, who slipped into the last space available for viewing the fabulous sight.

Jane interrupted her description of an ideal vacation with which she had been amusing her sister. "So we walked down the dune to the most perfect beach, and it was totally deserted. . . ." She paused to look over the rail. "Oh, my God," she said loudly. "It's Father."

EIGHT

SUSAN HAD GOTTEN FREE OF HER EQUIPMENT AND WAS lying on the bed with her eyes closed. Jed sat on the end of the mattress. "Thank God it wasn't him. At first glance, I thought—"

"We all thought," Susan corrected him.

"We all thought it was George Ericksen boiling away on the edge of that beautiful pool of water." Jed finished taking off his boots. "They still work," he said, wiggling his toes. "I was a little worried that I had killed them." He lay back on the bed beside his wife. "Anything interesting on that ceiling?"

"Hmmm."

"Susan? Are you okay?"

"Just thinking . . . You know, Jed—" she swung her legs over the side and sat up "—I can't figure out why anyone would play a stupid trick like that on Jane and Charlotte. It doesn't make sense."

"Sense?"

"Of course it doesn't," she corrected herself, ignoring her husband's confusion and flopping back down on the bed. "I don't know enough about the sisters—or the family. How could it make sense?" She stretched her arms over her head. "I wonder where Kathleen is. She'll be interested in this."

"Susan, I know what you're doing. You're investigating, but there's no reason to. No one has been killed—no one has even been hurt. And Kathleen is here for a vacation—just like we are. Maybe you should leave it alone this time, hon. After all, no crime was committed.''

''It isn't a crime to throw an effigy of someone into an ordinary pool of water, but I'm sure it is here,'' Susan argued. ''But that's not what's worrying me. What's worrying me is that whoever did it really wanted someone to think George Ericksen was dead.''

''It was the suspenders. All that white hair and those red suspenders. No one else looks quite like that around here,'' Jed said. ''Anyone who had ever seen George Ericksen would have thought it was him lying there—What are you doing?''

Susan was putting on the ski boots she had just removed. ''I'm going out.''

''What are you going to do?''

''Hang out, as your son would say. I just want to see what the rangers are saying about this afternoon. We're not eating until six-thirty tonight, are we? I have over an hour before then. . . .''

''You're not going to ski, are you?''

''Is there any other way to get around here? I'll be fine. You look as if you could do with a nap. Maybe you should set the alarm so you'll be up in time for dinner.'' She pulled skis and ski poles from where they had been dripping in the corner of the room. ''Did you ever think I'd get comfortable on these things?'' she asked, pushing the equipment in front of her.

''No,'' he answered as the door slammed behind his wife.

Five minutes later, Susan had stopped chortling with glee over how easily she had snapped her boots into their bindings and was wondering just what to do next. Her first thought had been to ski out to where the body had been found, but it was getting dark and she suspected that her newfound ability wouldn't get her there and back to civilization (as represented by the Visitor's Center) in daylight. Well, perhaps the Visitor's Center itself was as good a place to start as any. She swung her arms and skied off, only to be stopped by the sight of her son, skiing toward her in C.J.'s wake.

''Chad!'' she called to get his attention.

"Hi, Mom! Hey! You've learned to ski!" he called out approvingly.

"I told you she wasn't too old to learn," C.J. said.

"Thanks, guys. Where have you been today?"

"We went up to Fern Cascade. It was cool," Chad answered. "The trail is a little steep on the way up, and you have to herringbone almost until your legs fall off, but it's a great trip down. I only fell twice—and hit a tree once."

"Are you—"

"I'm fine," he insisted, knowing what she was going to ask—what any mother would have asked—without hearing it. "Did you hear about C.J.'s grandfather?"

"His . . . ?"

"Not really my grandfather—just a dummy made up to look like him," C.J. corrected the information.

"I was there when he—it—was found. In fact, I was wondering if it upset your aunts. For a minute, you know, we truly did think it might be your grandfather himself. The effigy looks very real, you know."

"Sure does. We just came from there. The rangers really had to work to get that thing out of the water."

"They didn't want to damage the sides of the pool by getting too close, but they had to make sure it didn't get waterlogged and sink to the bottom," C.J. said, continuing the story. "They told us how there's this ranger who knows all about geysers and fumaroles and stuff, and how, once in a while, he lowers the water level in the pool and it spits stuff into the air—stuff that people have thrown into it, like boots, tires, and other garbage."

Susan was impressed by all they had learned. "Do you know what they were going to do with it after they got it out? Did they tell you?"

"They were joking around about using the wig for a Santa Claus disguise at their Christmas party."

"Why are you so interested?" Chad asked. His mother's involvement in crimes had embarrassed and inconvenienced him more than once in the past. And in his adolescent view, she was embarrassing enough without playing detective.

"Just curious," she answered. "I'm going over to the Visitor's Center. I thought I'd look around in the bookshop before dinner."

"That's where they were taking the dummy." Chad sounded suspicious.

"Well, maybe I'll get a closer look at it," Susan said, trying to keep her voice casual.

"You know who might like to look at it? My grandfather!"

"I'm sure he would," Susan agreed, starting to ski away. The sight of George Ericksen meeting his effigy was something she didn't want to miss. "Oh, Chad," she called back over her shoulder, "dinner's at six-thirty."

She didn't think he heard. Well, that's what fathers were for. She swooshed through the snow toward the lights spilling from the two-story glass front of the building. The number of skis in the rack by the front door indicated something unusual was going on inside. She clicked her boots free, hung skis and poles on the crowded rack, and entered the Visitor's Center.

A large, open building paneled with pine, the Visitor's Center was divided into two parts. The auditorium was at the rear, while the front half looked out through large panes of glass toward Old Faithful. Susan glanced through the windows at the tail of steam rising into the air; she still hadn't seen an eruption. Three sides of the room were lined with shelves of books for sale and displays explaining various thermal activities. A small desk was located near the door, in a place convenient for tourists to question the ranger, who left his or her seat only to get up and throw a log on the wood-burning stove. On the floor in front of it lay the effigy. A dozen people stood around or sat on nearby benches. No one paid any attention to Susan as she wandered across the room and pretended to study the seismograph mounted on the wall.

"But it must have been someone who knew the old man. I can't see how they can deny that."

Susan was startled to hear voices close behind her: two

rangers had moved away from the rest and were conversing nearby.

"Don't be so sure. If it's someone who knows him, it must be a member of the family—and they're not so likely to admit that."

"So what do we do? Ask the family to cough up the money it cost to get the body from the pool? Call in the FBI for a full investigation?"

"Marnie's in charge here. I suppose she'll just warn them that this type of thing can't possibly be tolerated, and leave it at that. It was probably just one of the teenagers in the group, playing around. If they get a stern warning, it won't happen again."

Susan gasped and thought of her own children. She certainly didn't want anyone to think they were involved in this! She turned and walked purposefully to the group in the middle of the room.

"We can store it in one of the woodsheds near the staff cabins," Marnie was saying. "I sure wish Dillon would get here with those garbage bags. I should have told him to ask first at the Snow Lodge kitchen. If he went all the way back to his apartment—"

"Here he is," one of the young men standing close to the door called out as their driver from the previous day appeared bearing a box of double-thick plastic garbage bags.

"We shouldn't have all this nonbiodegradable stuff in a national park, but since it's here, we may as well get some use out of it," Marnie muttered, accepting the box. "We really don't need all that many bags."

Susan was surprised by the size of the pile of wet clothing. Looking closer, she realized the stuffing was gone: all that was left of the effigy was jeans, boots, wool shirt, those suspenders, and the wig and beard. "What was it filled with?" she wondered aloud.

"Newspapers. Crumpled newspapers." Marnie looked up from where she squatted on the floor. "Something else may have been used for the head. It fell off when we hooked the wig—it's probably at the bottom of the pool by now."

"It must have been dropped by the pool just a few minutes before we arrived," Susan said. "Otherwise, the papers would have been waterlogged and sunk, too."

Marnie stopped with one hand still in the bag she had almost finished filling. "I don't think so. It was on a ledge at the edge of the pool, not really in it. I think it could have stayed there for a day or so without falling further in."

"Or decomposing?" Susan asked.

"Probably. The water isn't very hot on the edges of the pools, you know."

"What are you going to do with the clothing?" Susan asked, having overheard her answer, but wondering what it would be officially.

"We're going to be asking if anyone can identify the clothing at the interpretive talks for the rest of the week, but I don't expect that anyone is going to come forward and admit to doing this. It was probably just a prank. Maybe someone will call a ranger and make an embarrassed confession, but I doubt it."

Susan started to speak, but the effigy seemed to come to life and stride into the room.

NINE

DESPITE THE FACT THAT HE HAD THE COMPLETE ATTENtion of everyone in the room, George Ericksen didn't speak as he strode across the floor, straight through the group, stopping only when he could kneel down beside the effigy. He touched the wig gingerly, then jerked it up with an angry gesture. There was nothing underneath. Susan thought the absence of a face, a skull, or anything similar startled him.

"I'm afraid the . . . uh, the head . . . escaped to the bottom of the pool," Marnie explained, continuing to fill the garbage bag.

"Disgraceful!" It was a bellow that a wild animal would be proud to have produced. "I understand that something dropped into a pool could cause a permanent change in the ecology of the feature. This is, as far as I'm concerned, an example of gross criminal behavior, and it should not be allowed to go unpunished. It is imperative that you catch the culprit." His voice became louder and more demanding with each sentence. "I insist on knowing what is going to be done about this!"

"Not very much," Marnie confessed quietly, standing up. "In the winter the staff consists mainly of interpreters and naturalists. We have very little time to investigate pranks. I'll make a statement at the talk tonight and post notices at various locations in Snow Lodge, but unless someone comes forward and confesses, we probably will never know who did this."

"Never?" George Ericksen looked up at Marnie.

"Probably not," she admitted.

Susan wondered if that was a look of relief that slid across George Ericksen's face. Or something else.

He stood up, rising over the ranger like a mountain over the plains. "I heard talk at the front desk about the cost of retrieving this . . . this thing. I would like to pay for that . . . uh, the rescue."

"You'll have to talk to my boss about it. He's park superintendent. I'd be happy to give you his number, if you like."

"Yes. I would appreciate that." George Ericksen picked up the largest garbage bag and flung it over his shoulder.

"You can't take that, sir." Marnie's tone left no room for discussion. Maybe George Ericksen had met his match.

"Excuse me?" He made the request sound like a threat.

"I need to keep that."

"May I ask why?"

"Regulation" was the brisk reply. She took the bag from his hand. Picking up the wig and beard, she slung everything over her tiny shoulder and started from the room. "I'll be back in a few minutes," she announced, without pausing long enough for anyone to stop her.

As she left, Phyllis Ericksen entered, closing the door behind her. "George?" She sounded anxious.

"I'm right here, Phil."

"I couldn't find you. I was worried."

"You worry too much," he answered like a belligerent teenager. "You've always worried too much. And you're always trying to get the entire family together to do things. If you are so worried about everyone getting to dinner, go ahead and sit down without me. Order me a steak and a bottle of that Chianti, and I'll join you all in a few minutes. Just make damn sure that I'm at the head of the table and that Randy person is at the bottom—as far away as possible. Understand?"

"I'm sure, if you would just give him a chance—"

"I will not learn to like him," he finished her sentence differently than she had planned. "I have very good reasons not to like that young man, and I see no reason to start learning to like him now."

"Of course, George. There's certainly no reason to start now." She turned and walked out the door.

"So how do I get in touch with this superintendent person?"

"The address is in the brochure that—" Dillon began.

"I don't want his address. I want his phone number. How long do you think I have to resolve this foolishness?"

"I'll get it for you," one of the younger rangers, standing near the desk, offered.

"Excellent." Susan got the impression that this sort of service was something George was accustomed to.

Marnie returned as George was putting the number away in the pocket of his inevitable plaid shirt. She was followed by Irving Cockburn. Of course, he was talking.

"This is very, very interesting—psychologically speaking.

The type of personality disorder that would lead someone to perpetuate such an episode . . . It could take years of therapy to discover the meaning of this." The heels of his cowboy boots clanked on the floor as he hopped along to keep pace with the ranger's stride. Susan noticed that he was only slightly taller than Marnie, even wearing a hat. Did he know how silly he looked? Apparently not.

"That's very interesting," Marnie said, smiling at him.

"Of course, I don't treat many people like that in my practice. I deal more with everyday neurotics—preferably rich ones who can afford my fees!" He chuckled, appearing to believe he had been clever. "I might be able to help you understand what happened here, though."

"That would be nice, but—"

Susan assumed that Marnie was going to explain that there would, there could, be no investigation, but she never got the chance.

"And what, exactly, do you think would cause someone to do this foolish thing?" George Ericksen growled. "I have a hard time coming up with an answer to that question. Except, of course, that it must have been done by someone with absolutely no respect for the environment."

"That's an interesting question." Irving answered the other man while looking at Marnie. "I believe it may be best explained to the layman as a classic case of projection. The person or persons imbued you with their own hostile feelings and then couldn't face the reality of their emotions and had to deny them—by drowning them, as it were."

"It's probably the mother," Susan muttered under her breath.

"It's always the mother," Marnie agreed quietly.

"Or, of course, maybe the person that did this had an urge to cleanse away these horrible things that he had transferred to the dummy—maybe he thought of it as giving the dummy a bath." Everyone looked up as Darcy Ericksen spoke.

"Where the hell did you come from?" his father roared.

"The stork, the cabbage patch, possibly, or impossibly, your hairy old loins." The reply was sharp. "Mother—"

"Is fussing around trying to gather everyone together for dinner," George Ericksen finished impatiently.

"No, she has gone up to her room to lie down. She has a headache. She asked me to come over here and tell you not to expect her for supper."

"So you're going to be your mother's errand boy now! I wonder what you would say if I asked you to do the smallest thing for me," George said sarcastically.

"But you don't ask the smallest thing from me, Father." Darcy smiled crookedly. "You ask me only to change my life completely for you."

"For your own good," George Ericksen roared.

"How did you manage to acquire all this wisdom about the lives of others? Exactly why do you presume to know what is right or wrong with me?" Darcy stuck out his chin angrily.

"I know what is natural and what isn't. I have spent my entire life studying what is natural. How could you presume to tell me anything about a world that I have lived in for forty-seven more years than you have? How could you possibly—"

But Darcy had spun around and was gone, slamming the door behind him.

"This is absolutely ridiculous. Have your boss call me— I'm in the main building at Snow Lodge. I'm on vacation, and I certainly don't need all these distractions. It's inexcusable," George Ericksen bellowed, following his son.

"Definitely in need of extensive family therapy. I would recommend sessions twice a week." Irving Cockburn broke into the silence that followed.

Marnie smiled at him weakly. "I better sit down and write my report about all this—before I forget the details."

"Will you be giving the talk again tonight?" the psychiatrist asked.

"No." Marnie moved to the desk. "But I'll be there."

"Then I'll see you. Maybe we could go out for a drink or something afterward." Irving beamed at her, and spinning on a heel so hard that he almost lost his balance, he propelled himself from the room.

"I get the feeling that he took his cousin to the senior prom," Susan muttered to herself.

"Only if his aunt paid the poor girl to go," Marnie surprised her by answering. The two women were near the side of the desk, apart from the rest of the room. The gathering, in fact, was breaking up, with people milling around or leaving for their evening meal. "I shouldn't have said that, but I couldn't resist it," Marnie added.

"I thought you were amazingly polite to him," Susan commented.

"We're trained to be polite. We have to answer the same question a million times a year with the same enthusiastic smile on our faces. That's part of the ranger's job." She sighed. "And most of the time, it's great. Most of the tourists are pleasant, polite, and wonderful to work with. But sometimes someone comes along like that Dr. What's His Name, who is so irritating. . . . I'm not being fair. He's not that bad, it's just that so much has happened today."

"You mean dummies aren't dropped into pools every day?"

"Not even every year." Marnie didn't manage to answer Susan's smile with one of her own. She seemed to feel that her mood needed an explanation. "One of my friends—a ranger that I trained with, in fact, was burned to death after falling into a pool like that one."

"My God."

"It was last summer. He was out by himself in the middle of the night. That's not terribly unusual—a lot of us get up in the night and check out a favorite geyser, especially on nights when there's a full moon. Anyway, he must have slipped on the edge of the pool somehow. He did manage to climb out, but not before his entire body was covered with third-degree burns. He walked back to the spot where a bunch of us were camping—it was about a quarter of a mile away. . . ."

"How . . . ?"

"Third-degree burns are fatal, but the victim feels no pain.

We called for a doctor—but there was nothing anyone could do. He—my friend—was dead less than ten hours later.''

"So for you, this hasn't been just a childish prank."

"Not entirely. But, of course, this isn't really very serious. Just a prank, like you said."

Susan had said it, but she didn't really believe it.

TEN

SUSAN HAD EXPECTED TO FIND HER FAMILY GATHERED and waiting for her in the wood-paneled dining room but instead, Jed was sitting by the window at a candlelit table for two.

"Where . . . ?"

"Right behind you, next to the door. You passed them as you came in," he answered her unspoken question.

Susan turned and saw her children and the Ericksen children sharing a table of their own. Chrissy and Heather sat on one side, heads close together, whispering. Chad and C.J. were across from them, apparently sharing a joke, their faces flushed with laughter.

"I spoke with Joyce, and we agreed that everyone could stand a vacation—the adults from the kids, and the kids from the adults. Their waiter knows who to bill."

"Where are Kathleen and Jerry?"

"They just got in from a trail. They left a message taped to the door of our room. They'll join us in the bar later." He looked closely at his wife. "Is anything wrong? I thought you'd be happy to get some extra privacy."

"I'm a little worried about what's going on in the Ericksen family, Jed."

"According to Chrissy, so is Heather."

"She talked to you about it!"

"Not in so many words. You know how the kids are about their friends' confidences. But she did say that Heather's family was having a pretty miserable vacation—something about her grandfather not liking one of her uncle's friends, and her grandmother being terribly upset by it all. I guess he's not the type of person to keep his feelings to himself."

"I'll say." Susan related the scene she had witnessed between George Ericksen and Darcy.

"Well, that explains a lot."

"You know, there's something else worrying me. There seem to be a lot of people who think that making the effigy and throwing it into the pool was the work of some kids—kids connected with the Ericksen family."

"You mean C.J."

"Yes, and that might connect Chad with this whole thing."

"So when was it dumped?" Jed asked.

"Well, I asked Marnie about that, and she thought possibly late this morning. The pool isn't very popular, so she doubts if anyone visited it between the ranger walk yesterday and the one this afternoon—except for whoever threw it in. She says there was just one set of ski tracks there before the tour arrived. She insists that it's something she noticed."

"Chad and C.J. were skiing on a different trail when that thing was dumped."

"You're sure? It's not that I don't trust Chad, but we don't really know C.J. at all and—"

"Yes, I'm sure." He accepted a beer from the waiter and took a sip before continuing. "Chad and C.J. took the trail up to Fern Cascade. Beth told me about it—I ran into her buying ski wax at the ski shack this afternoon. She and Jon passed them up there. It's evidently not a long trail, but you have to herringbone up for almost a mile. She said that she and Jon passed them early on the trail—what she said exactly is that it took the two of them about half an hour to do the three miles and that it was going to take the boys all after-noon.''

"So they couldn't have had anything to do with the ef-figy." Susan was surprised at how relieved she was.

"Not unless they were in two places at once. That pool must be at least three miles from Fern Cascade—as the crow flies. And it must be more like seven or eight on ski trails."

Susan gulped down some wine and looked around the room. "They all appear to be pretty relaxed now."

"The kids?" Jed looked over at his offspring.

"The Ericksens. Even Phyllis seems to be feeling well enough to eat."

The staff had joined three tables along one side of the room, and the entire family was sitting together. George Er-icksen was seated as far as possible from Darcy. Randy was missing. If Susan hadn't been present this afternoon, she wouldn't have suspected there was any conflict in the family. As she watched, glasses were raised and the entire group joined in a toast.

"Maybe whoever put that thing in the pool this afternoon got all of his or her hostilities out of his system, and now things have settled down."

"You sound like Dr. Cockburn," Susan told her husband.

Jed didn't appear flattered by the comparison. "He's a piece of work, isn't he? But maybe he's right."

"Well, I hope so, for all our sakes. This is supposed to be a vacation, after all. I don't particularly want to spend it in the middle of a family explosion."

"And you think one is coming?" Jed asked.

"There are an awful lot of exposed nerves around here. I really don't know what to think. I suppose that as long as the kids are safely kept away from the tensions, we may as well relax and enjoy the vacation."

"Good idea." Jed cut into his steak. "The kids are both planning on going to the talk tonight."

"Weren't you?"

"Well, I'm pretty tired and my legs ache. . . . ."

"But the topic is the exploration of Yellowstone. You said

that was something that interested you. And I would like to see what sort of reaction Marnie gets when she makes her announcement about what happened today.''

''You just said that you were going to concentrate on the vacation!''

''I can do that and wonder exactly what happened this morning at the same time,'' Susan insisted.

''I wonder how many people know about it,'' Jed said, frowning.

''Good question. There were around twenty people on the tour today, wouldn't you say?''

''Probably.''

''And others must have seen the rangers pull the thing out and bring it back here. . . .''

''They carted it back in a snowmobile. They're all over the place in those things. I don't think anyone pays much attention to them.''

''Well, they didn't exactly hide the clothing and stuff over at the Visitor's Center. Probably half the guests here know, wouldn't you say?''

''Possibly. I did hear some conversation about it at the front desk. And Beth mentioned it to me also.''

''When you were at the ski shack?''

''Yes. I was asking the boy who runs it which trail to take tomorrow, and she came up to me and asked me about the effigy. I didn't notice her standing in the corner when I came in, but she overheard me talking about it.''

Susan thought everything over for a while. ''Which trail did he suggest?''

''Well, I told him we were looking for a short trip, and he suggested the trails around Old Faithful Geyser. He said they're well marked and popular. And if the storm that's predicted comes in early, we can hurry back to the lodge.''

''Sounds good.''

''He suggested that we order box lunches tonight. The restaurant will have them made up and waiting for us in the morning. Then we won't have to come back unless we want to.'' He pulled a small booklet from the parka hanging over the back of his chair. ''I'll show you. . . .''

Surprisingly enough, his quiet words echoed from across the room, but in the echo, they were angry and abrasive.

''I'll show you. I'll show you!''

And Darcy Ericksen ran by their table, toward the doorway. He turned before leaving and repeated it, looking straight into his father's face. ''I'll show you! I will!''

With that, he was gone.

ELEVEN

''Is that pack too heavy? You know Chad offered to wear it.''

''I'll let him carry it for the second half of the trail,'' Jed answered, nearly running into his wife. ''It would help if you would let me know when you're going to stop.''

''When we're halfway there?'' she squealed, ignoring his suggestion. ''Are you telling me that we're not halfway yet?''

''Not at all. If I'm right—and I've been following the trail pretty closely on the map—we'll be halfway when we get to the bridge right here.'' He pointed to a tiny line on the sheet of paper he had pulled from his pocket. ''Well, almost halfway.'' He looked at his wife. ''You're not tired, are you?''

''No. I'm exhausted.'' She pulled her ski cap down over her ears. ''I thought today would be easier than yesterday, but I was wrong. I can't believe how much my legs and shoulders hurt this morning. Don't yours?''

''Mine ached last night. When I stood up after that talk, I felt my knees start to buckle.''

"It was a little strange last night, wasn't it?" Susan added, skiing slowly enough to talk as she went.

"To say the least," he agreed. "The tension in the Ericksen family was extraordinary. There's an awful lot of pain there."

"I was a little surprised to see Darcy back with the rest of the clan. After that exit from the restaurant . . ."

"You're right. It couldn't have been more than forty-five minutes later that they were all chortling together like nothing odd had occurred—except that their humor seemed a little strained."

"Strange," Susan mused, turning her skis to the side to climb a short hill. "This is going to be easier on the way back. It has to be faster to go down than up."

"Maybe." Jed wondered if his wife realized she had yet to ski down an incline without falling.

"Did you see that look on their faces when Marnie made the announcement about throwing things in thermal features? They looked as though it had nothing to do with them."

"Well, maybe it didn't. Maybe the fact that the dummy looked like George Ericksen was a coincidence. Maybe it was supposed to be Santa Claus with the beard and all—or maybe Paul Bunyan. Who knows?"

Susan thought she did know. She didn't doubt that George Ericksen was the person represented by the dummy. But she couldn't help wondering whether it was a joke or a threat. She was feeling nervous about the whole thing. She had had terrible nightmares last night, inspired, she assumed, by the story Marnie had told about her friend's death. In the middle of the night Susan had sat up in bed, upset and confused by images of a burned body lying at the foot of her skis. She couldn't seem to shake the feeling that image had produced. Not that the same appeared to be true for the Ericksen family. As she had told Jed, the Ericksens were acting as if nothing were wrong, in public at least.

Last night's talk was a good example. Heather and C.J. had left her children after dinner, saying, so Chrissy reported, that they had promised to spend the evening with their family. The Henshaws had gone to the Visitor's Center early—mainly because Susan had discovered, rising from dinner, that she wouldn't be comfortable until she was seated again. Her family sat in the middle of the third row and waited for the talk to begin. Other tourists came in, filling the chairs at the rear of the room. Marnie and two other rangers entered and were immediately accosted by Dr. Cockburn, who managed to involve them in conversation. Susan tuned out the hum around her and concentrated on her aching muscles. The rangers spent a few minutes convincing Dr. Cockburn to sit down; they were gathered at the front of the room, preparing to start the program, when the Ericksens made their entrance.

And it was some entrance. George Ericksen marched (yes, that was the word, Susan thought, remembering the scene) into the room, followed by his entire family. They were all smiling. And not talking.

The entire first row was open, and George Ericksen led his group there and dropped down in the middle. Phyllis sat on his right, and surprisingly, Darcy placed himself on his father's other side. The rest of the family joined them, with Heather and C.J. on either end. When Marnie came up to speak, they didn't blink an eye or even appear interested. The lack of response struck her as unusual, to say the least. Very unusual.

Marnie's announcement was intentionally matter-of-fact. She explained that a large and, she implied, rather funny object had been found in one of the thermal pools in the park, that it was the job of the National Park Service to see that things like this didn't happen, and that, while no one was anxious to upset anyone's vacation, they would be very interested in any information about this event. She added that, certainly, any and all information and the identity of the informant would be completely confidential. As with Marnie's handling of Irving Cockburn, Susan was impressed. And as far as she could tell, none of the Ericksens even blinked.

After the presentation of the evening's show (an interesting talk on the lives and deaths of early explorers in the park), Susan hung around to see if anyone approached the ranger. Except for the predictable presence of Dr. Cockburn, there were no stragglers. Apparently no one had any confessions to make. Irving Cockburn knew nothing specific; however, he generously shared his opinions and theories with anyone who would listen.

All in all, it had been a very strange evening. The Ericksens had filed out immediately after the program, except for Carlton and his family. The teenagers had gotten together as people do who, finding themselves in a foreign country, discover a common language among themselves. Susan and Jed stopped for a moment to speak to Joyce and Carlton about including all the children on the next day's trip. It turned out that the Ericksens were planning to travel on the same trails. But everyone agreed that the teens would be happiest together—and happier with Susan and Jed, who were slower skiers. The Henshaws had gone back to the lodge for a quick drink with Kathleen and Jerry and then fallen, exhausted, into bed.

The next morning Susan and Jed had discovered the disadvantage of traveling with their children and their children's friends. The youngsters made them feel old. Susan and Jed had ordered the teens to wait for them at various places on the trail, and accepted the abuse heaped on them for being "so slow." They would be coming to one of those points soon. Susan looked back to see how her husband was getting along. He waved a ski pole at her, and she slowed down.

"Are you okay? You've been awfully quiet," he asked, skiing up beside her. "You know, we're not really very far from the Visitor's Center—as the crow flies. If you want to, you could probably find a shortcut back." He again pulled the map out.

"No, I'm fine. I was just thinking. Aren't we supposed to be meeting up with the kids soon?"

"I told Chad and C.J. to wait at the bridge across this stream." He pointed to the beautiful rushing water, lined with thick banks of ice, that their trail had been following ever since the waterfall.

"Are we going to be forced to listen to a bunch of sarcastic comments about our skiing ability?"

"Probably—look, there they are."

The four children were sitting on mounds of snow piled up along the rails of the bridge. They waved excitedly when they spied Susan and Jed.

"Did you see them?"

"Do you believe how huge the male was?"

"Chad almost skied right past the mother and the baby— he would have, too, if Heather hadn't called out to him," Chrissy said, looking at her parents. "You did see them, didn't you?"

"See what?" Jed asked.

"The moose! The moose eating seaweed . . ."

"Aquatic plants, Chad, not seaweed," his sister corrected him. "We're a long way from the sea."

"The point," insisted Chad, "is not what they were eating, but that they were there. And whether Mom and Dad saw them."

"We must have missed them. Where exactly were they?"

"And how many were there?" Susan added.

"Three. A mother and her son in the middle of the water first, and then a little further on, a monstrous buck," C.J. answered.

"I don't know how you missed them," Chad added. "They were gigantic!"

"I spend most of the time watching the trail directly in front of the tips of my skis," Susan admitted. "It seems to help me balance."

"I think you're doing much better, Mrs. Henshaw," Heather said.

"Thank you. I think so, too," Susan agreed, and promptly slid off the bridge and into the snow.

"Sometimes she's better than others," Jed laughed, handing the backpack containing their lunches to his son. "Anyone thirsty?" he asked, helping his wife to her feet.

"Dying. I drank all the juice I was carrying in the first hour or so. Who would have thought you could get so dried out in such cold weather?" Heather asked rhetorically.

"There are some extra cans of apple juice in the pack, but don't forget that the trip back is going to be equally long."

"Maybe not. We've been mainly traveling uphill. So we should be able to do the return in a shorter time," C.J. suggested.

"In any case, we'd better get going. I'd say we're only halfway to the point where we were planning to lunch."

"I think I can. I think I can," Susan muttered to herself. Whether that worked or whether the realization that her lunch and another drink were waiting at their destination was the inspiration, make it she did.

"We weren't sure whose lunch was whose, so we just ate them in order. We left the two ones on the bottom for you— and two extra cans of juice," Chad explained, folding up the papers his food had been wrapped in. The kids had already finished their lunch when Susan and Jed finally arrived at the path overlooking the side of Old Faithful opposite the Visitor's Center.

"So where are you all going?" Susan asked, sinking to the spot Chad had just vacated on the broken branch of a large pine tree.

"We're going to ski up to the geyser," Chrissy said, pointing to the large cone rising out of the middle of a clearing in the snow. "We finished eating a long time ago. We were just waiting for you to get here."

"Well, have fun," Susan said. "There's a little steam coming from the cone. I wonder if we're in time to see an eruption." From here, she meant: she knew she wasn't going to ski one more foot than was absolutely necessary. "Thanks." She accepted the box lunch from Jed and opened it. "What is this?"

Jed peered at the sandwich in her hand. "Looks like peanut butter, banana, and trail mix on whole wheat. Probably very healthy."

Susan gazed at it doubtfully, but only for a moment. "I'm

starving," she confessed, putting a corner of the bread in her mouth. She leaned back against a tree trunk and chewed, looking about her. She had, she decided, truly been spending too much time looking at her skis and not at the extraordinary scenery. The sun was glistening off the snow; steam from the geyser twisted in a thin spiral up into the deep blue sky. As she watched, a large black raven, evidently startled by the kids skiing toward it, flew into the air, loudly cawing as it went. She took another large bite of the sandwich, chewed it, and sighed contentedly. This was living.

And then Chrissy called to her parents, telling them that Heather and C.J.'s grandfather was dead.

TWELVE

THE NATIONAL PARK SERVICE INSISTS THAT ALL VISITORS remain on the well-marked paths and wooden boardwalks provided. This is especially true for the areas around popular attractions. Old Faithful Geyser is, for many tourists, the focal point of the park, a must-see on their checklist of national sights. As such, it is surrounded by man-made barriers. On the side nearest the Visitor's Center and Snow Lodge, there are benches built in a semicircular pattern. In the summertime these benches are permanently filled with people waiting for the next regular eruption of the geyser. The weather makes this an impossible pastime in the winter. The far side of Old Faithful is bounded by wooden boardwalks, raised off the ground to allow water from the geyser to pass underneath.

George Ericksen's body was lying in the path of one of

these streams of water. The first ranger on the scene had had extensive first aid training and, luckily, a good stomach. Because George Ericksen, in death, in the natural world he professed to love so much, was only a carcass to the nearly starving scavengers struggling to live through the harsh wilderness winter. When she saw him, Susan was glad she hadn't finished her lunch.

Not that there was much time to think. Heather, surprisingly, took the death better than C.J., who had burst into tears and was willing to be comforted by Susan.

Jed worked to keep the ravens away from what they thought was rightfully theirs, and Susan led the sniffling boy over to a nearby bench, where his sister was waiting, her back resolutely turned to Old Faithful and the body that lay in its shade. "You two sit here. Help will come soon," she said, although she was sure of nothing of the kind. They had met only two other skiers on the way here, a young couple who worked at the lodge and who reported that they zip up, around the geyser, and back each morning for the exercise. Chad and Chrissy had taken off to find help, heading for the Visitor's Center, calling loudly, hoping to attract the attention of the people they could see in the distance.

"Susan . . ." Jed called out to her.

"I'm just going to go talk with my husband." She answered his call with a wave. "You can look after your brother for a few minutes, can't you?"

Heather stared off into the forest surrounding them. "Sure, Mrs. Henshaw. We'll be okay."

But one look at the girl's pale face convinced Susan otherwise. "I'll be right back," she assured them, miraculously skiing back up the slippery trail without falling.

"Do you have any idea if this thing is going to explode soon?" Jed asked her, shaking a pole at an approaching bird.

"Erupt. They don't explode, they erupt. . . ." She glanced quickly at the geyser and the body lying at its base. "Oh, my God!"

"You see what I mean."

And she did. George Ericksen's body was lying directly

in the path the water had taken the last time the geyser had erupted. And it was the same path the liquid would follow when it happened again.

"Should we move him?"

"That's what I was wondering."

"You're not supposed to move a murder victim. Not until the police or whoever is in charge—"

"But it will boil him. Not that the birds haven't already done a lot of damage to the body, but still . . ." Jed protested. "And we don't know that he was murdered, Sue."

"I suppose the same thing would be true in the case of a fatal accident," she mused, staring down at the points of her skis.

"There's no reason to assume that this is a murder," Jed insisted, trying to salvage their vacation.

"There is every reason to assume it's a murder," she argued, steeling herself for a second look at the body and the area. "Jed, don't move!"

"What?" He looked around anxiously.

"Look, we've been making tracks in the snow. We've probably destroyed valuable evidence." She looked at the crisscrossing lines from multiple ski tracks.

"I think it's a little late to worry about that. And we have to keep the animals away."

Susan sighed. He had a point. The ravens were flying around, and every once in a while a coyote peeked out of the forest. "It erupts every hour, so there's probably another coming sometime soon. Let's just hope that help arrives before then." Susan heard a sound behind her and looked around. "Jed! The kids' parents! That's Carlton and Joyce, isn't it?"

A second or two later, Heather spied them and called out, jumping up and waving her arms around. "Mom! Dad! It's Grandpa! He's . . . He's . . ." But apparently she couldn't bring herself to continue.

"We know. We saw Chad and Chrissy. We know," Joyce repeated herself, swinging her arms and pumping her legs even faster.

"Where . . . ?" Carlton began.

"Up here! He's up here," Jed called out, waving to attract attention.

Susan, relieved that Chad had made contact with someone, scooted backward on her skis, hoping to ease Carlton's path to his father. Carlton bettered his wife's speed and slid to a stop at the edge of the snow. The body was only a few feet away.

No one interrupted his moment of silence. "All that blood. It really is him. He really is dead." Carlton looked around. At Susan. At Jed. "I'm sorry. It must seem that I'm babbling. It's just that, after yesterday afternoon, I thought that perhaps your son was mistaken. That it was only another dummy."

"I'm afraid this isn't a dummy. I'm very sorry," Susan said, trying to console him.

"No, it's definitely my father."

Susan watched his reactions carefully, already considering suspects, motives. Carlton pushed the springs that kept his skis on, and walked toward the body. He raised one hand to deflect some spray that was now spurting energetically from the geyser; with the other, he gently touched the dead man's chin—the only part of his body available for touching, the rest being covered either with clothing or blood. "We have to move him," he insisted, without looking up.

"I don't think—"

"This thing has erupted over him once already. We'd better do something before it happens again!"

Jed looked more closely and saw that what the other man said was true. That, in fact, various places on the face bore unmistakable spots where the skin had been badly burned. And he felt a sharp sting when the now seriously splashing geyser threw burning liquid on his own face. There was a breeze blowing in their direction. Did the geyser get more active before or after an eruption? There was little time to worry about that now. Carlton Ericksen had decided to move his father, and he was doing it. Jed reached over to grab the dead man's feet, which were dragging on the ground, and they picked up the body and laid it gently on the boardwalk.

It wasn't an easy task: George Ericksen was a big man, and his clothing was water-soaked.

When they were done, Joyce joined them. Jed and Susan were silent as Joyce and Carlton looked at the dead man. Then Joyce stooped down, pulled a navy scarf from around her neck, and draped it across her father-in-law's face. Susan was relieved when the blood was out of sight. More relieved than she would have expected. It wasn't, after all, as though she had really even known the dead man—or liked what she had known about him. But who had wanted him dead?

She didn't have a lot of time to think about it; a familiar interruption was coming.

"It looks like there's a problem here. Anything a doctor can do?" It was Irving Cockburn, and he wasn't alone. On either side of him skied a young woman.

"There's been an accident. . . ." Jed began.

"We'll go get help," the tallest of the two women offered. The other nodded, and without a word from anyone, they took off.

"Looks like they're not very good in a crisis," Irving commented, turning to watch them. "Some people aren't, of course. And without medical training, they probably don't improve those particular skills."

Susan wondered if their burst of enthusiasm had been inspired by a desire to escape the company in which they found themselves. She knew that's the way she would feel.

"Did he faint? Is it hypothermia?" Irving Cockburn asked, taking off his skis and kneeling down beside the body. "This scarf might be keeping the sun from his eyes, but the man needs air. Of course, I'm only a psychiatrist (Susan thought he said this in the manner of someone hoping to impress by understatement), but I would have thought that common sense—" He stopped abruptly as the scarf came off George's face. "This man is dead!"

Susan found herself smiling at the indignation in his voice.

"And," he continued, "although it might be a little early to mention it, it appears to me that someone has killed him." With a shaking hand, he replaced the scarf.

A doctor who got nervous at the sight of blood? Susan wondered if that explained his choice of speciality.

"Although it could have been a bear attack. They're common in this part of the country, I understand."

Jed started to explain hibernation, and Susan, feeling slightly ill at her second sight of George Ericksen's wounds, decided to take a quick walk. It wouldn't hurt to look around, if she was careful to travel in already made tracks. Technically, of course, they were off the marked trails and breaking national park rules, but in the case of murder, she thought exceptions would be made.

When she returned to the group five minutes later, Jed was explaining that any claw marks to be found on the body were probably not made by bears. "I believe," Jed was saying, "that any marks were caused by the coyote that was here when we approached. And I really . . ." he added, looking at Heather and C.J., "I really think we should talk about this when the family isn't around."

"I don't think you have to talk about it anymore," Susan said, skiing up to them. "I've found the murder weapon."

THIRTEEN

A SMALL SHOVEL HAD BEEN USED TO SPLIT OPEN GEORGE Ericksen's skull. Susan and Jed were discussing it, sitting at their favorite corner table in the bar.

"I wouldn't have thought there were many around. Maybe a few that the rangers need to dig snowmobiles out of drifts, but still, only a few. Are you sure?" Susan asked.

"I've seen them hanging off the day packs of half a dozen

skiers—maybe more. I don't know what they use them for, but they're common equipment. You can even buy them over at the ski shack.''

"So anyone could have one," Susan said.

"Anyone." Her husband confirmed her analysis of the situation.

They were warming their feet in front of the fireplace by their table, discussing the day. Their children, deserted by their friends in this family crisis, had gone on a ranger hike. Susan and Jed were taking advantage of the time alone.

"How do you think the kids are dealing with this?" Susan asked, sounding worried.

"Pretty well. Neither of them was close enough to really examine the wound, thank goodness. And they don't actually know George Ericksen—they only met him two days ago. I think they're upset because Heather and C.J. are upset."

"Hmm. I was surprised by C.J. He didn't strike me as the nervous type—and he's been living in Europe for the past few years. It doesn't seem likely that he would be all that close to his grandfather."

"Surprised me, too, but Chad said that C.J. and his grandfather had a big fight last night. . . ."

"That might explain it. Nobody likes to think that their last words to someone were harsh."

"And it's not just that the man's dead, but that he was killed," Jed added.

"I wonder if it took more than one blow to kill him."

"Getting a little ghoulish now, aren't you?" Jed took his wife's hand.

"It seems to me that it could make a very real difference."

"Why?"

"Because it's a different type of crime if someone got mad and smacked him over the head with a convenient shovel, or if someone snuck up behind him and pounded him until he was dead."

"Maybe." Her husband sounded doubtful.

"One, of course, would probably be premeditated," Susan muttered. Jed smiled. He knew his wife had been reading a lot of mystery novels recently. "Although just heaving the murder weapon into the woods seems rather unplanned—to say the least. You know, I wonder why he walked there."

"You noticed the lack of ski equipment," her husband said.

Susan nodded. "And I've been thinking that somebody should probably search the woods and the trails nearby—and check out all the new tracks in the snow."

"True," Jed agreed, thinking that the influx of rangers, lodge employees, and curious tourists had probably obscured any unusual ski tracks in the area long before now.

"And I wonder who the people investigating will be. The local police seem unlikely."

"Maybe federal marshals. After all, national parks are on federal land."

"That's an interesting thought, but I'm pretty sure some of the rangers have police powers. I know Marnie does."

"Was she there?"

"I don't know. I should have noticed." Susan paused. "They really tried to keep us away, didn't they?" She thought back to the way her family and all of the Ericksens, with the exception of Carlton, who would have been impossible to contain, had been ordered, by a very young man, back to the area where they had eaten their lunch. Susan, in fact, had found her lunch box and sat down and consumed most of her sandwich. It was frozen, but she was so starved, it hadn't mattered. "I wonder why."

"It could have had nothing to do with the murder. They may merely have been trying to protect the area surrounding the geyser. All those people trampling around were certainly doing some damage. . . ."

"But it's murder," Susan protested. "That's more important than some tracks. . . ."

"In the first place, they weren't sure it was a murder when they arrived—no matter what they think now. And remember, protecting geysers is their job." Jed made his point and was silent.

Susan, too, held her tongue. She was thinking over the

morning, trying to remember exactly what had happened and who was where. It had all been very confusing. Some time after Carlton and Joyce had arrived and some time before Joyce and one of the rangers had gotten into the back of a snowmobile and ridden off with C.J. and Heather, the rest of the Ericksen family had appeared. She closed her eyes and tried to remember how they were grouped and in what order.

She was so accustomed to thinking of the family as a group. . . .

The problem was that they had arrived together—almost. She seemed to remember that the two women, Jane and Charlotte, had appeared before Darcy. And she might be right about that, but what about Phyllis? Had she been with Darcy? Unless she had skied out to Old Faithful alone. Or, possibly, all five had left the lodge together, and their order of arrival was only a result of their skiing ability. And where was Randy?

"Tired? Want to skip dinner?"

"Do you think George was hiking alone?" Susan asked her question without bothering to answer his.

"We haven't seen many people hiking alo—"

"He was alone yesterday when I fell down, though, so maybe he liked to be alone," Susan muttered.

"You're ignoring me," her husband announced. "And I'm getting hungry," he added.

"I should write all this down." Susan continued to talk and to ignore him.

Jed motioned to the waitress. Certainly they would serve some sort of munchies here.

"Good thinking." Susan applauded his action. "She'll be able to get us some paper," she added, and asked the girl to do just that.

"And a menu," Jed suggested before she could rush off.

"A menu? That's great. I'm always hungry here," Susan said.

"You want paper and a menu?" the girl asked, appearing to think they might continue to add items to the list.

"Exactly."

"No, we just want a menu," Jed said. "I'll go out to the gift shop and buy a notebook."

"That's an even better idea," Susan approved. "We'll probably need a notebook before this is over."

"We don't usually serve sandwiches this late in the evening," the waitress commented, handing Susan the stiff cardboard.

Susan glanced at the list of appetizers and ordered a hefty assortment.

"You've been skiing," the waitress discovered.

"Yes, how—" Susan began, her thoughts leaving the murder, and now looking for a clue to the girl's perception.

"Because you're starving. Nothing makes you hungrier than skiing."

"But you don't gain any weight because of all the exercise, right?"

"I've gained twelve pounds in the last two months, and I ski at least ten miles a day," the girl replied, leaving to get their order.

Susan had stopped thinking about that comment and had her Ericksens in order before Jed's return. "Just let me write this down and then we can talk," she insisted, grabbing the notebook from his hand and making her list. "There," she finished, writing Phyllis and circling it with a flourish. "Because I don't have any idea when she arrived or who she was with," she explained. "But I think I have everyone else in order. Let me show you; maybe you remember something differently. . . . Jed?" He wasn't paying attention. "Jed," she repeated.

"Sorry, Sue. I was thinking about something else." He leaned across the table to his wife and lowered his voice. "Has it occurred to you that the only person in the Ericksen family who is reacting to this situation normally is Heather?"

"No one else is upset?" Susan thought back to the shocked looks on the faces of the family as, one by one, they were informed of their patriarch's death. "Shocked, but not sad." She said her thoughts aloud.

"Exactly."

"But that might not be all that unusual. Maybe shock is the normal first reaction. Maybe sadness and all the feelings of loss come later."

"That might be true, except . . ."

" 'Except'?" Susan repeated.

"Except that I saw Jane and Charlotte in the gift shop just now, and they were giggling."

"Giggling?"

"Laughing, actually." He leaned even closer. "They were standing in the corner of the gift shop where those cards with the captions on the photographs of bears—"

"The ones that Chad thought were so funny?" Last night Susan had found her son laughing hysterically at a photo of a bear eating a picnic lunch.

"Exactly. Anyway, Charlotte and Jane were laughing rather more than you would expect of two young women whose father had just been killed."

Susan was silent, thinking about this. "People react differently to tragic events."

"They were laughing at the cards that showed the bears with skis superimposed on their feet—at jokes about skiing accidents."

"Those cards are pretty funny. And I suppose it could be a shocked reaction."

"But—"

"Mrs. Henshaw—Susan—my mother would like to speak to you."

"She . . ." Susan looked up into the earnest eyes of Darcy Ericksen, eyes filled with tears and rimmed in red.

"She would like to see you as soon as possible."

"Right away." Susan stood up, and took the young man's hands as tears ran down his cheeks.

FOURTEEN

SHE FOLLOWED THE BOY THROUGH THE LONG HALLWAYS of the lodge to a room on the second floor where, after knocking on the door and calling out, "Mother," he left her. Susan waited for the door to open. And when it did, she was surprised by his mother's appearance. Phyllis seemed in better control than her son.

"Mrs. Henshaw—Susan, I'm so glad you could come" were the woman's first words. Susan felt as if she'd been invited to have tea with a community group, rather than this . . . this what? she wondered. Exactly why was she here? But the tea party was beginning; if she wanted to discover any answers, she'd better pay attention.

"Won't you sit down?" Phyllis pointed to one of the twin beds in the small room.

Susan sat, wondering if she was sitting where George Ericksen had spent the last night of his life.

"Would you like something to drink?"

Susan, surprised, glanced in the direction Phyllis had pointed. She was even more surprised to find that the top shelf of the wardrobe had been converted to a small bar. In addition to a dozen heavy hand-blown glasses, Susan counted six bottles: two of expensive Scotch, one each of bonded bourbon, Myers rum, cognac, and a brand of liquor that she had thought was available only on one or two Caribbean islands. Back in their own room, she and Jed reserved that particular shelf for dirty laundry.

"My husband believed in maintaining certain standards

in his life. Even in the wilderness, there can be civilization, he used to say.''

Susan had visions of British aristocrats drinking tea from porcelain cups off damask linens in Kenya at the turn of the century. It didn't seem an apt analogy. "Of course," she agreed vaguely. "But I just had a drink with Jed, thank you. How can I help?" she asked, noticing that Phyllis didn't get anything for herself, nor was there a poured drink anywhere in the room. "Your son didn't explain. . . ." she continued. This time the vagueness was intentional. Maybe Phyllis just didn't want to be alone after this tragedy, maybe there were some chores (clothing to pack up? phone calls to make?) with which she needed help.

"We're going to stay at the lodge until the storm everyone is talking about has come and gone. I've spoken with the rangers, and it would be difficult, if not impossible, to leave right now. And I think George would have wanted us to give Heather and C.J. some pleasure." She wiped a tear from her eye and fell silent.

"I'm sure you're right," Susan said, more to fill the silence than because of any personal conviction. "What can I do for you?"

"I wondered," Phyllis began, "if you would tell me exactly what happened at Old Faithful today. I know I could ask Heather or C.J., but they're so young, and they certainly wouldn't be as accurate as you. Besides, they're really just children and they've been through so much stress already. . . ."

"Of course," Susan agreed. "You want to know what I saw?"

"Exactly. 'What you saw,' as you put it." Phyllis smiled encouragingly.

Susan felt as if she was being asked for "the facts, ma'am, just the facts," and she felt a little foolish trying to comply. She started with Heather's announcement of her grandfather's death, and ended with Phyllis's appearance. It wasn't an easy story to tell, but she did it slowly and carefully. It took almost half an hour, and when she was done, she wished she hadn't been so hasty in refusing a drink. Her throat was dry and her head ached.

Phyllis had leaned back against the headboard of the bed and closed her eyes for the last half of Susan's recital. At times, Susan noticed, the other woman had pressed her lips together tightly. Otherwise, there had been no movement, no response. After a few moments of silence, Susan sighed loudly. Phyllis opened her eyes wide, and she smiled gently.

"You're very observant."

Susan didn't know what to say, and Phyllis spoke before she had a chance to think of something.

"My grandson tells me that you're famous for solving crimes in your hometown in Connecticut."

Susan glowed slightly. Was it possible that Chad had been bragging about her? Was it possible that he found her something more than an embarrassment?

"I wonder if you could see your way to helping us? If you could help solve this crime?"

"I . . . I'm on vacation. And there will be other people . . . professional . . ." Susan protested, flattered but confused. "I really . . ." She struggled to put her thoughts in order. "I don't think this is anything I can do. I don't see how I can help you," she ended weakly.

"You could help. You could talk to whoever investigates this. You could just keep your eyes open, couldn't you?"

It flashed through Susan's mind that this woman had been reading the same mysteries she had. She glanced at the table between the two beds. The available literature was certainly more elevating than Agatha Christie. There were a few current books on the environment, a gigantic tome on thermal activity, and a bestselling scientific/philosophical work. Susan knew many people who had bought this book, herself included; she didn't know anyone who had actually finished reading it.

"I would be so grateful to you—our whole family would," Phyllis continued, wiping a tear from the corner of her eye. "Not that we'd expect you to ruin your vacation or anything. If you could just help us . . ."

"Well, of course, anything I can do . . ." Susan's voice dwindled. She should hire someone to follow her around and hit her over the head every time she made this particular statement. Then maybe she'd learn. "How stupid am I? Let me count the ways?" she muttered to herself.

"Excuse me?" Phyllis Ericksen seemed startled by this lyrical outburst.

"I'm sorry. I—" She was saved from inventing an explanation by a knock on the door.

"Come in."

Charlotte had gotten over her giggles. The face that appeared in the open doorway had mascara dripping down its pale cheeks, lips licked so free of makeup that they looked almost white, and a nose worn red, presumably by the crumpled tissues Charlotte clasped in her hands.

"Come in, my dear. Are you all alone? Where's Jane?" Phyllis put her arm around her daughter's shoulder and guided her to a chair. "You shouldn't be alone right now. Let me get you something to drink."

"I'll get it." Susan jumped up, wanting to be useful. She wasn't sure whether to leave or not. There was certainly no way for the other women to have any privacy in a room this size while she was present. She poured out a large brandy and handed it to Charlotte. "Maybe I should leave," she suggested, nodding to accept the thanks Charlotte offered.

"Well, I think . . ." Phyllis seemed not to know what to think. She looked intently at her daughter as she sipped the brandy.

"Did she say she would help us, Mother?"

Susan looked more intently at Charlotte this time. She appeared to be doing an Oliver Twist imitation, so humble and plaintive did her voice sound. This couldn't be real. She felt a moment's irritation that sparked an answer to their request. "Yes," she said slowly. "Yes." She spoke more quickly the second time. "I'd be happy to help in any way I can. Any way at all."

Phyllis Ericksen clasped both of Susan's hands firmly in her own. "Thank you. I know what an imposition this is—

what we're asking of you—and I truly don't know how to express my appreciation.''

"Maybe if you talk to Marnie Mackay—the ranger who's heading the investigation.'' Charlotte's appreciation appeared to be of a more practical nature.

"I don't think we have to tell Mrs. Henshaw what to do. She's done this before, remember,'' Phyllis admonished her daughter.

"Of course,'' Charlotte agreed quickly. "Thank you so much.'' She fell into line with her mother's spoken sentiments.

It was time to end all this. "I'd better get to work.'' Susan stood up, remembering too late that her feet hurt. She flinched, determining to ignore the pain—in public at least. "And I will talk to Marnie as soon as possible; I think your daughter is right. That's an excellent place to begin. But I had better get back to my room now. I want to make some notes . . . and things.'' She ended more weakly than she had begun, but no one appeared to notice.

"Wonderful. You'll let us know what you come up with, won't you?'' Charlotte asked.

"I think—''

"Just go about this the way you would any one of your investigations.'' Phyllis again appeared irritated by her daughter's suggestion. "And please let us know how we can help. My husband would want the truth about his death to be known. He was a very honest man. In a way, your investigation will be a sort of memorial to him.''

"I . . .'' Susan was saved from making up a final polite comment when Phyllis pulled a handkerchief from the pocket of her wool knickers and began to weep quietly. "I'll talk to you tomorrow,'' Susan promised, moving to the door.

"This has been a terrible strain on Mother,'' Charlotte said. "But I can't thank you enough. The entire family appreciates it,'' she added, almost pushing Susan from the room.

Susan was left standing alone in the hallway, trying to reconcile the anguish Charlotte was apparently feeling over her father's death and the conversation she had heard in the rest room yesterday. She walked, or rather limped, back to the bar where she had left Jed. He was sitting in the same place. The steaming mug in his hand was probably a different one.

"How many of those have you had?"

"It's coffee," he answered, standing up. "I've been trying to keep from falling asleep. Have you been with the Ericksens all this time?"

"Yes. Did we miss our dinner reservations?"

"Yes, but everything is a little topsy-turvy tonight, so we can go right in. The kids are in there already—telling Jerry and Kathleen about everything that happened today."

"C.J. and Heather?"

"They're eating in their rooms, according to Chrissy."

"Look, there are seats, we can eat with the kids," Susan said.

"We'd better not talk—" Jed began.

"I don't even want to think about the Ericksens right now," his wife agreed, smiling as she walked to her children.

FIFTEEN

SUSAN PROBABLY SHOULD HAVE FALLEN ASLEEP THE IN-
stant her head touched the pillow. After all, she had skied almost a dozen miles, found a dead man, and become involved in an investigation of his death. It had been a busy day, but she'd had a nap of over an hour and a half during the ranger talk. So when she lay down beside her already

snoring husband, she found she couldn't sleep. She hated lying in bed waiting for sleep to come. She glanced at the tiny travel alarm on the bedside table. Squinting, she could barely see the shining numerals. She'd give herself fifteen minutes. Then, if she was still awake, she'd get up and . . .

That stopped her. At home she'd go to the basement and run a load of wash, or sit down in the kitchen and make out a grocery list for next week; there were always chores awaiting her attention. And if that didn't work, she could drink a glass of Chablis in a warm bubble bath. But she was in the middle of a national park in the middle of winter; no chores, no bubble bath, and the closest wine was in the bar, which would require a trip outside, and she might find it closed at this hour. Susan sighed, punched her pillow, and rolled over. Sleep, damn it! she muttered.

It didn't work, and that didn't surprise her. Carefully, trying not to wake her husband, she got up and went into the bathroom. Long underwear dripped from the shower rod; wool socks were lying on the floor in the corner, their red dye oozing onto the white towels underneath; every spot on the tiny counter surrounding the sink was filled with hand cream, face cream, shaving supplies, brushes for hair and teeth, Ben-Gay, bottles of aspirin, and all the other necessities of life. This was no place to relax. She yanked on a flannel shirt that Jed had draped over the back of the door. It was large enough to cover most of her nightgown; she hadn't brought a robe. Back in the dark of the bedroom, she scrounged around and found one of the door keys. Quietly she left the room, tiptoeing out into the hall. After all, she thought, closing the door gently behind her, how many people would be awake and about at this hour? She turned and found herself face-to-face with over a dozen Japanese tourists. One or two giggled as they hurried on their way. Susan sighed, tried to smile graciously, and walked down the hall to the outside door.

The instant the door parted company with the jamb, she changed her mind about even a short look outside. It was well below zero, and frigid wind swirled around her naked ankles like dancing knives. She shut the door and spun around. This time she was alone. She walked slowly down the hall; she had noticed some public rooms at the end of the corridor opposite their room. Now was as good a time to explore as any.

There were three rooms. She knew at least one of them contained a soda machine; Chad had been asking her for quarters ever since they arrived at the hotel. She wrapped the shirt more tightly around herself and entered the largest of the rooms. It was unoccupied. A group of chairs and a sofa or two furnished the large room, as well as two vending machines, one for soda and one offering candy and packaged snacks. Susan rummaged in the shirt pockets; she was a little hungry herself. There was nothing else to see except for a bulletin board announcing the topics of the rangers' meetings, various ski trips, and other activities. Susan wished she had known about this sooner. Now that she had gotten into the routine of the place, all this had nothing to offer. She walked to the next room and found it empty except for a humming ice machine. She glanced out the window into the darkness. Who could possibly need ice with all this snow around?

The final room turned out to be a well-equipped laundry. One wall was lined with a half dozen washing machines; the other displayed an equal number of dryers. Susan smiled, noticing that the two farthest from the door were full. The spinning had stopped, and the owner had either forgotten or decided to wait till morning to pick up his clothing. She'd know who it was tomorrow; he or she would be the one wearing very wrinkled clothing.

So what was she going to do now? There was always the upstairs of the lodge to be explored. But she had heard footsteps over her head out in the hall; it sounded as though people were awake up there. Did she really want anyone else to see her dressed like this? Did she really want to lie in bed, waiting to sleep? She started for the stairs, only to be met by a couple more outlandishly dressed than herself. And they didn't appear to be the least bit embarrassed about it all.

"If you hit me one more time, I'll push you into Old Faithful the next time it goes off!" threatened a voice from the second floor.

"You and who else?" This jibe was followed by the appearance of a young man in his late teens or early twenties wearing a one-piece red union suit and bright blue wool socks. His long hair fell over his shoulders. In one hand he carried a ski pole with a bright red bandanna tied to one end.

"I mean it, you dirty rotten—" The girl stopped her threatening when she reached the bottom of the stairway and saw Susan there. "Oh . . . ." She appeared not to know what to say, then she looked down at herself, as if wondering, for the first time, what impression her clothing would make. She was wearing a union suit, also, only hers was international orange, and she had accessorized this remarkable garment in the following manner: A green bandanna was tied around her neck, a neon pink fanny pack accentuated her admittedly small waistline, the purple and gray hiking boots on her feet had red socks peeking out of their tops, and on her head she wore a cowboy hat remarkably similar to that affected by Dr. Cockburn. She seemed happily unaware that, somewhere in New York's most prestigious cemetery, fashion editors were turning over in their graves. "Hi! We didn't mean to disturb anybody." She smiled.

"I'm sure you didn't." Susan smiled back, trying to convey the message that she, too, had been young once.

"We'll be more quiet," the young man promised, putting his arm around the girl's shoulders. "Why don't we go to bed now, hon?"

"Do you really think that's more . . ." the girl began, starting to giggle again.

Susan hurried on up the stairs, leaving them to their antics. Wondering what she was going to run into next, she stopped at the top and peered around the corner and down the hall. There was no one in sight. She didn't know whether to be disappointed or relieved. She walked slowly down the corridor. Someone was snoring in the room next to the stairwell, and farther down the hall a baby was crying, possibly the

same one she had seen earlier riding happily on his father's
back while he skied along the trail. Susan spent a moment
thinking about Kathleen, who was skiing all day and nursing
Bananas most of the night—she had looked exhausted at dinner and had again skipped the lecture. When Susan got to
the end of the hallway, she finally had to admit to herself
why she hadn't been asleep. The last five rooms, divided on
either side of the hallway, belonged to the Ericksens. For
some reason, the senior Ericksens were staying in the main
lodge, and the rest of the family was here.

She slowed down and stared at the five doors. She was
positive of the location, as there had been some room shifting
two days ago when her children and Heather and C.J. had
decided to regroup. To keep the Henshaws together on the
same floor, two very nice couples had agreed to switch rooms
to the second floor. Susan and Jed has assisted their move.
And out of curiosity, she had noted which rooms belonged
to which Ericksen. She leaned against the wall now, thinking
about it.

On the right side of the hall, the room closest to her was
occupied by Charlotte. Next was her sister Jane's room, and
at the end of the hallway, by the other set of stairs, was the
room shared by Darcy and his friend. Where was Randy?
she wondered briefly. She hadn't seen him all day. She stared
at the three rooms. Light coming from under Darcy's indicated that he was still up. There was no light from either of
his sisters' rooms. On the other side of the hallway, both
rooms were dark. The nearest belonged to Joyce and Carlton,
the other to Jon and Beth.

Susan sighed and realized how sleepy she actually was.
She mentally shook herself. This was no way to find out
anything. She was acting foolishly. Time to go to bed. She
had a lot to do in the morning, and she was going to do it
without ruining her family's vacation. She started down the
stairway and would have gone back to her room and to bed
if the door to Darcy's room hadn't opened, if she hadn't
heard the voice. And maybe she shouldn't have been eavesdropping, but it's very difficult to resist such an opportunity,

especially when her own name was mentioned in the first sentence anyone spoke.

"Do you think this Susan Henshaw will really be able to help us, Charlotte?"

She assumed the voice was Darcy's.

"I think she was thrilled to be asked. I think she'll do just what we hope—"

"Shouldn't we—"

Was this Jane? Susan wondered.

"We shouldn't do anything except what she asks us to do. Mama wasn't very happy with me when I volunteered information, and I daresay she is right. Mrs. Henshaw is bound to ask a lot of questions, and we should answer as well as we are able."

"Whatever you say," Darcy agreed, speaking slowly. Susan imagined him looking down at the floor.

"This is harder on you than on the rest of us," one of his sisters commiserated. "Are you going to be okay? Is there anything we can do?"

"No, I'm fine. Yesterday I really didn't think I was going to make it, but today . . ." He paused, and Susan could almost feel his deep breath. "Today I woke up and knew what I had to do. I'll be fine. There will be time to mourn later."

SIXTEEN

IT WAS AN ENIGMATIC COMMENT, NOT WHAT SUSAN needed to lull her back to sleep. But there was nothing for her to do at this time of the night . . . except, of course, the laundry. There were those wet socks and a couple of cotton turtlenecks. . . . It wasn't a hot bath, but anything was better than wandering the halls like a lost soul. And she had a lot to think about. She hurried down the stairs and back to her room.

She unlocked the door quietly, but Jed's snores were assurance that she didn't have to worry about waking him up. It took but a few minutes to gather the laundry, grab her wallet, and leave. She tiptoed down the hall to the laundry room, hoping the Japanese tourists were snug in their beds. The laundry room was damp and warm, and as Susan filled the machine, she felt herself getting sleepier. She leaned against the humming equipment and looked through the circular windows into the stationary dryers. She was going to need to use one of those machines herself. Not having nerve enough to merely dump the load on any convenient space, Susan opened the door of the dryer closest to her machine and began folding the still warm clothing.

Whoever had abandoned his or her clothing had excellent taste and an ample income, Susan thought, examining labels from some of the most exclusive ski shops and men's stores in New York City. She ran the fine Egyptian cotton of an elaborate pullover through her fingers; it was almost a pleasure to fold them. There were nearly a dozen sweaters, and they made a colorful pile when she was finished. She was admiring her work when Kathleen walked into the room.

"What are you doing here?"

"What are you doing up at this hour?" Kathleen answered her question with a question.

"I couldn't sleep. Too much has happened today, I guess. But what about you? You're not even staying in this building! Why are you up and dressed at . . ." She paused, planning to check her watch before she realized that she wasn't wearing one.

"At one-seventeen A.M.," Kathleen read off her wrist. "I'm here to get something to eat from the machine. The dining room is locked up, the gift shop deserted, and I'm starving. I finished feeding Bananas ten minutes ago, but

I knew there was no way I was going to get any sleep unless I had something to eat, too. So here I am.''

Susan glanced at the churning washing machine. ''So let's go see what those machines have to offer,'' she suggested.

''I'm hoping for peanut butter cups,'' Kathleen confessed.

''Or Almond Joys,'' Susan said, following her friend down the hall.

''No one does laundry in the middle of the night,'' Kathleen insisted when they were seated on the couch, munching candy bars.

''Someone else did. I just finished folding his stuff,'' Susan argued. ''Besides, where else could I go? I didn't want to wake Jed up by turning on the light and reading—and there are others up,'' she added, and explained about hearing the Ericksens.

''I noticed the lights on in the rooms on the end of the second floor. I didn't know that was where the entire family was staying, though.''

''Not the entire family. Phyllis Ericksen is in the main lodge.''

''Surely they wouldn't leave her alone tonight,'' Kathleen said, picking the chocolate off the top of her candy and popping it into her mouth.

''Probably not.'' Susan was silent, thinking about the conversation she had heard earlier. ''Maybe Joyce or Carlton is with her.

''Phyllis asked me to help investigate the murder tonight,'' she added.

''How did she know you had experience with this sort of thing?''

''Evidently Chad told C.J. about it. I was surprised.''

''Surprised?''

''Surprised that he had been bragging about me. Usually he's pretty negative about anything I do—or have done.''

''I'm going to have some potato chips,'' Kathleen said, getting up and heading for the machine. ''Are you going to help her?''

''Sure. Oh, I'm not going to get so involved that it ruins

our vacation, but I'll do whatever I can. Don't you think I should?'' she asked when Kathleen didn't answer immediately.

''Probably. I was just thinking about what a strange family they are.'' She ripped open the chip bag. ''Even more now that they're all together.''

''What do you mean?''

''Well, we got here three days before you did, remember. And the elder Ericksens arrived the same afternoon.''

''And you noticed them right away?'' Susan asked.

''They stand out in a crowd,'' Kathleen said.

''What did they do?''

''It's not really what they do, but how they do it. You know, some people just act like they expect attention.''

''Did you talk with them at all?''

''Sure. We all sat together in front of the fireplace in the lobby the first night. Phyllis fell in love with Bananas. She said he was one of the handsomest babies she had ever seen and that he reminded her of her youngest son when he was an infant.''

''That's Darcy,'' Susan mused, taking a chip from the bag that was offered. ''He's really what used to be called 'the apple of her eye,' isn't he?''

''I guess so. She talked about nursing him, and how I should enjoy my son now, and that her heart was broken when her husband insisted on sending the boy to nursery school very young. . . .''

''She complained about her husband?'' Susan asked, surprised.

''Not really. She said that he was, of course, doing the best thing for his son. She actually made a big effort not to sound like she was criticizing.''

''Because George was around?''

''I don't think so. George, Jerry, and that pretty girl ranger were busy looking at maps of the ski trails and talking about wax and stuff. I don't think any of them was paying attention to what we said.''

''Did you talk about anything else?''

"She explained about the family reunion—that they were all getting together to celebrate their anniversary. I thought that was a little strange, to tell the truth."

"Why?"

"Do couples usually celebrate their anniversary with a family party?"

"Why not?"

"Well, you would think they would want to be alone together, wouldn't you?"

"I would, but our families are with us all the time. Phyllis and George's children and grandchildren have been living all over—even in France. It's probably a great treat to see them all together." Susan didn't end as positively as she had begun. After all, how many families celebrate anniversaries with a group squabble? A drowned effigy? A murder? So much for the great treat idea. "Whatever they were expecting, this wasn't the reunion that they planned, was it?" she ended.

"Maybe not. But someone planned on having this happen," Kathleen insisted.

"The murderer."

Kathleen nodded her agreement.

"One of the family." Susan peered into the now empty snack bag.

"More than likely."

"I wonder which one." Susan got up and headed back to the snack machine. "Want something else?" She waved at the selection available.

"Sure. How about more chips? Or those cheese things?"

"Why not both?" Susan suggested, laughing and pouring quarters into the machine. "You know, there aren't a whole lot of suspects for this murder. . . . I counted seven. It might not be difficult to figure it out."

"Phyllis, Jane, Charlotte, Darcy, Carlton, Jon . . . unless you count Joyce . . ."

"I was including Randy . . . although maybe we should include Joyce."

"Randy . . . the lover who has disappeared," Kathleen mused.

"He hasn't been around. . . ."

"Oh, he's disappeared, all right. I was talking with one of the maids who cleans here—a very nice girl—and she said that all the staff were talking about it. Evidently he just vanished. The assumption is that he skied out of the park—he left everything but some clothing and his equipment behind."

"You're kidding!"

"No. There was that huge fight at dinner. . . ."

"Yes. We were there, remember?"

"And the next morning the maid noticed that Randy was gone. Darcy was more than a little upset and ran around yelling and questioning everybody—that's how all the help knows about it—but he hasn't returned."

"Why do they think he skied out?"

"Well, the snowcoaches are booked for months in advance, so he didn't go that way. And you can't rent a snowmobile in the park, you have to rent it outside or bring in one you own, and he was supposed to be a strong skier. . . ."

"But to ski fifty miles!"

"Tough, but not impossible. And he might have hitched a ride on a snowmobile, come to think of it. . . ."

"We should find out," Susan insisted.

"You're right."

"You're going to help me investigate!" Susan grinned.

"I can't resist," Kathleen answered with a smile. "Besides, this time I'll get to be Hercule Poirot. You'll run around and do all the legwork, and I shall sit back at the lodge and use the little gray cells—and nurse Bananas."

SEVENTEEN

" 'TIME TO MOURN LATER.' THAT'S PRECISELY WHAT HE said." Susan was sitting up in bed, blankets wrapped around her knees, talking to Jed while he shaved in the adjacent bathroom.

"And you think—"

"I think this was a planned murder, a family-planned murder," Susan said, not giving him a chance to finish his sentence. She bounced up, with more energy than she usually felt in the morning. "You know, Jed, this may be a lot like *Murder on the Orient Express*."

"I remember that movie. . . ."

"It's a book."

"I only saw the movie." He wiped the last of the shaving cream off his face with a washcloth, and peered around the corner at his wife. "That's the one where everyone in the family gets together to kill one person—they all stab him, right?"

"Yes . . ."

"But only one blow killed George Ericksen. . . ."

"Not exactly like the book, Jed. I didn't say that."

"But . . ."

"What I'm thinking of is some sort of conspiracy. A murder that was planned by a group of people, carried out, and covered up by the entire group."

"But if they're trying to cover up, why ask you to help solve it?" He pulled a heavy wool sweater over his flannel shirt.

"Because they think I'm going to screw up the investigation in some way, or that my investigating will interfere with the official one, or something like that. They think I'm an incompetent bored housewife, with some sort of delusion that I can actually solve crimes. They're banking on my bungling it."

"How can that be? They didn't know you were going to be here to bungle up everything."

"What?" It was more a shriek than a question. "Are you saying that I can't solve crimes? Don't you remember—"

"I remember. I just don't understand how they could have planned on you . . . getting involved."

"Jed, of course they didn't. They just found us here, and probably Chad told them about my investigations in the past, and they were smart enough to take advantage of the situation." She frowned. "Why people think housewives are stupid . . . well, the only way to prove them wrong is to solve this," she muttered, more to herself than her husband. "Kathleen and I were talking about it last night."

"Hon . . ."

"I know. We're here on vacation." She smiled brightly at her husband. "Don't worry. I'll just poke around a little, ask a few questions. We'll still have our vacation." She glanced at the clock. "Look at the time. I'd better get dressed if we're going to meet the kids for breakfast." She started to do just that, getting up and yanking open drawers. "Why don't you check on the kids?"

"Good idea." He headed out into the hall, completely undeceived by his wife. She was going to investigate, and she was going to do it seriously. One of the things that had impressed him about her when they first met was her determination, her ability to get things done despite obstacles. It had gotten them through more than one crisis in their lives; of course, it had also caused one or two. He frowned, almost running into Chad, who, since turning thirteen, had found it difficult to walk slowly.

"Hi!"

Jed looked at his son. It wasn't like him to sound perky in the morning. "Hi, Chad. Where's C.J.?"

The boy's shoulders slumped. "Who knows? Probably moping around somewhere."

"Well, Chad . . ." his father began.

"I know. I know. He's had a terrible shock, his grandfather's been killed, et cetera, et cetera. It's just that he's so upset. I swear, Dad, he cried all night. I don't know . . . maybe I'll act like that when Pop dies, but . . . Oh, I don't know." Chad hung his head.

Jed put his arm around his son's shoulders; luckily, the boy hadn't come into close contact with loss before, and he didn't know how to accept it. "He'll come out of it. Everyone deals with death in his own way. But, you know, it shouldn't have to ruin your vacation. We could ask the Ericksens for another room switch. I'm sure they'd understand. . . ."

Chad took a deep breath and looked his father straight in the eye. "I don't desert my friends when they need me. I'll stay where I am."

Chrissy and Heather's appearance put a stop to the conversation before Jed had time to decide whether Chad's response was admirable or just immature.

"Hi, Dad . . . Chad. Where's Mom? Aren't we going to breakfast? I'm starving."

"Good morning, Mr. Henshaw." Heather's greeting was decidedly subdued; she was old enough to understand that certain things were expected of her in this situation. " 'Bye, Chrissy. I'll talk to you after breakfast."

"Okay. See you in the lobby in about an hour," Chrissy agreed, as Heather turned and headed up the stairs. "She thinks she should be with her family right now," she explained to her father.

"That's what C.J. thought," Chad said, not to be outdone by the older teens.

"So where is Mother? I'm really hungry."

"Right behind you," Susan said, appearing in the doorway, skis in hand. "I thought you didn't eat breakfast."

"All this skiing is making me hungry," her daughter explained. "Are we going to ski over to the restaurant?"

"I don't see why not."

"Good idea," Jed chimed in. "I'll just get my skis. . . ."

The next few minutes were obviously going to be spent sorting through equipment. "I'll go get a table for us all," Susan volunteered, hurrying away before anyone could ask her help in their search for shoes, mittens, and all the other items one's family can't find without Mother. They should learn to do these things for themselves, she decided. Besides, she was hoping for a chance to speak with Kathleen; they had gotten tired before there was time to formulate a plan last night.

"You mean this morning," Jerry corrected her as she mentioned her errand, slipping in beside him at a large table. "I thought I was dreaming when Kath walked into the room carrying her skis at two A.M.!"

"We—"

"She's not getting enough sleep, Sue. The baby keeps her up all night, and she absolutely refuses to give up skiing during the day. . . ."

"She looks wonderful," Susan insisted, managing to interrupt.

Jerry stopped being the concerned husband long enough to beam at Susan. "She does, doesn't she?"

Susan just laughed, waving for the rest of her family to join her. "I assume we're all eating breakfast together, aren't we?"

"Kathleen thought it might be a good idea. I came down early to get the table. I was afraid that we were taking the space reserved for the Ericksen family, but the waiter said that the lodge was arranging for them to eat privately."

The Henshaw family's appearance was followed by Kathleen, cuddling little Bananas. Chloe followed, an infant seat, crocheted afghan, and half a dozen stuffed toys dangling from her arms.

"Guess who's starting cereal today?" the proud mother asked.

"I'm not giving up my sausage and French toast for anyone," Jed answered factiously, handing a bright red plush lobster that had fallen on the floor to Chloe. "I assume this is part of your burden."

"Oui, monsieur."

Susan wasn't delighted with the shy smile Chloe gave her husband. Or his response.

"Why don't you sit down right here." He pulled out the seat next to him. "And we can just pile Bananas's toys on the windowsill," he suggested, helping to stow the equipment away.

"Oh, Chloe, if you're going to sit there, I think I'd better trade with Jed so Bananas and I are near his things. You don't mind, do you, Jed?" Kathleen asked, oblivious to what she was doing. "And if Susan could sit on the other side of me, we won't bother anyone with our little nursery . . . and we can talk," she ended in a whisper to the other woman.

Susan sat down, not looking at her husband. It was so tacky to gloat.

"What are you going to do today?" she asked Kathleen, after giving her order to the waitress.

"I've been thinking about spending some time in the lobby—it gives Bananas such an opportunity for mental stimulation." She winked at her friend. "And I want to offer my condolences to Mrs. Ericksen. She only has her family here, which might be difficult for her, and she was so nice about Bananas. I feel it would be rude not to say anything, don't you?"

"Absolutely!" Susan was sure Kathleen would use the opportunity to gather information.

"What are you . . . ?"

"We're going to Mystic Falls," Jed announced, not allowing Kathleen to finish her question. "Chrissy, Chad, and I were just talking about it," he added with a look at his wife.

"One of the rangers told us that it's a beautiful trail," Chrissy insisted. "He might even be up that way today—at least that's what he said," she ended.

"If it's what the rangers recommend," Susan said without even smiling at her daughter's latest crush.

"Mystic Falls . . . I heard . . . overheard . . . some people talking about that place while I was walking Bananas in the hallway last evening." Chloe was very enthusiastic. "They said it was the most beautiful place they had been in the park. And that it was a nice ski trip up there!"

"Well, this is your morning off," Jerry reminded her.

"If you would like to go with us . . ." Jed offered.

Susan now regretted the space between them.

"Oh, I would love to. If you don't mind." She looked anxiously at Susan.

What else could she say? "We'd love to have you."

EIGHTEEN

"I'VE BEEN ON SKIS SINCE I WAS A LITTLE GIRL. IN THE part of Switzerland where I was brought up, this is the way we traveled to and from school and how we did our chores in the winter."

"You certainly look comfortable—which is more than I can say for any of us." Jed followed his self-deprecating remark with an embarrassed grin.

You should be embarrassed! Susan kept the accusation to herself. It wasn't like Jed to act so infatuated with children— truly a girl young enough to be his daughter, as the cliché said. Susan stopped pushing herself and dropped behind her family. Heavy snow was falling from a gray sky, and as the rest of the group skied out of sight, Susan was left alone in the woods. She could hear the sound of nearby water rushing between rocks and ice floes, kept moving by the warmth of a nearby hot spring. There were gentle plops as snow piled on frozen branches, and bent them low enough to drop their load onto the ground. Her skis *shush shush*ed along the parallel tracks in the snow between tall ponderosa pines. And suddenly nothing mattered. Not the Ericksens, not the murder, not her children's adolescent angst, not Jed and Chloe. She was in the woods, and it was beautiful. She was smiling happily when a buffalo strolled onto the trail in front of her.

She had been in the park for three days, she had read about the dangers of wild animals several times each day, rangers had been insistent and persistent, bringing up the subject repeatedly, warning and explaining. Now, faced with over a ton of shaggy brown animal less than twenty feet from her, she had no idea what to do. Fortunately, neither did the animal. Or maybe Susan appeared a little eccentric in her carefully chosen outfit. He looked her straight in the eye, snorted, then turned and walked back the way he had come.

Susan watched his tail disappear through the trees, becoming aware of how her heart was pounding—and that there was something behind her. She forgot the skis on her feet and tried to spin around, succeeding only in falling. Expecting to discover another wild animal, she was overwhelmingly relieved to look up into the eyes of Darcy Ericksen.

"Are you okay?"

"There's a buffalo," Susan answered idiotically.

"I saw it. Poor thing. It didn't look like it was going to survive the winter, did it? Too old and too worn-out for this climate. Probably can't walk through the high snow anymore and has to stick to the ski trails to get around while he tries to find food."

"You feel sorry for him!" This was a different outlook on her experience.

"Yes. I know it's sentimental—that good old Mother Nature renews herself by weeding out the weak and the old. But I feel badly when I see something like that. My father would have told me I was being foolish. And maybe I am." He stared at the ground.

"I was very sorry about your father. We all are," Susan said, wondering if he was sad for the buffalo or for his father. Certainly the conversation she had heard last night had not been that of an intensely mourning son. She noticed his hands were shaking. "Are you okay?" She asked him the question he had asked her. "Are you out here alone?" She looked around. Wasn't shaking hands one of the first symptoms of hypothermia? And she knew Darcy wasn't a skier. . . .

"I'm fine. It's just that it's been a . . . a difficult week." Suddenly he looked at her with anguish in his eyes. "I can't understand it. . . . I can't understand where Randy has gone."

So it wasn't his father's death causing his distress. "Have you heard from him since he left?" Susan asked.

"No. I've called and called—" he paused "—but nothing. All I get is that damn cheerful message on the answering machine. 'Randy and Darcy are out having fun—or in having fun. Let us know who you are and maybe we can have fun togeth—' " He couldn't go on. "We live together, you know," he added.

"You seemed to be very close," Susan said softly. Darcy was leaning against a tree trunk now, and his shaking had become more intense. She was beginning to realize that she had to get him out of here. It was below freezing, certainly too cold to stand still for any length of time, and she had no idea how long Darcy had been outside. They had to turn around and get back to the lodge. She looked up the trail to the spot where she had last seen her family; they were probably more than a mile ahead. What would they think when she didn't catch up at their next rest stop? They would come back to see if she was in trouble, of that she was sure, but if they didn't find her in a short time, they couldn't be sure she had returned to the lodge. What would they think? Where would they go? She glanced at Darcy; he was shivering. The decision was made for her.

"Do you have a pencil or paper with you?"

"What?" He looked at her as though she were hallucinating.

"Something to write on. I want to leave a message for my family."

"Oh." He scrambled through his pockets. "No. Just this." He held up an extra ski glove. "I was pretty upset when I left. I just wanted to get outside. I didn't think about bringing anything. I'm awfully thirsty."

"Here." Susan gave him two small cans of apple juice that she had carried in her tiny belt pack. He needed them more than she did. She could always wet her throat with some snow. If only she could use it for paper and pencil, she thought, finding nothing more than a few tissues, Chap Stick, and sunscreen in the pack. Snow . . . She ripped a stick off one of the trees and used it to shape a few letters in the drift at the side of the trail.

"Gone back to lodge," Darcy read through chattering lips. "But they will pass right by. They won't see it."

"Yes, they will," she insisted, unwinding the long red scarf from around her neck and using it to underline the message. "It's sheltered under these trees; they will be here before the snow fills it in," she said hopefully. "We'd better get along. I'll follow you. We'll probably be back in front of the fireplace before they find this." She hoped she sounded more confident than she felt. Darcy looked terrible, but obediently he pushed off. And at the speed he was going, she would have little trouble keeping up.

They skied the mile or so back to Morning Glory Pool slowly but without stopping. Darcy paused as they passed a place similar to where his father's effigy had been found, and Susan thought he was upset by the location until she realized that he was exhausted and having trouble keeping his balance. The trail widened here, used daily by the many lodge guests, and Susan skied up beside the young man. His face was pale, but there were none of the white patches that, she had read, were the first indications of frostbite.

"Are you cold?" Susan tried to ask the question casually.

"My feet are freezing."

Susan remembered one book she had read recommending that cold feet should be tucked under the warm armpits of companion skiers. Her armpits were more than warm, she thought, realizing that she had been sweating profusely. Should she suggest such drastic action?

"It's beginning to snow more heavily. They're not going to find your note," Darcy announced.

"They've probably read it already," Susan said with substantially more cheerfulness than she felt. They weren't going to find the note. They might not be heading back to the lodge. She tried not to think that she had left her family to wander around in the forest looking for her. She had no choice but to keep going now. "I'm hungry. Let's hurry," she urged, trying to make it sound like a casual request. Darcy was looking worse by the minute. She knew she couldn't ski and hold him up at the same time. And she couldn't leave him alone here; there might be animals around, trying to keep warm in the steam pouring from the earth. . . . She was being so stupid!

"We can stand in the steam to warm up. Let's take a break over there by that geyser." She pointed with her ski pole to a spot where the trees overhung a small vent with steam pouring from the ground.

"Good idea. I'm feeling pretty rotten."

Susan looked at Darcy, surprised that he had thought he was keeping his condition from her. What a nice boy he was.

They huddled in the warmth for a while, thawing out as they rested. Darcy even took off his gloves and held his hands directly in the steam.

"Is that a good idea?"

"They were beginning to get numb. I was having some trouble holding on to the poles," he admitted.

Susan noticed that he was still breathing hard. How long should they rest? she wondered. Darcy was leaning back against a tree, his eyes closed. "Maybe we should get going. It isn't much farther," she urged, having no idea if she was lying or not. She hadn't recognized anything since they passed Morning Glory. Could they have taken the wrong trail? If there was more than one trail, it was certainly possible. She had just followed Darcy without considering that possibility. How stupid of her!

"I don't think I can go any further. Maybe you should ski back without me. If I rest here for a while, I'll be all right."

Susan knew that wasn't true. "No. I won't leave you. We'll ski back together," she added in her best *I'm the mother and know what is good for you* voice. It didn't work any better with him than it did with her children.

"No, I can't do it," he protested.

"Darcy!" Susan grabbed his jacket and tried to get his ever-wandering attention. "If you stay here, you could get hypothermia. You could die."

"That's okay," he insisted. "It really is okay." He looked at her earnestly. "Without Randy, I don't have any reason to live."

NINETEEN

"I DON'T KNOW WHAT I WOULD HAVE DONE IF YOU AND Chad hadn't found us then," Susan called out. She was sitting in a tub of warm water, speaking to her husband through a crack in the bathroom door. A very thin crack, as she didn't want any heat to escape unnecessarily. She had been in the bath for almost half an hour, but she still felt a chill in her extremities. "Darcy was ready to faint, and I couldn't leave him—but I couldn't do anything for him there. . . . What is that?" she asked as Jed walked into the room with a glass in his hand.

"Brandy. It was sent over from the bar. Drink it down. It's good for you."

"It was nice of you to order it," Susan said, taking the glass he handed her.

"I didn't. Maybe Kathleen or Jerry did—or someone at the front desk who saw the shape you were in."

"Did I look that bad?"

"Pretty close to exhaustion. And Darcy looked even worse."

"Where is he?"

"In his mother's room. She was trying to find a doctor to look after him—but some of the rangers have extensive first aid training and are probably able to deal with any problems he may have."

"He's so upset," Susan muttered. "I was a little shocked."

"Well, his father . . ."

"It's not his father he's upset about. He's worried about where Randy's gone."

"Who's to say that he didn't just go back home?"

"Evidently Darcy has called home—they live together—and he keeps getting the answering machine. It was upsetting him terribly."

"There are probably a hundred places Randy could be—with other friends or relatives—and maybe they had a fight and he's at home listening to the answering machine, but not picking up."

"Of course, that's possible." Susan didn't sound as if she believed her own words.

"Are you thinking of getting out of there before you turn into a prune? It's almost lunchtime."

"Lunch! I'm starving!" Susan stood up immediately, grabbing two towels from the rack at the same time.

"I could possibly ask for something to be delivered—under the circumstances, I'm sure the lodge would comply. Then you wouldn't have to go out in the cold right away."

"Oh, Jed, I don't mind. I don't think I'll bother to put on skis again, though. Just hiking boots and gaiters." She was already pulling on a clean turtleneck. "I think I'll have bean soup to start, and maybe some nachos. I wonder if there's a table available near the radiators. . . ."

"We'll find you one," Jed said, smiling at her enthusiasm. "I'll just run down the hall and tell the kids what we're doing."

"Great. Tell them I'll be dressed and ready to go in five minutes. I really am starving!"

The air did feel colder than before when, almost fifteen minutes later, she made the short hike to Snow Lodge. Snow was falling steadily now and she shuddered, thinking what might have happened if Chad hadn't spied her scarf or if the message had no longer been legible when he did.

"Didn't you wonder why I turned back?" she asked, thinking of all the questions she hadn't had the energy to ask.

"What we wondered was who you were with," Jed answered.

"How did you know I was with someone?"

"Ski tracks. There was no way only one person could have chopped up the snow so much," Jed answered. "And there were two clear tracks of Darcy's skis—they're the same length as mine. That's a good six inches longer than yours."

"I never thought of that." Susan walked through the door Jed held for her.

"You were busy, remember?"

"Yes, I . . ." Susan looked around the large lobby of the lodge. She must look worse than she thought; everyone was staring at her. She pulled off her knit hat and hurried toward the restaurant.

"Mrs. Henshaw. We were hoping you would feel well enough to come for lunch," the hostess chatted as she led them to their table. "The chef just finished the corn and chicken chowder, and it's wonderful," she advised before leaving them. "Have a nice meal."

"Thank you, we will." Susan smiled back. "Isn't it amazing how they know everybody's name? I hadn't noticed before."

"I don't think they know everyone. Susan, you saved Darcy's life, you're the heroine of the day."

"You certainly are. And we're impressed; three days ago you couldn't ski, and now you've become a one-woman rescue team."

The voice came from behind them. Susan turned around. "Jerry. Kathleen. Why don't you pull up that table and we can all sit together?"

"You can take my seat," Chad offered graciously. "C.J.'s waving to me over there. . . ." He explained this sudden burst of excellent manners.

"Thank you, Chad." Jerry held out the chair for his wife and borrowed a spare from another table for himself. "So tell us all about your adventure. Everyone in the lodge is talking about it."

"All I did was get Darcy out of the woods and then follow him about halfway back here. If I hadn't been found by the rest of my family and Chloe, I'd probably be suffering from frostbite—or worse—right now. I don't think I'm the real hero here."

"Chloe said something about a message and a scarf," Jerry said. "But Bananas is having a difficult morning and was crying so much that we didn't really get the full story."

So Susan explained to the Gordons what had happened, and then to the waitresses who gathered around while presumably taking their orders, and then to Charlotte and Jane, who appeared right before the chowder arrived. The sisters thanked Susan for saving their brother's life and wanted to hear the story from the beginning.

"Thank heavens you stopped when you did," Charlotte exclaimed when Susan had finished. "Darcy probably would be dead by now if you hadn't."

"How is he?" Susan asked, picking up her spoon.

"Some of the park rangers are looking after him. He has frostbite on his nose and one of his ears and was still cold when we left the room, but there's no serious damage, and even the frostbite is mild."

"That's good to hear," Jed said, giving his wife a chance to eat her lunch.

"How's your mother?" Kathleen leaned across the table and asked.

"She's fine now. She was frantic earlier, of course," Jane said, pushing her silky velvet headband deeper into her curls. "Why?"

The sisters exchanged looks. "Well," Charlotte began, "Darcy and my mother had a fight this morning—"

"My sister is exaggerating," Jane interrupted. "Darcy and Mother are still connected by some sort of invisible umbilical cord. They don't fight in the sense of screaming and yelling. They disagree vehemently. They exchange wounded looks."

"Jane!" Charlotte glared at her sister. Evidently some of the family disagreed more vehemently. "When Darcy left the lodge this morning, he was very upset. And Mother was very upset. And I know she would have been devastated if something serious had happened to him."

"After Father's death, I don't think she could have taken another tragedy," Jane agreed. "My mother is much more fragile than she appears, you know. We all have been very worried about her."

"Darcy is terribly upset," Susan said. "He mentioned something about Randy leaving—as well as his father's death. Maybe he shouldn't be allowed to go out skiing alone."

"We would never have let him go if we had known. Never!" Charlotte shook her hair vehemently. "He just stamped out of the lodge and skied off into the snow—at least that's what Mother said. We were in our rooms."

"If it is what I said, it's true." Phyllis Ericksen appeared behind her daughters.

"Mother! No one thought that you weren't telling the truth. . . ." Charlotte protested, apparently horrified at causing her mother more distress.

"I know that, my dear. I'm not accusing anyone of anything. It's been a long morning, and I'm afraid I don't know what I'm saying." She turned to the Henshaws. "My son is going to be just fine. I wanted to come down and let you know—and, of course, thank you for saving his life."

"Oh, I don't think . . ." Susan began to make self-deprecating noises.

"No. I'm sure that's exactly what you did. I don't believe Darcy planned to return from his little ski trip this morning. He would not be alive now if it weren't for you." A woman with exceptional posture, she straightened up even more. "I thank you."

With that, she turned and walked from the room. Jane and Charlotte exchanged another group of significant glances and got up to follow their mother.

"You know, maybe it would have been better if he hadn't come back. I don't know how she's going to take this," Jane said as they followed her.

"Did she say what I think she said?" Kathleen asked, choking on a corn kernel.

"They think he did it," Susan said. "They all think Darcy killed his father!"

"Just because he objected to Randy? I don't think so," Jed argued.

"Why not?"

"In the first place, this couldn't have been the first time that George Ericksen objected to his son's choice of life-style—after all, Darcy isn't sixteen. This has probably been known for a long time."

"And in the second place?" Susan asked.

"What the girls were just saying about the relationship between Darcy and his mother—he wouldn't want to hurt her. And killing his father was bound to do that."

"Think of Oedipus. Think of Freud," Jerry urged, getting into the discussion. "It isn't unheard-of."

"A Greek play and a psychological theory aren't evidence," Jed argued. "I don't see the poor kid as a murderer. He had a fight with his family about his choice of life-style, his lover got mad and left. Those are rotten things to happen, but not reasons for murder."

"I think—" Jerry was interrupted by a large commotion out in the lobby. Shouting and yelling were heard, and a woman screamed. Chad, who had been sitting closer to the doorway, ran over to their table.

"They found Darcy's friend. And he's dead."

TWENTY

"WHAT ARE YOU THINKING ABOUT?"

"What?" Susan turned, looking at Kathleen with a blank expression.

"Susan, you've been sitting here staring at a tiny trickle of steam coming from a geyser cone for almost fifteen minutes. You must be concentrating on something—as well as risking freezing to death," she added, pulling her hat down over her ears.

"I am cold," Susan admitted. "Want to warm up with me at the Visitor's Center?"

"I think that would be an excellent idea."

"I was sitting there trying to picture Darcy as a murderer," Susan said, following Kathleen down the path.

"And?"

"And I still don't see it."

"But now that Randy has been found . . ."

"Surely no one thinks Darcy killed Randy!"

"I don't know what anyone thinks. All the tourists are in a state of shock. The rangers aren't talking anymore—not even to be polite. Anyone who asks any questions is told that the matter is under investigation and they are not allowed to speak of it. I know: I tried asking a few questions of a few people."

"Darcy would never kill Randy!"

"I agree. But what if George killed Randy, and then Darcy found out about it?"

"And then killed his father. Is that what you're suggesting?"

"I think it's possible. There's certainly motivation there. His father disapproved of his life-style, publicly humiliated him, and then killed his lover. Except for a will leaving Darcy millions of dollars, I don't know what more a person could ask for in the way of motivation—or what more the police will ask for," she concluded, stamping the snow off her boots and opening the door for her friend.

"Maybe, but that doesn't explain a lot of things—the effigy of George Ericksen, for one," Susan insisted.

"Why couldn't Darcy have put that there? Or maybe Randy did, and George found out, and that's why he killed him?"

"He killed him in revenge for a practical joke? I don't think even George Ericksen was that sensitive. . . ." Susan began.

"But we don't really know very much about George Ericksen, do we?"

"No. In fact, we don't know very much about the entire Ericksen family, but we're going to find out—unless they leave the area."

"I was wondering about that, too," Kathleen agreed as they moved closer to the warmth of the wood stove. "But they can't leave the park."

"How do you know?"

"I asked Betsy. . . . Is that the name of Jon's girlfriend?"

"Beth."

"That's right: Beth. She was sitting alone in the lobby before I came out to find you. I went over and expressed my condolences, and while I was at it, I asked if the Ericksens would be leaving the park."

"And?"

"And she said probably not. It seems that all the snow-coaches are booked up months in advance and it would be impossible for that many people to leave without inconveniencing a lot of other people. . . ."

"What about snowmobiles?"

"I was getting to that. Usually they could rent a number of them to come into the park and pick them up, but this snow is the beginning of a major storm, and it's considered too dangerous right now—maybe in a few days or if the weather forecast is wrong. But for now, they're stranded here."

"And we may only have a few days to sort through all this and discover the answer," Susan mused.

"If we're going to do it."

"Of course we're going to do it. Do you think I saved Darcy Ericksen's life just so he could stand trial for a murder he didn't commit?"

"But you don't know that he didn't do it," Kathleen reminded her.

"And they don't know that he did."

"Anyone ever tell you that you're stubborn?"

"I know. It's just that I've been thinking and thinking, and I cannot believe that Darcy did it. He seemed so genuinely worried about where Randy was—he wouldn't have been worried if he had known that he was dead, would he? And he would have known if he killed his father in revenge over his father killing his lover. . . . This is getting a little complex."

"True."

"Did you have a chance to talk to anyone about the Ericksens this morning before Darcy got lost and Randy was found?"

"Yes, I did." Kathleen looked around the room. A half dozen tourists were thawing out or waiting for the next tour to begin. Two rangers stood by the information desk discussing whether the coming bad weather warranted rearranging the afternoon's schedule of events. No one was paying attention to two women warming themselves by the stove. "I spent a fair amount of time with two different people," she started, lowering her voice so they wouldn't be overheard. "First Bananas and I talked with the maid who cleans the senior Ericksens' room in the lodge. She's just a young girl, taking a break from college to earn some money for tuition, but she seems quite bright and a pretty reliable witness. . . .''

"So what did she tell you?"

"She said that Darcy has moved in with his mother. I don't know if it means anything. If they are very close, the family may have felt it better that Phyllis have someone with her, and who better than her favorite son?"

"True. But could he stand being there if he was the one who killed his father? Probably not," Susan answered her own question.

"Or maybe his mother knows that he did it and she is trying to protect him," Kathleen suggested. "That is just as possible, you know."

"Protect him?"

"Maybe keep him nearby so that he doesn't say anything to incriminate himself."

"That's crazy. Next you're going to suggest that she wanted him to stay with her because he's a compulsive killer and she's afraid if she leaves him alone, he'll massacre everyone in the lodge. Phyllis Ericksen loves her son, but she also loved her husband—"

"Why did you stop?"

Susan was remembering the argument she had heard between George and Phyllis. But all couples had arguments, she reminded herself. "I was just thinking about George Ericksen. So what else did she say?"

"Not much, just something a little weird . . ."

"What?"

"She said that she thinks that it's bad for Darcy to be with his mother. That she thinks—that is, the maid thinks—that his mother drives him crazy."

"Why did she think that?"

"She was nervous about mentioning it. But she explained that whenever Darcy spent much time with her, he got frantic. I asked her to be more specific, and she was hesitant to continue. But when I had convinced her that I was worried about Darcy, she told me that twice she had seen Darcy leave the room terribly upset. The first time was before six this morning, when she came on duty. She was walking down the hall when Darcy ran out of his mother's room and down the hall to the laundry room. She went by and said he was furiously smashing his fist into the cement wall, crying horribly.''

"My God."

"She waited in the hallway until the sobbing had stopped and he seemed to have gotten himself under control, and then she went in and tried to cheer him up with some small talk about cleaning or something—they're pretty much the same age, remember."

"And did it work?"

Kathleen shrugged. "She said that he seemed a little more relaxed when she left, but that a few hours later she was walking by the room, and he was screaming at his mother and then he dashed out again. That was when he left this morning, and you know how he was when you ran into him in the woods.''

A ranger came over to add another log to the fire.

"Got to keep this thing going with a storm coming in."

"Will we lose our power?" asked a man joining the group. Susan looked up at Call Me Irv. He had turned in his cowboy boots for ski boots, but the hat remained the same.

"Very unlikely. We used to be without power for much of the winter up here, but there's a new generator and new underground wires, and we have pretty good emergency backup equipment, so we don't worry too much." He slammed the door of the black stove. "But we also like to be prepared. It doesn't pay to get too cocky with Mother Nature."

"But if we did lose our power . . ." The doctor followed the ranger back to the desk, asking worried questions as they went.

"What an obnoxious man," Susan commented.

"That's the other thing I wanted to tell you. Guess who the doctor was who examined Darcy this morning?"

"How would I . . ." She looked across the room. "Not Dr. Cockburn. He's a psychiatrist, for heaven's sake!"

"He went to medical school." Kathleen shrugged. "And maybe the fact that he's a psychiatrist is a plus for Phyllis."

"Why?"

"What if she thinks Darcy killed his father and she's working on making sure that his defense is incompetence by reason of insanity? It is possible," she added when Susan didn't say anything.

"I suppose so. But just because she thinks he did it doesn't mean that he did."

"It must be someone in the family, Sue."

"There are a lot more people in that family," Susan insisted.

"I won't argue with that."

"I think we should try to talk to each one of them today. After all, they want me to investigate, so I'll just go ahead and investigate. Jed and the kids are going to look for moose on a ranger-led ski trip, so I'll just go over to the lodge and start knocking on doors."

"Jerry could go with Jed, so if I feed Ban, I'll be free for a while, too. What do you want me to do?"

"Good question. Do you think they know that we investigate together?"

"No one has mentioned it to me if they do. I suppose we could assume that they don't. Why?"

"I'm sure they think I'm completely incompetent, but if they find out you were once a detective in the state police and that we work together, they may change their minds."

"So we won't tell them, and we'll hope they don't find out. I can keep asking questions, though."

"Fine. Too bad the rangers aren't talking, isn't it?"

"Maybe there's another way to find out what they know. The staff live together, you know—rangers and kitchen help and everyone else. I'll try to make more contact with them."

"Good thinking. I'll talk to each family member and take some notes—that way I can report what I learn to you—and you can get as much information as possible. Where shall we meet?"

Kathleen glanced at her watch. "How about my room in

two hours? If we're done then, fine. We'll just decide what to do next. If one of us still has more people to talk to, at least comparing notes may help us know just what to ask.''

''Good thinking.'' Susan stood up and stretched. ''It feels good to get organized, doesn't it?''

''Yes.''

''You know, maybe the first thing you should try to find out is just where they found Randy's body.''

''Oh, I know that. Everyone was talking about it back at the lodge. You must have left too early to hear the announcement. He was found by the corner of one of the cabins near the ice cream shop. The body was totally frozen and covered with a pile of snow. He had probably been there ever since he vanished.'' She looked at Susan, who had resumed her seat. ''Sue? Are you okay?''

Susan looked up at her, horror on her face. ''I skied into him the other day, Kathleen. I ran into his body. Only, it was soft—it wasn't frozen. He must have just been murdered. He might not have been dead. Maybe . . .'' She caught her breath, forcing herself to utter the thought. ''Maybe if I had investigated further, I could have saved him.''

TWENTY-ONE

''MY HUSBAND IS AN ALCOHOLIC—ALTHOUGH HE HASN'T had a drink in years. I'm very proud of him. But he was once totally out of control; any stress at all could set off a major binge. And most of the stress came from his family. That's one of the reasons we've been living abroad.'' Joyce Ericksen shifted uncomfortably on the chair where she sat, and looked across the room at Susan.

Susan had parted from Kathleen more determined than ever to find out who had murdered George Ericksen and Randy. Leaving Kathleen in the lobby, she had run into Joyce Ericksen, who, she discovered, was anxious for a chance to talk. Very anxious. It turned out that the one person in the Ericksen family whom Susan would have considered the least likely suspect had an excellent motive for murder.

"You see," Joyce explained, "it was his family that made Carlton crazy, and when he was crazy, he drank. And that made him more crazy." She stared at the floor for a few minutes and then continued, her voice trembling. "Yesterday he had the first drink he's had in years—years," she repeated. "And it was all that man's fault. George Ericksen was a horrible, evil man! And he did terrible things to Carlton! But my husband didn't kill his father. He couldn't do that! You must believe me!"

"Why don't you tell me about it from the beginning," Susan urged. "I'd like to help, but I really don't know very much about the family."

"I can only explain from my own point of view. And I'm afraid I'm prejudiced." Joyce had regained control of herself.

"Prejudiced?"

"I hated George Ericksen. Sometimes I think I've grown to hate the entire family."

"Look . . ."

"It wasn't always like this," Joyce went on. "When I met the Ericksens, I thought they were the most extraordinary family ever. And they were. They were enchanting." She smiled at the memory, picking at the end of her long braid.

"Carlton and I met during my sophomore year of college. We fell in love almost immediately, and he took me home to meet his family in June, after school ended. They're from Chicago, you know, from one of those big suburbs that line the lake north of the city. But they had a fabulous summer house up in Door County, Wisconsin. It was actually set in the middle of a cherry orchard. It had been a long winter that year, with a late spring, and there were still blooms on the trees the day we arrived. As we drove up to the house, Phyllis, Jane, Charlotte, and Darcy came walking toward us through rows of pink blossoms, and I thought I had never seen anything so beautiful. To a kid from a small town in northern New Mexico, they were quite a revelation.'' She smiled. ''I remember thinking that they looked like an illustration in a book of fairy tales I had as a child. And about as real, I discovered later. But when George came down the steps of this gigantic log cabin dressed in jeans, a faded chambray shirt, and bright red suspenders, I was totally, completely enchanted.

''That night, after my first sophisticated dinner ever—fabulous beef bourguignonne, salad with fresh herbs, homemade French bread, and strawberries and cream—was the first time I ever saw Carlton drunk.''

''You mean he drank too much whenever he was with his family?''

''Not always. Not in the beginning. I only remember one or two times that first week. Although I was just twenty, and I'm not sure I would have recognized the symptoms of a secret drunk—but I learned them later, I can tell you that.''

''When did you get married?''

''The next year. Carlton got his degree and was accepted for graduate school in Chicago. I transferred to Northwestern. We rented a tiny apartment with a large bay window near campus, and all hell broke loose—as they say.'' She sighed. ''At the time, I was so young, so immature, and so insecure that I assumed everything was my fault. But it was the drinking. And living so close to his family.''

''I don't understand,'' Susan said, feeling guilty about intruding on what was obviously still a very real pain to this woman.

''I think I do, but I honestly don't know how to explain. Naturally we saw the family from time to time. And I think they were wonderful at first.'' She looked out the window at skiers who were passing by. ''I say I think because I'm not really sure. George and Phyllis helped us move into our apartment. George spent a day spackling and painting the walls, and Phyllis brought over her sewing machine, set it up on a card table—our only table—and made us beautiful batik curtains from fabric she had brought back with her from Thailand that summer. They were extraordinary: gold, purples, and reds printed in stars and moons and flowers.''

"They sound remarkable.''

"They were, but they were also very ornate—and our tastes ran more to Danish modern when we were young. In fact, Carlton hated them, not only the way they looked but because they blocked out almost all the light in the apartment. He didn't say anything, though, but George guessed what his son was thinking and pulled him aside the day they went up, and insisted that his mother never ever find out how he felt. He really made a big deal about it, and—and what I came to think of as the inevitable happened.''

"Carlton got drunk.''

"Roaring. I . . . I don't think I could believe it at first. We had been given a magnum of champagne as a wedding gift, and he sat in our only chair in our only room and drank the entire thing—and then threw the bottle at those curtains.'' She shook her head. "It took me days to wash out the stain and sew up the rip he made in them. And I would swear that Phyllis peeked at that spot every time she came over. I hated those curtains and was thrilled when the damn things rotted. Naturally, it took years. We moved and moved, and each time Phyllis would come over and alter them and then rehang them on new windows. And she would see the patches, and George would glare at Carlton, and Carlton would get drunk, and I would sew up the new rips. I got pretty good at patchwork back in those days.'' She started to laugh, surprising Susan. "I actually got interested in handwork, patching and repatching that batik. I taught patchwork and quilting and fancy stitching to a group of women in Paris. And it all started back then.''

"Along with Carlton's drinking.''

"Yes. I began to dread all the inevitable family occasions—holidays, birthdays—and in a large family, there are a lot of occasions.''

''Carlton got drunk at them.''

''Every single one. I remember a party for Darcy. It was his ninth or tenth birthday, and he was crazy about *Star Wars* figures at that time.'' She paused. ''Anyway, Carlton got completely plastered, put on an old black cape that his father had worn as a young man, and claimed to be Darth Vader. Darcy loved it and insisted he be allowed to stay costumed no matter what his parents said. So Carlton ran around the whole house, going outside and scaring the ponies that had been hired to give the kids rides, and finally passing out in a pile of hay and manure by the driveway. It didn't thrill Phyllis and George.''

''No, I guess not. But why did you stay with him? Why did he stay near his family?''

''I stayed with him because I loved him—and even then I knew a Carlton who was sober . . . the Carlton who wasn't with his family. But why he stayed by his family is a more difficult question to answer.

''I've thought about it for years. Maybe the answer is simple; and maybe hate is more powerful than love, and Carlton hated his father and mother. Or maybe he was more insecure than most adult children and he needed parents longer than most people. I thought they were destructive; I thought that for years. Now I don't know. All I know is that when Carlton is with his parents, he becomes self-destructive. I don't know why. But I don't think it's gotten much better over the years. Our answer was to leave. First Carlton worked on the East Coast and we saw them rarely, but then George retired, and he and Phyllis became more mobile and visited the family around the country. So Carlton got a position at the Sorbonne in Paris. Phyllis doesn't fly, so Paris is farther away for her than for most people.''

''And you hadn't seen them for . . .'' Susan began.

''Seven or eight years. The kids have been back to the States at least once a year, and have stayed in contact with their grandparents, and aunts and uncles. Carlton stopped drinking almost a decade ago—I don't think C.J. probably even remembers seeing his father drunk—and Carlton keeps in touch with the rest of his family through frequent letters and less frequent overseas phone calls. I know it's a strange situation, but my family is together, and my husband is productive and sober. Being normal isn't that important anymore.''

"And everything was fine until this week."

"Yes. Everything. I was a fool to agree to this trip."

"How did it get arranged?"

"I really don't know. We moved back to the States, thinking that Carlton had the drinking under control. And we saw his parents as we passed through Chicago in the fall, and everything was fine. Then George called about a month ago and explained that Phyllis really wanted the whole family together for their fiftieth wedding anniversary. We talked it over and talked it over. Phyllis called once or twice urging us to go. It seemed that everyone else had agreed to the plan, so in the end, we did, too. Yellowstone Park isn't a place with any family connections; there's a lot to do here, so no one has to spend more than dinner with the family. . . ." She shrugged. "We really thought Carlton could handle it."

"And then . . ."

"And then the same old things came up." She shook her head, and Susan thought there were tears in Joyce's eyes. "Carlton began so well. The first night here I turned around and he was standing next to his father in the lobby and they were laughing together." A tear fell down her cheek. "I'd never, ever seen them enjoying each other—not for a single moment. It was wonderful. I was sure we'd made the right decision.

"The next morning, I noticed a fifth of vodka wrapped in wool socks in Carlton's drawer." She stopped again, and Susan wondered if she was going to be able to continue. But after a moment, she did. "He didn't drink it until yesterday. I don't think he drank anything until yesterday. But I know enough about drunks to know that no one knows anything about them when they're drinking.

"But Carlton was upset over all the fighting about Darcy and Randy—we all were. And the dinners and evenings together were longer and more difficult than we had ever thought they could be. I am so thankful that your family was here—it kept our kids out of all this to a certain extent. But Heather knows her father is drinking again, and she's worried about that as well as the murders. . . . Damn it, I would give anything to live the last month over. I wish we could go back to the beginning and decide not to come. But that's the thing about this family. They are so damn difficult to say no to."

"Why?" Susan asked gently.

"I don't know. George talks about how hurt Phyllis will be, and Phyllis says not to worry about her, but that it's George's feelings we should be concerned with, and in the end, people seem to do things they don't want to do. Talk to the other kids—they'll tell you the same thing. It's insane. But Carlton would never have killed his father!"

"Then who did? It has to be a family member, Joyce."

But Joyce was crying too hard to answer.

TWENTY-TWO

LIKE HER SISTER-IN-LAW, JANE ERICKSEN FOUND SUSAN and suggested a talk. Unlike Joyce, she was calm.

"Mother has this idea that you could help find Father's murderer, and she wants all of us to speak with you," Jane explained, settling back on a leather couch in the corner of the lodge's lounge. Today she was wearing plum leggings and a green, purple, and gold tunic with gold chains around her arms and neck. She tucked her long, elegant legs underneath her and slung one arm gracefully across the back pillows.

Susan sat down, waited, and admired the performance.

''I really cannot believe that someone in our family killed Father. I know that's what that tacky little ranger Marnie thinks, but she must be wrong. After all, I've known these people my entire life!''

Susan refrained from mentioning that someone had had a lifelong relationship with most murderers. She was beginning to wonder if Jane was reading from a prepared speech. She sounded more like her always-in-control sister, Charlotte. Until now, Susan had regarded Jane as the more impulsive one, but she suspected that she was going to have a difficult time finding out what she needed to know. So she sat back to listen to what Jane wanted to tell her.

''Father could be a difficult man. I'll be the first to admit it. He tended to be overly involved in the lives of his children. I think we would all agree to that. But it was his concern for the family that caused problems, and we all knew that and understood it. and even . . .'' She paused and ended more stridently, ''and yes, we even loved him for it.''

Well, it was good to know that Jane was a rotten liar. That would make Susan's work easier. A little easier. Now all she had to do was find out the truth and why Jane was so diligently lying to hide it. Just because Susan didn't see Jane as the killer didn't mean that she wasn't just that. Anyone could have hit George with that shovel and killed him; no special strength was needed.

''It was the most difficult for Darcy, of course,'' Jane was continuing. ''He's the youngest, and in some ways, the most special. . . .''

''Why?''

Jane seemed surprised by the question. ''Well, because he's the youngest . . .''

''You said that.'' Susan was beginning to grow impatient.

''So he was always the baby of the family,'' Jane continued, glaring at her. ''And, of course, now he's the last to be a grownup. Our parents have moved out of the lives of the rest of us—more or less." She ended less confidently than she had begun.

"And the rest of you aren't gay," Susan reminded her, having no idea whether or not it was the truth.

"My parents are, like most of their generation, a little conservative about that type of thing. I do think that my father would have come to accept Darcy as he is in time. I was talking to my mother about it yesterday, and she agreed. . . ."

"Darcy is obviously your mother's favorite," Susan said, and then reminded herself that interrupting was not the way to get information.

"Well, maybe."

Who wants to hear that one's sibling is more loved than oneself? Susan wondered if now Jane would have to end this speech and say something significant.

"What you have to understand is that we are a very close family. We had our problems, like all families. Right now, Darcy's choice of life-style is putting a lot of stress on us, but we would have solved that just like we've solved problems in the past. No one would have killed anyone over . . . over anything."

"But someone did. . . ."

"How do you know Father wasn't killed by some freak who hated men who wore red suspenders? There are a lot of psychopaths in the world, and they certainly could be in Yellowstone National Park." Jane was getting angry . . . and anxious?

"And Randy?" Susan pushed.

"A rejected lover," Jane flashed back.

"It's a lot of coincidence." Susan kept her voice quiet.

"But it is possible!" Jane insisted. "Now, listen, Mother asked you to help us, not hurt us. You don't know all the pain this family has suffered over the years. And if you did, you'd try to spare us any more." She glared at Susan.

"Maybe it would be easier for me to find out what I need to know if I asked the questions and you just answered," Susan suggested, wrongly assuming Jane would never agree to that. ''And why don't you start by telling me about the problems the family has had in the past. It usually helps if I have as much background as possible about everyone involved.''

Jane didn't say anything, staring through wide, crystal blue eyes.

''For instance, Joyce tells me that Carlton is an alcoholic,'' Susan said, priming the pump.

Jane played with the delicate gold chains around her left wrist, taking her time before saying more. ''As I said, we are a large family. I don't think the fact that one of us abuses alcohol is in any way a reflection on the rest of us. . . .'' And then she lost control. ''You really are a ghoul, you know. Do you like collecting information on people's weaknesses? So what if one of my brothers is gay and the other is an alcoholic? What business is all this of yours?''

''Your mother asked me to investigate these murders,'' Susan reminded her. ''And no, I don't collect information about people because I take some sort of perverse enjoyment in discovering their weaknesses. I do it to help people. It always helps people to know the truth.''

''You're going to have to grow a mustache if you're going to insist on these Hercule Poirot imitations,'' Jane said, almost smiling. ''But I understand what you're saying, of course. In fact, I don't see how we can survive as a family unless we know who killed Father. Which one of us killed him,'' she amended sadly. ''So what do you want to know?''

''How important is your family to you?'' Susan asked the first question that came to mind.

''A lot. I don't think most of my friends are as tied to their families as I am to mine. Though large families may tend to be more connected than families with fewer members.'' She stopped playing with her jewelry and looked up at Susan. ''I've given this a lot of thought from time to time. Ours is a family of alliances. Some of the alliances changed over the years, and some remained static. For instance, Charlotte and I are only one year apart in age. In some ways we might have been twins. We look similar, we like the same things, and so we formed our own unit inside the family. And even now, when we live on opposite sides of the country, we stay in close touch. We vacation together about once a year. Once we even discovered that we had dated the same man—an airline pilot who flew the red-eye—although not at the same time," she explained.

"And did the rest of the family work like this? Are there other groups within the main group?" Susan asked, thinking vaguely of a social psychology course she had taken her sophomore year of college, and that she now, when it might come in useful, had completely forgotten.

"Not exactly. Carlton and Jon have similar talents—they were always interested in science, for instance. But their ages were too far apart for them to be close when they were children. So Jon inherited Carlton's rock and bug collections, and his chemistry set, I think. But there's a fifteen-year difference in their ages, so . . ."

"That's really unusual, to have such spaces between children. How old are you all?"

"Let me think. Carlton must be forty. I'm thirty-one, Charlotte is thirty. Jon is twenty-five (we celebrated his birthday over Christmas), and Darcy is just twenty-one."

"Your parents did some interesting spacing of children," Susan commented.

"My mother had at least two miscarriages between Carlton and myself—maybe more. We never talked about it. And I knew she had a baby that died within the year after Charlotte was born. I don't remember it, but I can vaguely remember going to visit its grave when I was a child. I don't even know if it was a boy or a girl; all that was carved into the granite was Baby Ericksen—it might have been any of us. Anyway, she also had a miscarriage between Jon and Darcy. I was six or seven at the time, and I can still remember how upset she was. Probably that's the reason she and Darcy are so close.

"They're the other group within the family, I guess. She has always adored him, and he has always adored her. Even during Darcy's adolescence, he rebelled against my father, not against Mother."

Susan was a bit overwhelmed, trying to imagine the cumulative pain of a woman who had suffered so much loss over the years. And who once again was grieving. She was sure it didn't get any easier.

"I've always admired my mother; she's been through so much. And now . . ."

"And now?" Susan prodded.

"I have a horrible feeling that she thinks Darcy killed my father."

"Why?" Susan asked.

"She's not really grieving for Father. Her first reaction, almost her only reaction so far, has been to hold Darcy closer than ever. He's moved in with her. And she refuses to leave the room unless she's with him. And the times that he has left without her, she's been frantic. Charlotte was with her this morning after Darcy stormed out, and she says that she thought Mother was going to go mad, she was so worried about him."

"I suppose it's my turn to talk, isn't it?" a voice interrupted.

Charlotte had joined them.

TWENTY-THREE

CHARLOTTE SAT DOWN ON THE HEAVY TRUNK THAT served for a coffee table. She was wearing black wool slacks, a shell pink silk shirt, and a black vest displaying elaborate vines embroidered in gold thread. Where, Susan asked herself parenthetically, did these sisters get their clothes? And if this was their idea of casual, what did they wear when they got dressed up?

"Mother is still busy nursing Darcy, so I took this chance to get away," Charlotte explained to her sister. "How does this work? Do we tell her what we think she should know, or does she ask the questions and we answer?"

"Whichever you prefer," Susan explained, before Jane could answer. "Although usually I ask the questions." And she preferred to ask them when she was alone with the other person, although she didn't say so.

"I had just finished explaining about the age differences in our family and how many children Mother lost," Jane added.

"She's lived with a lot of loss, but I don't know how she's going to survive this," Charlotte said. "No matter what has happened in her life, no matter what terrible tragedies she has lived through, Mother has always had Father right by her side. We'll all do what we can, of course, but for Mother there's only Darcy—and he's pretty fragile himself. There's no way she can depend upon him now, no matter how much she tries."

"Maybe . . ." Susan hesitated, knowing that neither woman would want to hear what she was going to say. "Maybe she isn't depending on him. Maybe she's trying to protect him."

"I think that's true. She's trying to make sure he doesn't kill himself," Charlotte said, nodding to her sister. "That's why she was so worried when he skied off this morning." She turned to Susan. "My youngest brother is very high-strung. I think the murder of his lover and the murder of his father have been too much for him."

Susan, who had been thinking of Darcy in the roll of murderer, not mourner, didn't know what to say next. Of course, Darcy could be both murderer and mourner. "Is Darcy usually . . . umm, more stable than this? I mean, Charlotte said he's 'high-strung,' and being gay is difficult in this society, and . . ." She decided to stop before they could construe her questions as insulting.

The sisters exchanged a look that Susan wished she could interpret. Charlotte spoke first.

"What I meant when I said high-strung is . . . I think we should tell her, Jane," she insisted, interrupting herself and reaching out to her sister.

Jane nodded. "Yes. I think we should."

Susan sat quietly, waiting for Jane to begin.

"Except that it's not all that easy to explain."

"Maybe the beginning," Susan suggested gently, falling back on a cliché.

"Where's that?" Jane asked, apparently honestly.

"I know where it begins for me," Charlotte surprised them by saying. "Back with the ink." She gave her sister a look best called significant.

"Go ahead and tell her. Maybe it's time someone knew the truth about us." Jane turned just enough to look out the window. Susan hoped she wasn't going to get to watch each Ericksen dissolve into tears, one after the other.

"It's a silly story in some ways. It wouldn't be worth telling—or would have been forgotten by now—if it hadn't started a whole string of events. . . . But I'm getting beyond the beginning right away. Anyway, the story starts about fifteen years ago when Darcy was just a little more than five years old. My parents had an argument. Not a knock-down, drag-out argument, just a run-of-the-mill screaming contest like most married couples have occasionally. It would have been over with and forgotten if Darcy hadn't been awake later than usual for some reason and overheard the whole thing. He . . . he got mad at Father, presumably for upsetting Mother, and he went to Father's desk, found some permanent ink that Father used to identify specimens, climbed to the top of Father's dresser, and poured the entire bottle of ink into a pile of a dozen white linen shirts that Father always had made in London. It ruined the shirts, of course. And some of Father's work was on the desk, and that was destroyed, too. I don't remember the reaction, but the family story goes that Father was furious."

"But knowing Father, I've always wondered if he was a

little proud of Darcy. It was the type of act that showed what Father might have called spunk," Jane added.

"True. But remember, we were barely in our teens. We're working entirely on memory."

And family myth, Susan added to herself. "I gather this was only the first time something like that happened" was what she said aloud.

"Just the first of many," Jane agreed. "You see, even as a small child, Darcy was terribly attached to Mother. If he saw her unhappy, he did something about it. Actually, there were some very funny things . . . like when my mother complained that one of the women she did some sort of volunteer job with was working her too hard, and the next time that woman came over to the house, Darcy threw a ball at her, screaming that she was a slave driver. He was very young then, of course."

"But as he got older . . . ?" Susan asked.

"As he got older, he got more and more sophisticated." Jane sighed. "It really was remarkable. I understand the lengths some children will go to, to get and keep their parents' attention, but for Darcy it was easy: he charmed my mother."

"And your father?" Susan was hesitant, but she had to ask.

"He wasn't so successful with Father," Jane admitted. "Certainly, though, it was partially Father's fault."

"Definitely," Charlotte agreed. They exchanged looks again.

"You see, Father is somewhat sexist. Up until Darcy's birth, he had two sons, both of whom were interested in science, as he was, and two daughters, who are more interested in the arts. Darcy is an artist. He was from the first time he put a crayon on a piece of paper."

"Your mother said he is very talented."

"Oh, he is," Charlotte agreed. "He goes to art school, and he's certainly one of their best students."

"But it's more than that," Jane added. "Darcy looks at the world through the eyes of an artist. He sees little relevance in Father's facts, and classifications, and natural laws. To Darcy, reality is only the beginning. Everything is processed through his imagination and becomes something special. It's not just his art, he lives life like that. You know, my mother's the same way.''

''And your father didn't object to it in a woman?''

''Well—'' Jane paused, apparently trying to find the right words ''—my mother was always able to find an outlet for her creativity in domestic things. She's a fabulous gardener, not because her plants grow well but because she invents gardens that are rare and special. In Wisconsin one summer, she spent weeks creating a garden within a garden. She literally worked from dawn until dark until she had a tiny plot, complete with a miniature waterfall that was a minuscule reflection of the larger garden around it. And our homes were always decorated with great imagination and flair.''

''And her cooking is extraordinary,'' Charlotte said. ''Not just good, but presented wonderfully. I remember one of my birthday parties when everything was shaped like a star—from cakes and cookies, to the tablecloth, and all the decorations. She even made each guest a crown of stars to wear. My friends were overwhelmed.''

''And Darcy takes after your mother?''

''Yes, but the problem was that Darcy always wanted to help Mother with all her projects. And Father thought it was effeminate.''

''And . . . ?''

''And was always insulting about it,'' Charlotte said. Susan thought she was getting mad. ''Father has been making cracks about toughening up Darcy as long as I remember. And, of course, it never worked. For instance, Darcy was wonderful at sports: soccer, baseball, all the games kids play. And Father would have been so happy to go and cheer him on. . . .''

''But it didn't work out?'' Susan asked.

''The first soccer game of the season in third or fourth grade, Darcy made the game winning goal. My mother had insisted that the whole family be there to watch, and we all dashed onto the field after the game to congratulate Darcy. He looked so sweet in his striped shirt with white shorts and knee socks. . . . Anyway, Father walked slowly across the field and came up to Darcy with a big smile on his face. He said something like 'It's about time you made me proud of you.' Darcy never played soccer again,'' Charlotte added. ''If it was for Father, he just wouldn't do it.''

''Unless Mother insisted. He would do anything for Mother,'' Jane added.

''It's true,'' Charlotte agreed. ''Mother has been keeping the peace between them for years.''

''Have there been any other conflicts like this in the family?'' Susan asked, thinking that one sounded like more than enough.

''Not really,'' Jane answered quickly. Maybe too quickly.

''I suppose we all rebelled in adolescence. But nothing unusual. As long as we were getting good grades in school and not doing anything to publicly disgrace the family, the rest of us were allowed a fair amount of freedom and we went our own way,'' Charlotte said.

Susan stood up, sensing that no one was going to say anything more right now. Neither woman had mentioned that their older brother had changed his whole life, going so far as to change continents to avoid his family. She wondered what else they weren't mentioning.

TWENTY-FOUR

IT WAS BETH WHO MADE SUSAN REALIZE HOW LITTLE THE Ericksens were affected by Randy's death.

"I keep thinking about Randy" was the way she put it. "It must be terrible to die among strangers."

Susan wondered if Beth was thinking that she was also among strangers. Beth's next comment, that "Randy and Darcy hadn't been together long," gave Susan an opening.

"Had you met him before this trip?"

"Once. In New York City. Jon and I were there after Christmas. He was visiting me. I grew up in New Jersey, and my family still lives there," she explained. "Jon has been living in the city since last fall. He was on some sort of work-study semester. I don't think he knew Randy before then. Randy just graduated from NYU last year, and he's been working for an ad agency since then. By Christmas they were sharing an apartment."

"Randy's?"

"I don't think so." She stopped for a minute. "Now that I think about it, I'm really not sure. But I do know that Phyllis had done a lot of the decorating."

"Really?" Susan didn't know many grown-up children whose mothers had decorated their first apartments. Not that she didn't know a lot of mothers who were dying to try. In her own home, her children had insisted on displaying their own taste in their individual abodes. The results were interesting: Chad was living in the middle of a montage of long-haired rock musicians. It would have given her nightmares, but he loved it. Chrissy's room was covered with posters of her favorite artists' work and piles of books; Susan actually enjoyed putting away laundry in there.

"Yes, and she did an incredible job. It's just a tiny fourth-floor walk-up in the Village—two rooms only, but she turned the bedroom into a fantasy, fabric on the walls, pillows everywhere. She even bought them an antique sleigh bed. . . ."

Susan didn't listen too carefully to Beth's description of the wonders of Darcy's apartment. She was beginning to tire of the works of Phyllis Ericksen. Actually, she was beginning to get tired of everything here. She was hungry again and could use a cup of coffee. She had suggested to Beth that they talk in the restaurant, but Beth had explained that she was waiting for Jon.

"Even in Jon's dorm room . . ." Beth was saying when Susan returned to the conversation. "You should see it."

"I'd like to. What do you think about the murders?" she asked, trying to return to the subject that really interested her.

"I . . . I really don't know," Beth said. "It all seems a little unreal somehow. First the fake body turning up in that pool, and then George dying, and now finding Randy's body—it's almost too much."

"It's not the vacation you planned."

"No, it certainly isn't. I'll admit I was worried about this trip. I'd never met Jon's parents, and I didn't know how they would feel about me or the fact that we're living together. . . ."

"And how did they feel?"

Beth looked surprised. "I don't think they cared one way or the other. Oh, they were very polite," she added, seeing the puzzled look on Susan's face. "They said all the right things and made me feel comfortable and welcome and, I suppose, like a member of the family. It's just that I felt like they were doing it automatically. Like it didn't matter who Jon brought on this trip . . ."

Like Beth wasn't anything special, Susan thought. "Are you and Jon planning to make your relationship permanent?" she asked.

"You mean, are we getting married?" She shook her head. "I thought so. And I'm not a girl who assumes that if a man sleeps with her, he's going to marry her, if that's what you're thinking. . . ."

"I wasn't. . . ."

"It's just that, until this trip, Jon was acting like marriage was what he wanted. When we were in New Jersey, he even kidded my parents about wanting grandchildren. We haven't made definite plans, but we've talked about what type of wedding we would like, and where we would live if Jon was lucky enough to find the position that he wanted. . . . I wasn't imagining it, Mrs. Henshaw, Jon was planning to marry me!"

"And that changed when you got to the park? Or after the murders?"

"Almost right away. Maybe the first night, in fact. We all met in George and Phyllis's room for a drink before dinner. I had met Phyllis as soon as we arrived—she was waiting to meet the snowcoach that we were on. . . ."

"And George?"

"She explained that he was skiing, told us that the whole family was going to get together at five o'clock, and gave us their room number. She was very sweet and welcoming. To tell the truth, I was relieved."

"Meeting parents is difficult," Susan suggested, remembering her own past.

"Yes, and Jon had always talked about his childhood as though it was a happy one—you know, a summer home, parties, and trips to neat places. My family is very working-class; we didn't do things like that when I was young. . . ."

"But you think now that it wasn't such a happy time?"

"I don't know." She spoke slowly. "We spent the night before we came here in Jackson Hole, and we were eating dinner in a Mexican restaurant when I noticed that Jon was awfully quiet. At the time, I wondered if he regretted bringing me along on this trip. And maybe he did."

"I don't think so." Susan tried to comfort her with clichés. "He appears very attached to you. . . ." But did he?

"Then he said something about how different his family was from most other families. He didn't explain, but it made me remember the opening line of *Anna Karenina*—you know, about happy families being all alike, but unhappy families all being unhappy in different ways? That isn't exactly how it goes, but—"

"I remember. So you started to wonder if his family life wasn't as ideal as you had imagined?"

"Exactly. And when I asked Jon about it, he changed the subject. That's not like him. Usually he likes to talk. So I was a little nervous by the time we got here."

"You didn't show it on the way." Susan commented.

Beth laughed. "Wanna bet? I don't even know what book I was looking at!"

"How have things gone since you arrived?" Susan asked. "You said something about that first night?"

"It was odd. You know, so much has happened that it's difficult to remember that it was only a few days ago."

"I know."

"Well, I was a little nervous when we got to their room. Jon made a big deal about how his father hates people being late—I don't think the first thing you should know about a person is what they don't like, do you?"

"No," Susan agreed, thinking that Jon was an inconsiderate, or possibly insensitive, young man.

"So we got there at exactly five o'clock, and there was Phyllis, who introduced me to Jane and Charlotte, and gave me a glass of wine. And then George came in, a little late himself. I was surprised by that, and Phyllis made a comment about it, but to be honest, it was a relief to find out that he wasn't perfect. And he was very, very nice. He can be the most incredibly charming person . . . could be, that is."

"But he wasn't always."

Beth sighed deeply. "No, not always. But from the first night, he was mad at Darcy. I really don't know what happened. One minute he and Phyllis were standing in the middle of the room, typical hosts, and suddenly he was glaring at his youngest son."

"And Phyllis?"

"She was standing right beside him, a fixed smile on her face and, unless I'm very much mistaken, tears in her eyes. I think she knew then that the reunion was going to be a disaster—and that she could do nothing about it. Jon says that no one can control his father."

"Really?" She wondered who had tried. "You think George just couldn't accept that Darcy's gay?"

"I guess so. But I don't understand it. Jon said that Darcy has been very open about his sexual preference since he went off to college. And that was four years ago. I think everyone should have adjusted to it by now. And Randy was a perfectly acceptable person—actually a little dull and middle-class for someone like Darcy, was what I thought when we all met in New York.''

"But evidently George couldn't deal with it.''

"And that was making things miserable for everyone. After twenty-four hours with his family, Jon was becoming a nervous wreck, Carlton and Joyce were keeping more and more to themselves, Jane and Charlotte were bickering, and, of course, most of the people here know that Darcy and his father were feuding. And that scene in the dining room was only the tip of the iceberg—they were sniping at each other every time they met.'' She fell silent. "Do you think George Ericksen killed Randy, and when Darcy found out about it, he killed his father?''

"I don't think so,'' Susan said. "But I think that's what everyone else thinks.''

TWENTY-FIVE

Jon joined Susan and Beth in the lobby, but insisted that Susan speak to Heather and C.J. before talking to him. Susan agreed, thinking that the entire Ericksen clan appeared to be cooperating with her. She was impressed—and worried. Jon had explained that he thought his niece and nephew were truly upset by the murders. Susan didn't want to say or do anything to make it worse. She wouldn't even have spoken to them if they hadn't asked for an interview. She didn't like children being involved with murder.

"They seemed nervous, and I didn't know what to do, so

I bought them hot chocolate. They're waiting at one of the small tables in the back of the bar," Jon said. "No one will be able to overhear you there."

"I'll find them," Susan assured him, hurrying into the restaurant. She glanced at her watch as she went. She was supposed to meet Kathleen in forty-five minutes. She hoped to speak to Carlton, Darcy, and Phyllis before then. Probably, though, talking to the kids wouldn't take very long. They undoubtedly could use some reassuring and a little TLC.

Or maybe more than a little, she thought when she arrived at the table where C.J. and Heather sat. Neither of them had touched their chocolate, and they both looked scared to death.

"Hi, I—" she began, sitting at an empty chair.

"We need to talk to you urgently, Mrs. Henshaw," C.J. interrupted. Then he was cut off by a kick from his sister.

"My grandmother says that you're helping investigate these crimes. . . ." Heather took a deep breath. "So we thought we should talk to you right away. . . ."

"We know something," C.J. interrupted again.

"I think you'd better let me tell her!" Heather gave her brother a stern look.

"Fine." The word indicated agreement; his tone didn't.

Heather glared at him, but withheld comment. "We've never been involved with murder before, but we know something about it—"

"She means that she reads mystery novels," C.J. interrupted.

"Why don't you let Heather explain, and then, afterwards, you can tell me everything she leaves out," Susan suggested.

"Fine," the boy agreed. "Well, go ahead," he directed his sister.

"C.J.'s right—all we know about this comes from books, but some of the things in those books make sense, Mrs. Henshaw! And we've been thinking about where everyone was when Grandfather was killed."

"I've been wondering about that myself," Susan said.

"Well, we were skiing ahead of you—"

"C.J.!"

"Okay, you tell her."

"My brother's right. We were ahead of you, and, well, we weren't as tired as you were, so we might have noticed more," Heather said.

"And?"

"Well . . . ." Now that she had Susan's complete attention, Heather seemed to forget what she wanted to say. She fumbled in the pocket of the anorak she wore. "I'm afraid I'll make a mistake. C.J. and I made a list. . . ."

"Good idea," Susan encouraged. Both children seemed very nervous.

"Here." Heather held out a piece of lodge stationery.

Susan read it carefully.

Grandfather
(Jane, Charlotte, Darcy)
Jon and Beth
Heather, C.J.
The Henshaws
Joyce, Carlton, and Phyllis

"What are the parentheses for?"

"That's because we know Aunt Jane and Aunt Charlotte and Uncle Darcy were there before us, but they . . . ." C.J. seemed unable to go on.

"Because they weren't skiing together all the time and they may have arrived separately," Heather explained. "Jon and Beth were different. We saw them ahead of us a few times, though, so we're pretty sure they got to the geyser together. Although I guess we weren't being exactly accurate," she ended doubtfully. Then she looked up at Susan. "Does it help?"

"Yes, very much." Susan's answer was more definite than she felt. The evidence was building in favor of Darcy as the suspect. But could Darcy have killed his father with his sisters present? Or one of them with the other two around? Or Jon and Beth?

"We don't think there is any way that anyone could have

gotten ahead of the other and killed Grandfather," C.J. added.

"What?" Susan looked at the boy, realizing for the first time what a terrible strain these children were under. C.J.'s face was white, and he was nervously shredding a napkin. Heather's hands were shaking, and she had licked chapped skin from her lips.

"We looked at all the maps," his sister explained. "And we tried to figure out the times and everything—even for a wonderful skier—and there is no way that someone like, say, Grandmother could ski ahead of Mom and Dad, kill Grandfather, and then ski back. Not that she would! I don't want you to think that we think—" Tears were dripping down her cheeks.

"No," Susan stopped her. "Look, this is a horrible thing that's happened in your family. You're both too old to ignore how serious it all is, and I can't tell you that everything is going to work out easily, but it's obvious that you're thinking about how you can help, and I don't know what else there is to do."

"Will you come to one of us if you have any questions about this?" Heather needed reassurance.

"Definitely." She was glad to see that they were relieved. It was, after all, frequently easier to be part of something than to sit on the sidelines and fret. "In fact, this is going to be a big help to me. Thanks." She folded the paper carefully and put it in her parka pocket.

"So you kids are helping with the investigations, are you?" Susan turned around and discovered that Jon had joined them. Heather and C.J. looked uncomfortable. Maybe they were thinking about their list and what they had just told Susan. Certainly, going by that, Jon qualified as a major suspect in his father's murder. But motive?

"Your parents have come in," Jon continued. "They're at a table by the window."

Heather hopped up. "We'd better get going."

Her brother didn't argue.

"They're having a tough time," Jon commented, watching them leave. He sat down in the chair Heather had just vacated. "In truth, we all are."

"We live in a civilized world. We don't know how to react to murder," Susan said, resuming her seat.

"I suppose we should add 'thank God' to that," he answered. "What sort of a world would it be where people have practice reacting to murder? Someplace that makes *A Clockwork Orange* look like a faculty cocktail party? In the room the women come and go talking of cyanide and arsenic pills? Don't mind me. My father always said that I'm over-educated. When I get upset, I babble." He leaned across the table. "You're talking to all of us. I know, Beth told me. How can I help you?" He brushed his long, sandy hair out of his eyes as he spoke.

Susan thought about how his female students were going to love those sincere gray eyes.

"I'm really only trying to get some background on your family, Jon."

"Who wanted to kill Father? It's a difficult question. I think the answer is, all of us at one time or another—but I think we're all reasonable people. Meaning, of course, that we might want to, but we wouldn't actually do anything. Who was it that said murder and civilization don't mix?"

"I have no idea," Susan said honestly. Whoever it was, of course, had been wrong. Modern history had proven more than once that some civilizations' very foundation was murder. "But people do get so angry that they lose control," she suggested.

"But to murder someone?" Amazingly, Jon seemed to find it a new thought. "I'm fairly sure most of us would stop short of murder."

"Someone didn't," Susan reminded him grimly.

He agreed reluctantly. "Everyone outside of the family seems to think that Darcy did it," he added sadly.

"You don't?"

"I . . . I find it difficult to believe. Darcy was mad at Father, furious, in fact. But Darcy is truly a gentle soul. He does not have the psychology of a murderer. I'm sure of that!''

Susan wasn't interested in his inexpert opinions. ''This must be very difficult for Beth,'' she suggested, to change the subject.

Jon looked surprised. ''Beth? Why Beth? She isn't even involved, for heaven's sake. It's my mother we should be worrying about. She is much more fragile than she appears, and Father did a good job of protecting her from some of the harsh realities of life. It's definitely Mother I'm worrying about,'' he repeated.

TWENTY-SIX

''I'M TERRIBLY WORRIED ABOUT MOTHER.'' CARLTON WAS to echo his brother's words a few minutes later. ''She insisted that I speak to you as soon as possible, so I hurried to find you. I'll do anything I can to ease her horrible anxiety. So please, ask me anything.'' Carlton rubbed his forehead with a nervous gesture Susan had noticed before. ''I know Joyce explained to you that I'm an alcoholic.'' he continued before Susan could speak. ''She says that she told you the whole history of my drinking and why we moved to France. I suppose you think I'm a weak person to have to leave my family in order to stop drinking. And I suppose I am really. I thought, though, that I had it licked. But this reunion was too much—and I knew it was going to be too much. That's why I brought the vodka,'' he added softly. ''I should have made some excuse. . . .''

"But terrible things have happened, and you're not drinking now." Susan tried to comfort him.

"You're being nice," he said, almost smiling. "But I have it back under control, and we do have other things to worry about. My drinking is self-destructive, but my father's death threatens the entire family. So why don't you ask me whatever it is you need to know?"

"Fine. Maybe you can help me with a few facts. Who ate breakfast with your parents yesterday morning?"

"I did. And Joyce, too, of course," he answered, as she expected.

"And did you talk about the ski trip?"

"Yes, some. Although, actually, my father tried to keep the conversation focused on the ski trip, but my mother wanted to discuss Darcy."

"Darcy?"

"Well, where Randy had gone and how Darcy was so devastated . . ." He stopped to think. "Of course, no one knew then that Randy was dead."

"Except for the person who killed him."

He looked at her, startled. "I guess you're right. Unless he was killed later, after Father."

"It's possible, but not likely," Susan said, remembering the lump in the snow and thinking that she should check this out with whoever was acting as medical examiner. "Your mother was concerned about Darcy." Susan returned to the subject.

"Yes. I guess all the guests here knew how poorly my father and my youngest brother were getting along. And Darcy, of course, was on edge because Randy had apparently vanished the day before. And my father was still upset that Randy had even been brought to the reunion—although he didn't appear terribly happy that Randy had left. My mother, I'm afraid, was caught between them." He stopped a minute, hand on forehead. "It wasn't an unusual dilemma for her. And I don't think she ever got used to it. She's always said that she could never stop caring enough to make living with either of them easy. She was very upset that morning," he added. "Not as upset as she is now, of course, but truly distraught. She had looked forward to this reunion so much. I think the fact that it wasn't going well was very painful for her.''

"Did she and your father usually ski together?" Susan asked.

"I don't know about usually. They probably were together about half the time. Father enjoyed going off on his own. He said he felt a certain peace when he was alone in the wilderness. And my mother likes to ski fast, so she usually goes out with a group and then gets ahead and circles back. Actually, my mother is a much better skier than my father. When I was a child, I can remember her flying by the entire family, blond hair falling to her shoulders from under her ski hat. My father used to hate it. But they were both aware of safety, and they traveled together much of the time. I suppose it's just unfortunate that they weren't together that morning.''

"They planned on skiing separately?"

"Yes. Father was anxious to get going, and Mother urged him to go on without her. I think she probably wanted to check up on Darcy and didn't want Father to know. He probably would have said she was worrying too much. They expected to meet at the east side of Old Faithful for lunch—near where Father was found, in fact.''

"And you and Joyce?"

"We skied with most everyone for a while. We started off with Darcy and my mother. But she got ahead almost before we left the lodge's parking lot. And then Jane and Charlotte caught up with the three of us. They ended up going ahead. Darcy had trouble with the bindings on his skis, and we helped him get fixed up, so we did get rather behind the others. I know Jon and Beth passed us, but then we passed them while they were taking a detour to look at some moose. I think we got there about the same time.

"You're trying to figure out who could have gotten to Father first," he said.

"I . . ." Susan began, swiftly deciding not to mention that she had gotten this information from his children earlier.

"Well, I've been thinking about that, too. And it seems to me that any of us could have done it."

Susan opened her mouth, but remembered it was better to listen than to talk.

"You see, we were all separated from each other at one time or another, and, of course, the geyser basin is a mass of trails. Anyone could have gone ahead and killed Father and then circled back to the rest of the group."

"What?"

"Yes. It's possible. At least, I think it's possible."

Susan didn't say anything, trying to reconcile this with what Heather and C.J. had reported. Who was wrong here? And was it intentional? Was someone lying? Was one person in the family more likely to lie than the others? "Why do you think you're the only person in the family who married?" she asked, deciding to concentrate on background.

"I don't know." He seemed surprised by the question. "I've never really thought about it. I'm the oldest. And, I suppose, the most conventional, the most responsible—except when I'm drinking," he added ruefully. "I guess I still think of all my brothers and sisters as children—which they're not, of course. Darcy is just twenty-one, and Jon four years older, I guess. They're both still in school—maybe their lives are still too unsettled to think about serious, permanent relationships. Jane and Charlotte are both at least thirty, though. I don't know why they're not married. They do both seem to be enjoying their life-styles. They have good careers and appear to make excellent salaries. They've both traveled extensively—I know they each came to Paris annually when we were there. Maybe they just haven't met the right man."

"So neither of them has ever been married?"

"Jane was married for a few months her senior year of college. It was a very short marriage, though. I was living on the other side of the country. Heather was in nursery school or kindergarten, and I think C.J. was just a baby. I don't really remember now. I do recall that Joyce and I were still trying to figure out what to send for a wedding present when we got word that the marriage had ended.''

"You didn't go to the ceremony?''

"I don't think there was one—at least not one to which the family was invited. . . .'' He looked over Susan's shoulder. "Here's my wife. She might remember this better than I do. She's the one in the family who enjoys the ceremonies.''

Joyce sat down in the chair between them. "Remember what?'' she asked, waving away a prompt waiter.

"Jane's wedding.''

"She didn't have one,'' Joyce answered immediately.

"Why not?'' Susan asked.

"I don't actually know. You would have to ask her. I thought, at the time, that she was afraid to make any sort of public announcement for fear her parents would put off the whole thing.''

"Because they didn't want their daughter married before she finished college?'' Susan asked.

"I don't know about that. But they certainly didn't want her married to him!''

"What was wrong with this young man?'' Susan asked. "Or wasn't he so young?'' she added, thinking how many young girls were attracted to older men.

"Oh, he was young, all right. Probably nineteen or twenty. That wasn't what upset Phyllis and George. They were not, however, happy that Jason had dropped out of college in the middle of his freshman year and had been busy since that time trying to get a break in the rock music world.'' Joyce laughed a little. "I met him once. He was into what I think is called punk rock. His hair was bleached white. He wore a half dozen safety pins in each ear—which matched the hundreds on his jeans and leather jacket. George roared with anger every time he mentioned the boy. And Phyllis didn't mention him—she just sat around with a sad look on her face and tears ready to spill from her eyes. Jane, of course, loved it. She shaved off most of her hair and dyed what little she had left bright green. She went wherever Jason's band went, and she became active in some sort of anarchist political group. She really found an alternative to her parents' life-style.''

''So they ran off to get married and presented it as a fait accompli to her parents?''

''That's how I understand it.''

''But Jane was too old for her parents to force her to get a divorce,'' Susan said.

''Oh, yes. No one claims that they tried. As I understand it, they invited the happy couple to stay with them over the Christmas holidays, and two weeks later, Jane and Jason left in separate cars and went their separate ways. You should ask Jane if you want to know more about it.''

''And that was the last anyone heard of Jason?''

Carlton laughed loudly.

''Hardly,'' his wife said, a big smile on her face. ''In fact, his face is plastered all over one wall of C.J.'s bedroom. His hair is black now, and so long, it almost touches his waist, and he's moved up from the safety pins to chunky silver and turquoise jewelry, but it is still Jason. And now he's the lead singer in one of the biggest heavy metal bands in the country.''

''What does Jane say about this?'' Susan asked.

''We don't even know if she knows,'' George answered. ''We didn't mention to C.J. that his hero was almost his uncle because we didn't want to stir up old hurts for Jane.''

''It is interesting, though,'' Joyce added. ''You see, this particular band has a big social conscience—they sing about the homeless, the environment, war, and politicians. Jane used to be very liberal and very political. Of course, now she's a businesswoman, and we don't know how close to her heart those issues are, but Jason has, in his own way, done something that she would have been very proud of at one time in her life.''

''How remarkable,'' Susan commented, pausing for a minute. ''And Charlotte?''

''She's never been married,'' Carlton explained. ''I don't know if she has ever even been serious about a man for a long time, or if she's lived with anyone.''

"If she has, she's kept it quiet from her family," Joyce suggested.

"Are you the only person that George and Phyllis have accepted into the family?"

"I don't think it's quite like that," Joyce said. "I would assume that they're very happy with Beth. They just want their children to be happy—and like a lot of parents, they can only imagine that their children would be happy in a lifestyle like their own. I can't say that Carlton and I are so different, in fact."

Susan thought about her own children. Certainly she would be more comfortable if they chose to live as she and Jed did—but she didn't think she would be able to force them into it. There was one last question. "If the murderer is someone in your family—" she began.

"Who is it?" Carlton finished the question for her, sadness in his voice. "I thought about it all night. It's an ugly question. It's an ugly idea, and it's hard to think that someone you're related to might be a murderer."

"But you've lived away from the family for a long time. I thought you might have more perspective than any of the others," Susan said. "Or Joyce?"

"I can't imagine," Carlton said, "but—" he looked at his wife, and she nodded at him "—but everyone in the family seems to think that Darcy did it."

Susan thought they both looked utterly miserable.

TWENTY-SEVEN

Phyllis stared out the window at the geyser's steam curling up into the sky. "I felt it was important to see you alone. There are things you should know that no one else knows—or suspects. I . . . I appreciate your willingness to leave your family and meet me here."

Susan had been startled to discover Darcy standing behind her almost immediately after his oldest brother's pronouncement. But Darcy apparently hadn't overheard anything to upset him; he had only requested that she meet his mother at the Visitor's Center as soon as possible. Carlton and Joyce had urged her to leave immediately, and she had done just that, putting on her skis just a few hours after she had sworn she was taking a break from this particular form of exercise. She quickly skied across the path to the tall building. While wondering just what Phyllis was going to say, once again she had missed Old Faithful's hourly eruption.

"You know, this really isn't a very good place to meet. There are too many people who might overhear us."

Phyllis's comment made Susan feel guilty, as though she had been the one to suggest the location.

"Why don't we ski around the geyser basin and talk? I . . . I haven't been outside since my husband's death. I think the change might do me a lot of good."

"Of course," Susan agreed. "But, you know, maybe you should tell Marnie—she's been put in charge of this investigation. The storm is making it impossible for anyone to enter the park right now, and Marnie had some police training before becoming a ranger. She knows about this type of thing.''

"No. I don't think I could do that. She's so young, and I'm afraid she wouldn't understand. If . . . if I tell you anything you think she should know, maybe you could tell her. It would be much, much easier for me,'' Phyllis insisted, moving toward the door.

Susan followed her outside to the rack provided for skis.

Phyllis had snapped her shoes into their bindings before Susan had pulled her skis from the rack. Susan hurried as much as she could, remembering George Ericksen's comment over her ineptness.

"Don't rush. I really don't have any reason to hurry now that George is gone.''

Naturally Susan ignored her words, and just as naturally, the task took longer than it would have if she had taken her time. "This is the first time I've done any cross-country skiing,'' she admitted when, skis finally on, she attempted to follow Phyllis along the icy path toward the Old Faithful Lodge. "I thought that old building might be open,'' she added as the two women skied in front of the gigantic log structure.

"Too big to heat,'' Phyllis suggested, glancing at the peaked line of the roof.

"Probably,'' Susan agreed. "You said you wanted to talk to me right away,'' she reminded her gently.

"Yes. I think you've spoken with all of my family—except for Darcy.''

Susan was having trouble keeping up, and she fell behind even more when she realized that Phyllis had been keeping track of her investigation. "Yes, I have,'' she admitted.

"Who do you think did it?''

"I . . . I honestly have no idea,'' Susan answered.

"Do you know who had the . . . the opportunity to do it? Who was at the geyser at the time of the murder?''

"I'm not sure right now. It's possible that anyone could have done it—except for C.J. and Heather, who were with my kids the entire time.''

"I spoke with that girl ranger you mentioned—Marnie something—and she says that the doctor who examined the bodies was positive that Randy was killed at least a day before my husband." She slowed down for Susan to catch up. "I had hoped that maybe Randy had killed George and then he himself was killed. I guess that's a strange type of wishful thinking."

"Did you have any thoughts about who, in that case, would have killed Randy?"

"No." Susan wondered if the answer came too quickly to be true. "I just thought," Phyllis went on, "that a judge or jury would understand why a person would kill someone who killed their father. Don't you?"

An answer seemed called for. "Yes. I guess so. Is that what you thought happened?"

"I said I *hoped* that's what happened."

They skied past a group of elderly women. Susan noticed that none of them could resist peeking at Phyllis. No wonder the poor woman had been spending so much time in her room.

"You said you wanted to tell me something—something that other people don't know," Susan reminded her companion.

"It is very difficult to talk about your children."

"Yes, I can understand that. If you've changed your mind . . ."

Susan left the statement unfinished.

"No. You . . . the people who are investigating this murder . . . There are some things that have to be known." She took a deep breath. "My son . . . Darcy . . . tried to kill himself."

Susan, working hard to keep up, didn't say anything.

"He was young at the time—although I suppose that isn't much of an excuse. . . ."

"How young?"

"A senior in high school. Or, more accurately, the summer before he left home and went to college."

"I suppose that is a very trying time in the lives of some children.. . . ."

"Darcy's whole life has been trying. He was an unwanted child—unwanted by my husband, that is. I adored him. His birth was the most difficult of all my deliveries—and I have never had an easy time giving birth." Susan thought of the miscarriages that she had learned of this morning, but didn't speak. "The very moment I saw him, cuddled up in the incubator, his finger in his sweet little mouth, his head covered with blond hair, I knew I had been right to insist that we have this one more child. I named him Darcy after the hero in *Pride and Prejudice*, and he has lived up to that name: he's handsome, charming, sensitive—"

"You'll have to slow down a little. I can't keep up," Susan said, hating to interrupt but finding it more and more difficult to hear.

"I'm . . . I'm sorry. It's hard for me to realize that I'm going too fast."

"You were talking about Darcy," Susan prompted when Phyllis didn't continue immediately.

"I was trying to explain. I wanted you to understand about him. He's a remarkable human being. I know that you're thinking I'm his mother and I love him, but he really is something special."

"I don't believe that old saying about a mother's love being blind."

Phyllis gave her a grateful look and slowed down even more. "Well, his father has always had a difficult time with him. George thought four children were enough and that I was a little too old to be pregnant—and I appreciated his concern, and loved him for it." She stopped and stared at a bubbling stream that ran by the side of the trail. "But in this instance, I misjudged George. I thought he would love the baby once he was born, but that wasn't to be. Even in the hospital, I saw Darcy rejected by his own father. George came each day, of course, and he brought flowers and vanilla milk shakes—my favorite—and he gave me a fabulous ruby ring to celebrate the birth. He always gave me a beautiful piece of jewelry when each of our children were born. But he ignored Darcy. He didn't even go to see him in the nursery. And when the nurse brought him in, George just passed him to me for feeding. Even then I thought things would change, that once I got home with the rest of the family, George would grow to love Darcy as much as I already did."

"And that didn't happen?" Susan asked, relieved to stand by the stream and ask questions without gasping for breath.

"George was especially busy with research the first year of Darcy's life. He was also traveling all over the world to speak at conferences and symposia. Maybe, if he had been home more, it would have happened. But to answer your question, he didn't ever really bond with Darcy. I'm afraid that, in some very important ways, Darcy grew up without a father."

"And as he got older . . . ?"

"Darcy grew up, and if anything, they grew farther and farther apart. Darcy was so different than our other boys—and so different from George. George was a scientist, a sportsman, an outdoor enthusiast. And Darcy is an artist, with an artist's personality and interests. He's creative, introspective, sensitive. He and George just don't . . . didn't live the same life."

Susan thought back to the suicide attempt. "And this hurt Darcy in some way?"

"No, of course not," Phyllis surprised her by answering. "Darcy was a naturally happy child, and I tried as hard as I could to shield him from his father's disinterest. But I'm afraid I didn't succeed," she ended, taking her ski poles in her hands.

"It was terrible, always watching the two people I loved most in the world misunderstand each other and hurt each other through those misunderstandings." She pushed off, and Susan followed. "I was always hoping things would get better, that George would become more open-minded, or Darcy would grow up enough to give in more easily to his father's wishes, but it never happened. And then, the summer before he left for college, George and I came home from dinner at a friend's home and found Darcy in the downstairs bathroom with bleeding wrists. He had taken one of the scalpels that George used for dissecting specimens and used it to make deep slices in both wrists.''

She was quiet for a moment, and Susan respected her needs.

"But we got there in time and my child was saved," she continued. "I thought he was too fragile for it, but Darcy insisted on going off to college less than a month later. And he's done very well there. He's so talented that all his art professors just have to respect him, and he has a lot of friends . . .''

"When did you find out that he was gay?" Susan asked, when Phyllis didn't appear anxious to continue.

"He announced it that first Christmas vacation. Although, of course, I had suspected it for some time. But George just couldn't accept it—I don't know why either. I guess it was some deep-seated prejudice that couldn't accept such a thing in his own son.

"Anyway, Darcy went back East early that December. And he has worked to stay away from home ever since. It's been very, very sad.''

Susan thought about Beth's description of the apartment in New York City that this woman had apparently decorated for her son. "But you've seen him. I mean, you haven't waited for him to come home to see him.''

"Oh, yes. I've visited him in college or wherever he's been living for the summer as much as possible. Darcy has urged me to do so over and over. I felt like he needed his family, even if he hasn't managed to have a good relationship with his father all these years.''

They skied together for a while before Susan gathered the courage to ask the question. "Why do you think I have to know this?''

"Because I can't ignore the fact that everyone thinks Darcy is the murderer. And, Mrs. Henshaw, you're the only person who can help my son!''

TWENTY-EIGHT

Susan didn't see how she was going to help Darcy. In fact, she couldn't even find him. She had gone to the room he had shared with Randy, to his mother's room, had wandered the lobby and restaurant of the lodge, and she hadn't found him. She had checked the ski rack, and his equipment was there. She then left messages at the front desk, with most of his family, and with the hostess in the dining room. Maybe Darcy would find her.

"At least, that's what I'm hoping," she explained to Kathleen, flopping down on the bed in the Gordons' room.

"This isn't a very large place. If he hasn't gone off on his skis, he'll be close at hand," Kathleen assured Susan, holding the baby over her shoulder, hoping to produce a burp.

"Unless he's feeling suicidal again," Susan answered, and then proceeded to explain what she knew about Darcy's past.

"I'm surprised they leave him alone," Kathleen commented, putting Bananas down in his portable crib.

"Unless they hope he kills himself," Susan said, almost to herself, leaning over to pat the baby.

"Do you think they might?"

"Everyone seems pretty sure Darcy did it. And I suppose, if he did take his own life, at least they wouldn't have to worry about who the murderer is anymore. Even Phyllis, who obviously adores Darcy, isn't saying he didn't do it!"

"Sounds to me like she's trying to get a light sentence for him," Kathleen agreed. "In fact, I was going to talk to you about that. Dr. Cockburn stopped me in the hall earlier today. . . ."

"You're kidding. You couldn't avoid him?"

"I didn't want to when he explained that he was very, very concerned about Darcy—you know, I think he is the most pompous ass I've ever met. Dr. Cockburn, not Darcy. Anyway, it seems Mrs. Ericksen has spoken to Dr. Cockburn about her son—informally, so he felt it was ethical to speak with outsiders about it."

"And?"

"And he all but told me that he's sure Darcy is crazy."

"What?"

"He didn't put it like that—you know how psychiatrists talk." She stopped for a moment, pulling a patchwork quilt over her sleeping son. "Actually, come to think of it, he doesn't talk like most psychiatrists talk."

"What do you mean?"

"He's not very discreet. He talks too readily about his cases and his theories."

"But he's no one's doctor here, is he? He really doesn't have to be discreet, does he?"

"No. And it's more than that. He's too positive. Back when I was working, we had a number of psychiatrists who advised the police and prosecutors about suspects—and they were never positive about anything! I swear, there was nothing you could do to get one of those doctors to give a completely firm answer. They were always adding comments about their opinion only being an educated guess or that people weren't completely predictable. Dr. Cockburn is just the opposite. He appears to be absolutely sure of the truth of his opinions. I've never run into anything like it."

"But he didn't actually say that Darcy is crazy, did he? That doesn't sound like a diagnosis."

"No. He said that Darcy was a very unstable personality and was not responsible for what he did."

"He just came up to you and made an announcement about Darcy Ericksen?"

"Almost. I was walking back from the laundry, where

Bananas and I had been washing his last clean pair of pajamas, and he asked if I had time to speak with him for a few minutes—very formally, in fact.''

"And you said that you did.''

"Sure,'' Kathleen said. "I even invited him to my room.'' She grimaced. "Naturally, he felt he had to make an inane comment about us being alone together in a hotel room. For a person who specializes in human behavior, he doesn't seem to have much sophistication about his own life. Which is neither here nor there, is it?''

"So he went to your room,'' Susan prompted.

"Yes. And after he made these dumb comments, he said that he had been talking with Mrs. Ericksen about her son and he had come to some conclusions. Which is when he explained about Darcy being unstable and not responsible. He almost blurted out a complete diagnosis—which I think we can ignore.

"But what we can't ignore,'' Kathleen continued, "is that he said Mrs. Ericksen asked him to talk to Darcy and then to tell you what he thought.''

"What?''

"Yes. He was only telling me about Darcy because he knew I was your friend and he thought it was imperative that you know about this as soon as possible.''

"I wonder why. Did he explain?''

"No. He said that he was going to be in the lodge until after dinner and that he would love to speak to you.''

"I think this all fits together. I think Phyllis is sure that Darcy killed his father, and she is trying desperately to set him up with the best defense possible. You know, I wonder just what she said to Dr. Cockburn.'' She stood up. "Look, I'd like to talk to him right away. I think I'll go look around. Maybe I'll run into Darcy while I'm at it. Want to come with me?''

"I'd love to, but I'm going to have to find Chloe first.''

"Where . . . ?''

"Her room is four doors down.'' Kathleen pointed in the

right direction. ''But she may be in the lounge. I told her that she wasn't going to be needed for a few hours.''

''I'll go look for Chloe, as well as Darcy and Dr. Cockburn. If I find her, I'll send her back with a message so you know where to meet me. Okay?''

''Perfect.'' She opened the door to the hallway for her friend. ''Good luck.''

''Thanks.'' Susan smiled as Kathleen closed the door gently so as not to awaken the baby. She counted doors down the hall, then knocked on what she hoped was Chloe's room. There was no answer. Sighing, she headed for the exit. She hurried down the hall, her hiking boots clunking against the industrial carpeting as she went. No one was coming in that way, and she pushed open the door, moving into the cold, crisp air.

It was snowing more heavily now, but Susan didn't notice. She was thinking over what she had seen through the open door of the last room on the right. In a room furnished with two double beds, Dr. Irving Cockburn had been sitting on one, apparently listening intently to Kathleen's au pair, who was sprawled out on the other.

Why hadn't she interrupted them? she asked herself. After all, she was interested in talking with the doctor. And Kathleen needed the girl. What had stopped her from knocking on the half-open door? Was it the degree of intensity in the look on Dr. Cockburn's face that made her feel uncomfortable? Or was it merely that they seemed such an unlikely couple? What could they possibly have to talk about?

She was shaking her head at her own stupidity by the time she got to the dining room. He was a single doctor, she was a beautiful young girl. What was going on in that room was normal. Susan had been foolish not to interrupt. Now Kathleen would be stuck in her room with a sleeping baby. . . .

''Hi! Find anyone yet?''

''How . . . ? Where . . . ?'' Susan had the sense not to turn quickly, but she was astounded to hear Kathleen behind her.

''Chloe came back to the room right after you left, so I

ran after you.'' Kathleen answered the unasked questions.
''What's wrong?'' she continued when Susan just stood there
with her mouth open.

''I just saw Chloe. She was lying on the bed in Dr. Cockburn's room.''

''What?''

''Shhh.'' Susan tried to quiet Kathleen's shriek. ''Let's go
in there.'' She pointed to the restaurant. ''I could use some
coffee, and I'll tell you about it.''

''They were together on the bed in Dr. Cockburn's room?
Were they dressed?'' Kathleen asked.

''Shhh!'' Susan insisted on waiting until she was seated at
a private table before discussing it. ''That's not what was
going on. You're missing the point!''

''I hope so,'' Kathleen said, sitting down across from her
friend. ''I know he's a doctor, but I think Chloe can do better
than that. Besides, he's too old for her. I feel responsible—''

''Would you shut up? We'd both like some coffee,'' she
added to the waitress who had appeared at their side. ''I'm
not talking sex,'' she added when they were alone together.
''They were just talking.''

Kathleen put her napkin in her lap and looked closely at
her friend. ''So why are you making such a big deal about
it?''

''Because it didn't look right to me.''

''I didn't know you were such a stickler for propriety.''

Susan waited to answer until their coffee had been poured
and the girl had left, leaving the pot on the table. ''I'm not.
You know that! There was just something strange about the
way the two of them were together.''

''What exactly?''

''They . . . they acted like they had known each other for
a long time—like they were relaxed in each other's company,
not like they only met a few days ago.''

''Oh, that. That's Chloe. I mean, that's the way she is
about everyone. We only met her ourselves a week ago, and
already she seems like part of the family. It's wonderful!''
She sipped her coffee. ''With her looks and her personality,

that girl could find a place for herself anywhere in the world—and with anyone. I think you're making too much of this. That's just the way Chloe is.''

And a perfect description of most con artists. But Susan kept that thought to herself.

TWENTY-NINE

''So are you going to talk to Irv?''

''Who?'' Susan stared at Kathleen.

''Dr. Cockburn. He's who you started off to see, isn't he? And you saw him in his room.''

''Oh. Yes. I guess I should go back over to the rooms. . . .''

''You don't have to. He's here. . . .''

''Mrs. Henshaw. I thought I had explained to Kathleen that I needed to speak with you,'' Irving Cockburn said, and though as yet unasked, sat down in the spare chair at the table.

''I told Susan—''

''This is really very, very important. And it shouldn't have to wait,'' he continued, ignoring Kathleen. ''I've always been a person who believes in getting right to the center of a dilemma, dealing with it, and getting it out of the way. Believe me, a psychiatrist knows that things have to be dealt with.''

''I'm not arguing with you,'' Susan protested.

''We have to put the ghosts of the past to rest if we're going to make progress in our futures,'' he continued as though he hadn't heard her.

This from a man who apparently couldn't even pick out appropriate clothing for himself? He went on.

"When people start avoiding a therapist is usually the time they should be going to me . . . him."

Wonderful. He had arranged the world so that any avoidance of him could be attributed to the other person's neurosis instead of his own personality. Susan would have been amused if she hadn't remembered that other people's lives were involved here. "Aren't there any *hers*?" she asked sweetly.

" 'Hers'?"

"Aren't there any female psychiatrists?" She reworded her question.

"Naturally. We speak generically rather than sexually," he said grandly.

"Naturally," Susan parroted. "But you wanted to speak to me. A female, but not a psychiatrist." She gently nudged him back toward reality.

"Mrs. Ericksen wanted me to speak to you. I usually don't talk about my cases with strangers."

And with friends? "What did she want you to tell me?" was all she said.

"I don't allow others to dictate my prognosis."

"I didn't think you did," she lied, wondering when he was going to get to the point and who was paying the bill.

"We should start, I think, with the victim."

"Which one?"

"I believe that George Ericksen was the only real victim here. That other young man who came along with George Ericksen's son was the first victim of Darcy Ericksen, but although George was the second victim, he was the only true victim." He stopped. "You do understand?"

"You want to tell me something about George," Susan translated. Accurately, it turned out.

"He was a sick man. Sicker even than his son."

"You mean mentally?" Susan thought of cancer, heart disease, other possibilities.

"The greatest sickness of all." He leaned across and glared into her eyes.

Susan resisted the urge to laugh. "What *exactly* do you mean?"

"The overwhelming need to control the lives of others," came the pronouncement. "It's common enough. And it is probably even acceptable and encouraged in some functions of life—such as a guard in a maximum-security prison." He chuckled, apparently thinking he had been clever. "But," he continued sternly, "it can be the most destructive trait of all. A person who demands that their family, friends, and colleagues conform to their wishes has made prisoners of those who love him.

"I have spoken extensively with Mrs. Phyllis Ericksen, and I had come to the conclusion that George Ericksen controlled his family completely, and that led to his own destruction."

"You mean someone killed him to stop him from controlling their life."

"No. Someone killed him to escape the pain of his constant disapproval."

"So the person who killed him was the person he disapproved of most," Kathleen commented.

Susan nodded her head. "Darcy. But why—"

"That's not the point," the psychiatrist interrupted her. "The point is that he had no control over it."

"Darcy Ericksen had no control over whether or not he killed his own father?" Kathleen asked, sounding more like a police detective than she had in recent years.

"Exactly!" He beamed approval. "You see, he could not live up to his father's expectations and still be himself. He either had to kill himself or kill his father, thus becoming free to be whatever he wanted to be."

"A murderer." Kathleen was looking angry.

"You are missing the point, if you don't mind my saying so."

Susan kicked Kathleen under the table. "It's just that Kathleen and I don't understand this type of . . . of personality. You're saying that George Ericksen tried to control his family, and when he failed, his disapproval was so great that Darcy killed him to escape from it.''

"Exactly." Susan and Kathleen were confused. Cockburn had contradicted himself by explaining the same situation in two different ways.

"Did Phyllis tell you to talk to me?" Susan asked.

"Yes. She thought it imperative that you understand this. She told me you were investigating the murder for her."

"Yes."

"She has lost her husband, and now she is trying to save her son," he said.

"I can understand that." Susan felt for the woman. "But why is she so sure Darcy killed him? Why is everyone so sure that Darcy killed him?"

"Probably because he says he did. He made a confession over an hour ago."

Susan, Kathleen, and Dr. Irving Cockburn looked up at the earnest face of Marnie Mackay.

THIRTY

"I DON'T KNOW ANY REASON WHY YOU SHOULDN'T SEE him. The poor guy is just sitting there with this incredible look of pain on his face. But he probably won't talk to you. He's refused to speak with any of his family—they've all been trying to change his mind for the last hour."

"That's how long you've had him in custody?" Susan asked. She was skiing as fast as she could to keep up. Marnie Mackay had already explained that Darcy had come to her, saying that he had killed his father and he was turning himself in. "He came to me because, apparently, he didn't know what else to do. So I told him that he was under arrest, and we turned the warming hut next to the Visitor's Center into a temporary holding cell, arranged a schedule of rangers to guard him in their off-duty hours, and . . . and that's it. With this storm coming in, it's really all we could do. We called the FBI and the police station at Jackson, but until this storm lifts, no one is coming in and no one is going out."

"And he refused to see anybody—even his mother?"

"Yes. We told her immediately, of course, and she came over, but he insisted that he didn't want to speak to her. And it is his right, you know. We certainly can't insist that he see his mother—or anyone in the family, for that matter. They've all tried, and they've all been turned away." She shrugged. "I sure hope you can convince him to talk. The poor guy looks like he's going to explode from the pain inside him. I don't think I've ever seen the face of despair before—it's a lot like my worst nightmare."

"Is he safe?" Susan asked. "I mean, he can't hurt himself, can he?"

"No. We took away his Swiss army knife and his belt, so he couldn't do anything. The hut's heated by a wood stove, but there's a ranger watching through the window at all times, as well as one at the door.

"We told him he could make a statement now or wait till the storm clears and make it to whoever is sent in to take care of this case. He chose to wait. So that's really where things stand right now."

"I know how this looks, so this sounds like a stupid question, but do you think he did it?"

"No. I guess I don't." Marnie stopped, and Susan skied up to her side.

"Did you tell him that?"

"No. I'm in charge right now. I didn't think it would be appropriate to comment. Look, most of the rangers get a certain amount of police training these days. The national parks reflect the world outside their boundaries, and we have our share of crimes like anyplace else, and I spent some time training to be a police officer before coming to the Park Service, but I'm not thrilled to be handling this alone. Unfortunately, the weather isn't giving me any choice. And I don't want to do anything to screw this up—for Darcy Ericksen or for the National Park Service.

"And that's why I came to you. Someone has to do something for that kid—and you were the only person I could think of."

"But first I have to get him to talk to me."

"I'm afraid so."

"You said that the rest of his family has tried—alone or all together?"

"Each and every one came over individually, starting with his mother. And he refused them all."

"How . . . ?"

"They all wrote him a note, a ranger took it in, he read it, and then he refused. That's all." She skied off.

"So what am I going to say that will convince him to see me?" Susan followed the ranger.

"Good question," Marnie called back over her shoulder. "Think quick. We're almost there." She waved a ski at a minuscule log cabin almost hidden in a grove of ponderosa pine. A park ranger, snow covering his heavy down jumpsuit, stamped his feet in place by the door.

"Looks cozy." Susan was relieved that Darcy, who had suffered so much these past few days, was spending time here where silvery smoke curled from the stone chimney, and red and white checked curtains hung at the windows.

"There are cabins like this one all over the park," Marnie explained. "We keep fires burning in them all winter so hikers, skiers, and anyone else out in this weather can always find someplace to keep warm." She turned her skis to stop. "Thought of anything to say?"

"Do you have a paper and pencil?"

"Sure do." Marnie handed them over. "Good luck."

"Thanks."

"Is that all?" Marnie asked almost immediately, taking

back the paper on which Susan had written only five words before folding it in half.

"That's all I can think of."

Marnie gave the note to the ranger at the door, exchanging a few words with him before he went inside the cabin.

"I thought he could use a few minutes to warm up," Marnie came back to her. "He says Darcy is looking worse. . . . Hey! He's waving us over. Maybe it's good news."

"I don't know what you did, but he's agreed to see you," the ranger announced happily. "Sure hope you can help him. He needs it."

"I'll be in the office at the Visitor's Center. Please come see me when you get done," Marnie asked quietly as Susan took off her skis and leaned them up against the side of the building.

Susan agreed before entering the door the man held open for her. The cabin was sparsely furnished with a half dozen wooden benches arranged to be as near as possible to the large, black wood-burning stove. A door at the back of the room announced that a bathroom was behind it. A bulletin board hung on one wall, carrying many of the same announcements and messages that Susan had seen elsewhere in the park. A topographical map of Yellowstone was pinned on the wall near the door. Darcy was sitting by the stove, biting one of his fingernails.

"It tells where people have spotted various animals this winter," he explained, seeing her glance at the map. "The colored pins stuck in it stand for different kinds of animals— like green for moose, red for bison, blue for snow goose—"

"Trumpeter swan."

"What?" Darcy seemed startled by her words.

"The blue stand for trumpeter swan," Susan explained. "It says so on this chart here." She pointed at a sheet of paper swinging from its own pin on the wall, and was relieved to see the beginnings of a smile on the young man's face. "I'm glad you could see me."

"Do you believe what you wrote here?" Darcy asked,

throwing the piece of paper through the crack in the stove door.

"You don't?"

"I thought . . ." He sighed loudly. "I don't know what I thought."

"Why did you confess to the murder? You didn't kill your father, did you?"

"I wanted to. I really wanted to. I really thought he killed Randy." He started crying.

Susan waited a moment for him to calm himself before she asked her next question. "Do you know that for a fact, or are you just guessing?"

"Who else could it be?"

"I don't know," Susan confessed, "but any one of a number of people could have done it, couldn't they?"

"But why? Only my father hated him."

"Are you sure? You couldn't have known everything about his life now, could you?"

"No, but—"

"Maybe you should tell me what you do know about all of this. From the beginning. It's the only way I'm going to be able to help you," she added as he hesitated.

"I guess . . ." He stopped to take a deep breath. "I guess the beginning was the day we arrived here."

"When was that?"

"We got here the same day you did. Randy and I came in on one of the morning snowcoaches. Charlotte and Jane did, too. We had all met in Jackson Hole the night before. We arrived on different flights, and Randy and I were staying in a different hotel, but we had arranged to meet for dinner in a restaurant that Jane knew about. My sisters have known that I'm gay for five years or so, but they hadn't met Randy before. . . ."

"And you all hit it off?"

"Yeah. I was very nervous about bringing Randy along, and I'm afraid that I tried to drink away my fears. . . ." He almost laughed. "We all had a great time that night."

"And the next day?"

"Until dinner on the next day, we were fine," he answered. "The drive here was fun—maybe a little bumpy for someone suffering from a first-class hangover, but Mother was here to meet us all. And we all got together for lunch. . . ."

"Where was . . . ?"

"My father was out doing some exploring on his own."

"And your mother had met Randy before?" Susan remembered what Beth had reported.

"Yes, a few times. We live together in New York City, and Mother loves to come to the city, attend the art exhibits, and tour the galleries every few months. She even helped decorate our apartment, which was sweet of her," he added, a little doubtfully.

"Each generation has its own taste," Susan muttered tactfully.

"True." Darcy frowned. "But she's around so often that we really don't want to offend her and put anything away. . . ."

Susan wondered what version of the batik curtains Phyllis had foisted off on her son and his lover. "Your mother liked Randy?" was all she asked.

He surprised her by not answering immediately. "I think so. She's met a few of my other . . . other lovers . . . and she's never acted like she didn't like any of them. And she was the same with Randy."

"Was he different for you? Were you more serious about him than anyone else?"

"He could have been, I think. I'm older and more settled now, but who knows what will happen in the future?"

"Your father hadn't met Randy, though?"

"No. I told my family that I was gay my freshman year of college. But my father choose to ignore that information, never recognizing the men I've lived with, even going so far as to ask things like when was I going to meet a nice girl and settle down and get married?"

"He didn't respect your decision?"

"He didn't respect anything about me. I was born a disappointment to him. And I'd been letting that rule my life. After telling him that I was gay, I spent the next three and a half years pretending not to be—at least as far as my father was concerned. Maybe Randy wasn't different, maybe our relationship wouldn't have lasted, but I was different. I was standing up for what I was. The invitation to this family fiasco included what my mother chooses to call significant others. Jane and Charlotte chose to come alone. Jon brought Beth. I brought Randy—and look what happened. Poor Randy's dead. Father's dead. Mother is close to some sort of breakdown—and all because of me.'' He looked at Susan. ''You see, I do wish that I had killed him.''

THIRTY-ONE

''THAT,'' SUSAN BEGAN IN HER MOST MATERNAL VOICE, ''is simply not true. You did what you had to do, and if someone reacted to that with murder, it's not your fault. And certainly not your responsibility.''

''But—''

''No buts. No one can drive another person to kill. It's the killer's decision—and his responsibility. Now tell me exactly what happened when you introduced Randy to your father.''

''We all met for drinks in my parents' room. Randy and I got there a little late. To tell the truth, we stopped at the bar for a little liquid courage. Not that we wouldn't get enough to drink—my father has always been very liberal with his alcohol, I'll give him that.''

''And . . . ?''

''And we were the last to arrive. My parents were standing

together in the middle of the room, with Carlton and Joyce close by. They all looked over when we walked through the door.''

"And . . . ?"

"My father said something to my mother, but I couldn't hear what, then Mother's eyes filled with tears, and my father glared at Randy, then at me. . . ."

"But what did he say?"

"Father didn't speak at times like these. . . ."

"Times like what?"

"Times when his children disappointed him—at times like that, he just growled."

"What did he growl?" Susan continued to question.

" 'How could you do this to your mother?' I think those were his exact words. My father was always claiming that my mother's heart was breaking over something I had done— even if it was something she had told me to my face that she had accepted. He was like that about everything—my being gay, an artist, moving to New York." His words came out as sobs. "Don't you see? I love my mother, and my father used those feelings to try to blackmail me into being someone I'm not—and someone my mother wouldn't necessarily like. It's unconscionable."

Susan thought so, too. "Did you say anything to either of your parents?"

"Well, I didn't have to introduce Randy to my mother, and my father was rather obvious in his repugnance of my lover, so I just went over to Carlton and Joyce. They seemed willing to be friendly to Randy, and that's all I really cared about at that moment."

"But you all went to dinner together that night."

"Yes. And I actually did get the opportunity to introduce Randy to my father. I had to, for Randy's sake," he added.

"And you were all together that night at the ranger talk, weren't you?"

"Yes. Doing the family thing. You see, Randy doesn't have any family—well, just an elderly aunt who was his legal guardian. His parents died in a plane crash when he was only a year old. His aunt put him in boys' boarding schools and summer camps as soon as he was old enough. He loved the idea of family. Probably because he never had one," he added ruefully.

"Randy didn't admit to himself that he was gay until he graduated from college. He spent years and years hiding from his feelings. His life wasn't very happy. You know, he was really looking forward to this trip. He . . . he said that he thought it might be the only chance he ever had to go to a family reunion."

Susan gave Darcy a moment to regain control before continuing. "And after the ranger talk?"

"I went to the bar and checked out who was there. . . . In other words, I was scouting out the place for family. I saw you and your husband, in fact. But the people I was trying to avoid weren't around, so Randy and I had a few hot buttered rums. And then we went to bed, too.

"The next day we got up early, had breakfast, and took that class in cross-country skiing. You remember?"

"Yes. Didn't you say something to Randy about how your father controlled your mother? I don't exactly remember, but it seems to me that some sort of comment was made."

"I don't remember specifically, but it's totally and completely true. My mother was ruled by my father. He set the standards of the family, and she had to live with them. For instance, he bought the cabin we had up in Door County without even telling her about it. My mother tells the story that she was away for a long weekend settling some details of her parents' will, and she came home to discover that they were the proud owners of two homes. That's not normal in a marriage, is it?"

Susan was a lot older than Darcy and less likely to divide the world into normal and abnormal. "But your sister told me that your mother loved that cabin, that she had designed a special garden of some sort. . . ."

"I didn't say that she doesn't love the cabin; she does. My mother has learned to make the best of a lot of things. In fact, it's a talent she has, a real talent. She has taken the life my father has given her and made something extraordinary out of it."

Susan thought that it didn't take a whole lot of talent to make something of a life that included two homes, five healthy children, and the income required to amply meet the needs of all. But then she remembered the stillbirth and the miscarriages. Money didn't cure everything. She decided to return to the original topic. "So you and Randy took the ski class in the morning. What happened in the afternoon?"

"We didn't make it till afternoon." Darcy's answer was almost a whisper.

"You mean . . ." Susan had temporarily forgotten the body under the snow.

"Randy and I left the class as soon as the instructor dismissed us," Darcy began. "Remember how he told everyone to practice by going around that circle near the parking lot?"

Susan nodded. She had traveled that path for almost an hour, trying to synchronize arm and leg movements.

"Well, Randy wanted to practice, but I was tired. And looking back, I know that I was nervous about meeting the family later in the day. I had run into Joyce at breakfast, and she told me that she was worried that Carlton was drinking again. And he had been dry for years! I guess I felt like everything was beginning to fall apart."

"And what happened then?"

"I had this terrible argument with Randy. And it was all my fault—it really was," he added, seeing she was about to interrupt. "I know myself pretty well, and I know that I blame other people when things get to be too much for me to handle. And that morning things were getting to be too much for me. Amazing, isn't it? Looking back, I realize that everything was almost perfect then, but at the time . . . Well, hindsight isn't always what it's cracked up to be, is it? Anyway, I picked an argument with Randy. I told him that he was being stupid and enjoying this damn family reunion because he was selfish, that if he cared about me, he wouldn't be having so much fun. I said that he really cared more about having a family than being with me . . . and all sorts of other awful things. I get sick whenever I think about it.''

"You were upset. You said some things you shouldn't have. Everyone alive has done that. The only difference is that Randy died before you could tell him how sorry you were.'' Susan tried to comfort him.

"Yeah. I guess so. But what makes it worse is that Randy didn't even argue back. He just said that I was upset and he was going to practice alone for a while, and skied off in the direction of the woods.''

"And you?''

"I headed back to the lodge. I was upset and my feet were killing me. All I wanted to do was take a quick shower and get into normal clothing.''

"Did anyone see you?''

"I suppose people in the hall or something. I didn't see anyone from my family.''

"And when did you realize that Randy was missing?''

"He didn't come to lunch.''

"But certainly—''

"Randy was raised by a cranky old lady. He is, I mean was, absolutely reliable about things like mealtimes and washing behind his ears. We used to joke about it. So when he didn't come to lunch, I assumed that his absence was intentional—that he was purposely not coming. And then, when he didn't appear later in the afternoon, I thought he might have gotten so mad that he left the park. The snow-coach out of Yellowstone leaves around one each day. Since then, I've heard that all the seats are reserved months in advance—but I didn't know that then.

"That night I started calling the apartment in New York. It was silly, of course; even if he had left at one, he could never have managed to get to New York City from Wyoming in less than twelve hours. But, of course, it turned out that he wasn't going to be answering any more of my calls anyway.''

"Did you ever think he might be dead?''

"Actually, I did. I wondered if he could have been in a

plane crash or a taxi accident on the way into the city from the airport. It never occurred to me that he might be lying dead here in the park. I don't know why. That's not true—I do know why. Because Randy was very, very careful. He would never have skied off alone; he simply didn't take risks. So I thought of accidents. Or the possibility that he was so mad that he decided to hide—to stay with someone else or something like that. It never occurred to me that he might be murdered. Why would anyone want to kill Randy?''

"You thought your father had," Susan reminded him.

"You seem to be the only person who doesn't think so," he said, looking at the fire. "And let's face it, Father hated Randy. But even Father wouldn't kill someone just because he hated them. The world would be littered with corpses if that were true. Father didn't like a lot of people."

Susan digested that bit of information. "Your parents were the only ones staying in the main lodge, right?"

"Yes, the rest of us are in the building where you're staying."

"Did anyone else in your family talk with your father about his feelings, about what was happening?"

"I'm sure Mother did. In fact, we were talking about that last night. She insists that I did the right thing by bringing Randy here. Not, of course, that the murders were a good thing, but she firmly believes that Father would have adjusted to my life-style in time and that we could have had some sort of viable adult relationship."

"You don't sound convinced of that."

"I know it would never have been like that. I don't remember a time in my life when Father and I got along. And he's had years and years to come to accept me as I am. Why would he suddenly do so now?"

"But your mother—"

"Is an eternal optimist. Which you would have to be if you were married to my father."

Susan was silent for a moment. "Darcy, if you weren't your parents' son, what would you think of them?"

"Interesting question. I've asked it myself, in fact."

"And have you reached any conclusion?"

"Sometimes I love them. And sometimes I hate them, but that's not the answer you're looking for, is it?"

THIRTY-TWO

DARCY STARED UP AT THE CEILING FOR A FEW MINUTES before continuing.

"My mother is a very creative woman—and very domestic. She's the type of person who decides to paint the dining room, and two weeks later she's learned to stencil and to glaze, and she has created something wonderful out of a dull nine-by-twelve room." He paused again.

"And your father?"

"He's the one who noticed that there were fingerprints on the walls and that the repainting was necessary. Probably he blamed me for making them. Okay, I'm not being very objective, am I?"

"Not really," Susan agreed, although she still found the conversation revealing.

"The truth is that my father is not that bad if you don't have to live with him. He's well educated, he's led an interesting professional life—I mean, he's been all over the world doing research and giving speeches. He's one of the leaders in his field, in fact. He makes a decent living, although I guess a lot of the family's money comes from my mother. . . ."

"Your mother works?"

"No, her family has money. She's one of the Boston Applegates—it's an old shipping family, and she's always had money. There was a trust fund from her grandmother when she was twenty-one, and more money when her parents died.''

''And did your father have any trouble with that?''

''With getting money from his wife? Not a bit! He's always said that the first thing a college professor needs is brains, and the second is a rich wife.''

''And he had both.''

''Yes. And he had a family. If I were looking at this thing from the outside,'' Darcy said slowly, ''I would say that family was very important to my father—in a good way. He probably worked hard to include Jon and me in his life; I know he brought us presents and made phone calls from all over the world. But, in fact, I don't remember a lot. Jane and Charlotte were into their teens before I was five years old. And Carlton wasn't even living at home when I was born. I remember thinking that he had escaped and that I could do that, too.''

''Do what?''

''Go to college, get out of the house, make a life for my-self.''

''And you did.''

''Yes. My mother always insisted that, no matter what, each of her children must train for a career. Her parents didn't believe in women working unless they had to support themselves and their family, but Mother always said that everyone should be productive, and in this world, that meant earning a living.''

''An artist's life isn't always lucrative,'' Susan suggested.

''Now you sound like Father. He said that each of his children had careers, but that I was just acting like a spoiled brat when I decided to become an artist. I did think of getting a more practical degree, something like art therapy or a teaching certificate, but Mother thinks that I have enough talent to support myself, so I'm doing my degree work in fine arts.''

''Do you think your mother regrets not having a career?''

''Not really. I think she just realizes that the world she

grew up in doesn't exist anymore. Inherited money doesn't go as far as it used to. I think my mother was happy raising her children and keeping house.'

"Do you think your parents had a happy marriage?"

"Hard question." Darcy glanced around the small room as if expecting to find the answer written on a wall. "I don't know. Maybe they were happy before I came along. I . . . I seem to have put a wall between them." He looked straight at Susan. "You know my father didn't even want to have me, don't you?"

"I . . . I heard that."

"My mother told me that once. I was just a kid at the time, but I never forgot it."

"Why did she tell you?"

"I don't know. I think she was trying to tell me that I had to be good, that I had to please my father. I don't think it had to do with me completely. Possibly Carlton was drinking then, and one of my sisters was involved with a man that no one in the family approved of, Jon was going through adolescence like a crazy person, involved in drugs and not appearing at school regularly, but I remember that it was fall and I had been helping my mother rake leaves late one afternoon. I was happily piling up the leaves, thinking how spectacular the colors were, when I noticed that my mother was leaning against the trunk of an old maple that stood in the middle of the backyard, and she was crying so hard that her whole body was shaking."

"How old . . . ?"

"I think I was nine or ten at the time. I was terrified," he continued. "One of the kids in my fifth grade had a mother who died of cancer in the summer, and when I saw Mother like that, it was all I could think of. Anyway, I asked her if she was hurt or if I was doing something wrong, and she said no, that she loved me just the way I was. Then she told me that my father was very, very unhappy—I remember that she said 'very, very'—and that she and I must work very hard to make things right in the family.

"Well, I had spent most of my youth making my father

unhappy. He wanted me to be involved in competitive sports, he didn't like what I was interested in, he didn't like me taking art lessons—''

"Were they private lessons? Lessons with a private teacher?"

"Yes. I was identified at a very young age as being artistic and every Saturday, for truly as long as I can remember, I had private lessons. I suppose my parents fought over that, too. But if they did, my mother won, because I had those lessons.

"Anyway, that afternoon Mother sat me down and explained the facts of life to me—the facts of my life, that is. She told me that my father hadn't wanted me to be born, had all but ignored me in the hospital, had traveled so much the first few years of my life that I didn't even recognize him until I was over a year old. She told me that I had to be very, very good so that my father would love me as much as she loved me." Darcy was near tears. "But even though I was only a kid, I knew that I couldn't be myself and be a person that my father would love. I knew that I couldn't do it. . . .''

"But your mother loved you. . . .''

"Yes, I know. My mother has always loved me, and I know that has made it easier."

"Made what easier?"

"Being such a disappointment to my father."

"What happened after Randy disappeared?" Susan asked, regretting that she had to ask all these painful questions.

"Well, of course, I called everyone I could think of, and then I talked to some of the rangers here to find out if anyone had seen Randy join the afternoon trip out of the park, and then I had a horrible argument with my father."

"About Randy?"

"Yes, but not just that I had brought my homosexual lover to the family reunion. You see, my father had the balls to accuse Randy of making that damn dummy and dumping it into the pool. . . . Here was Randy lying dead under a snow-drift, and my father is accusing him of committing some petty crime. . . .''

"But your father didn't know he was dead at that point, did he?"

"I don't know. . . ."

"Presumably only the person who murdered Randy knew where he was."

"Aren't you going to ask?"

"Ask what?"

"If I think my father killed Randy. Isn't that the way it's supposed to go? I discovered that my father killed Randy and so I killed him?"

"We started out this conversation like that," Susan reminded him. "And I told you that I don't think you did it."

Darcy looked at the door through which he had thrown the note she had written.

"So why don't you tell me what happened between Randy's disappearance and finding your father, and maybe we'll figure out who did do all this."

"I ran into Father in the hallway outside of my room right after I had talked with the people at the desk about Randy. I . . . I was pretty upset, and I think I said something to him about how Randy was missing and he probably was glad about it. I was pretty nasty, in fact. Anyway, he was actually fairly nice to begin with. He said that he was sorry Randy was missing, but that he had probably left the park and I'd hear from him eventually. He suggested that I just go lie down in my room and try to relax, that getting so upset wasn't going to help anything. But he wasn't mean about it. I mean, I honestly think that he was trying to be kind."

"And you were very upset at that point," Susan prodded.

"Almost hysterical. Maybe I had some sort of premonition that something terrible had happened to Randy, I don't know. All I know is that I was horrible to Father. I told him that I was in love with Randy and that his attitude toward us was destroying me. I told him that he was trying to ruin my life. I told him that I hated him, that I would never ever talk with him again. . . . I was dreadful."

"And?"

"And that's when my father suggested that Randy wasn't

the person I thought he was, that Randy had made the dummy and put it into the pool. And that was so unfair. Randy didn't have a mean bone in his body. He was one of the kindest and gentlest men I've ever known. He would never do anything to hurt me or a member of my family. He just wouldn't!''

"And you told your father all that?"

"No, I just called him some names, and he said something about this not accomplishing anything and he left."

"And you?"

"I went into my room and actually did what my father had suggested. I was exhausted and I fell asleep."

"But you were at dinner that night."

"I only slept for an hour or so. Then, when I woke up, I realized that I was going to be late for dinner. You know, I almost didn't go. But I thought that if I stayed in my room, it might just make things worse. Randy and I had talked about it the night before, and he thought that the only way I was going to get through the week was to just do what I was supposed to. And I had decided that he was right—I even thought about how I would see him again in New York and I would tell him about how I did just what he suggested. . . . I'm not going to finish if I keep thinking like that, am I?"

Susan just smiled and put one of her hands on his.

"So I got up and changed my clothes and went over to the lodge for dinner. My family had left a place for me—my mother was seated between my father and myself, presumably as a barrier or some sort of neutral zone—and I sat down, apologized to everybody for being late, and ordered a drink."

"And then?"

"My mother—she was trying to be helpful, I know— whispered to me that maybe it was for the best that Randy had left, that now my father and I would have a chance to sort out our problems, and I . . . and I blew up. I shouted threats of some sort at my father and left the room."

"I was there. I remember."

"I guess everyone who was there remembers. People have been looking at me rather strangely ever since."

"But you were all back together at the ranger talk that night."

"Yes. My mother came to my room right after dinner and begged—actually begged—that I join the family for that. And I did. It was the last time I saw Father, in fact. I don't think I even said good night to him before going to my room. I had a terrible time sleeping, though. I was upset, and the hotel was very noisy—kids running up and down the halls and people chatting. I think I fell asleep around five A.M. And then I got up late. I was meeting Charlotte and Jane for breakfast; we had arranged it the night before. I stopped along the way to call one or two friends that I thought might have seen Randy, and later I joined Carlton, Joyce, and Mother for the trip around Old Faithful. Then we found out that Father had been murdered. . . ."

"Darcy." Susan called him out of the past. "Who did you ski with yesterday?"

"Everyone. I started with Carlton, Joyce, and Mother, and then Mother went on ahead. Jane and Charlotte skied with me for a while—I ran into them when they were watching the moose eating in the stream—and Jon and Beth passed by and then circled back to get the camera equipment they had forgotten. I don't actually remember the order all the time. I do know that I got to Father's body right after Joyce. You were there," he added.

"Yes. But I can't remember the order everyone appeared," Susan explained.

"I guess I haven't helped you very much, have I?" he asked as the door opened.

"Looks like you're going to have company," a ranger announced, entering the room. "Two more members of your family have suddenly remembered that they killed your father."

THIRTY-THREE

"I REALLY DON'T HAVE ANY CHOICE OTHER THAN TO TAKE all confessions as true. Although, of course, all three couldn't have murdered their father. At least, I hope they couldn't have. Frankly, I'm beginning to think I'm going crazy. Have some more herb tea." Marnie Mackay pushed a tall green thermos across the table to Susan. They were sitting together in the tiny, windowless office allotted rangers in the Visitor's Center. "They probably shouldn't be kept together, should they?"

"I—"

"But I don't know where else to keep them. I did think of confining them all to separate rooms in the lodge, with guards standing outside the doors, but that seemed a little too public. It isn't fair to the other guests to turn part of the hotel into a jail. So I told them not to talk to each other about the murder—not that they're likely to listen." She reached out and refilled her own mug with tea. "So which of them did it?"

"Or did any of them?"

"I was afraid you were going to say that," Marnie said. "What can we do? Wait until each member of the family has confessed except for one and then arrest that last person for murder?"

"Crazy, isn't it? What did Jane and Charlotte tell you?"

"Actually, I think it was Jane who did all the talking. She's the one with longer hair, right?"

"Yes, and she's the more vocal of the two," Susan said.

"They seem so alike—almost twins," Marnie mused.

"Oh, well, that's neither here nor there. They came to me, and Jane said that they had killed their father and they wanted to confess to the crime—just like that! As though two people confessing to a murder was an everyday occurrence. Although it may get to be, if this keeps up.'' She sipped her tea.

"They said they both did it?''

"Exactly. I asked how, and Jane said that they had both hit him with the shovel. They almost made a mistake there. I think Charlotte was starting to tell me that there were two shovels when her sister interrupted with this story of sharing the same shovel. Jane probably realized that I might suggest they produce the other murder weapon.''

"But you didn't act like you believed them, did you?''

"Are you kidding? Sarah Bernhardt couldn't act like she believed them. When I explained that I didn't see how I could accept their story, Jane said that I had no right to decide who the murderer of their father was.''

"I suppose they have a point,'' Susan admitted reluctantly. "I suppose they said they were confessing because they wanted you to know that Darcy didn't do it.''

"Exactly, although I wondered if this wasn't just their way of getting in to see him.''

"But they didn't know that you were going to . . . to store them all in the same place, did they?''

"No. But they might have just assumed it. I did ask one of the rangers to stay inside the warming hut with them. So they don't have much privacy, if that's what they were looking for. I don't know how legal that is, but with the temperature already below zero and still dropping, I can't risk having their guard freezing to death. I'll move them all in here after the program tonight. That will be easier for everyone. And we'll all stay warm and have a place to sleep.''

"You're going to stay here, too?''

"I don't see what else I can do. I'm officially in charge of this case. And I will be until someone else gets into the park. The snow isn't letting up, is it?''

"Worse than ever.''

"A few years ago it snowed here for six days in a row. Over forty inches fell. Dead animals all over the place. I can give a great lecture on natural selection and population decline among wild animals, but it still breaks your heart."

Susan shivered, despite the stuffiness of the little room.

"So you don't think Darcy did it?"

Marnie's question recalled her to the business at hand.

"No, but I can't tell you who I think did."

"I was afraid you were going to say that. You know, that obnoxious psychiatrist has been pestering me with his theories all day long—when he's not trying to convince me to go out with him. I thought he was going to drive me crazy, but I'm beginning to think that I'll take an answer from anywhere. Do you want to talk with Jane and Charlotte?" She changed the subject.

"Not now. I learned a lot from Darcy—not that it makes much sense right now—and I think I'd like to check in with Kathleen and see if she's come up with anything."

"Kathleen?"

Susan explained their relationship, asking that Marnie keep quiet about it.

"You know, one of the things I don't understand about these murders—one of the many things—is why Mrs. Ericksen asked you to investigate."

"Oh, that's simple. That's the only thing I do know for sure. She wants me to get involved because she thinks I'm incompetent. She thinks I'll confuse the issues so much that no one will ever know exactly what happened."

"You're kidding."

"No. Originally I was flattered that she had asked me, but then I began to consider her source of information. You see, she heard that I had experience from Chad, my son. I thought that he had been bragging about me. Then it occurred to me that I was dreaming. Chad is fourteen years old. He doesn't spend any time bragging about his mother these days; in fact, he does the opposite. If Phyllis Ericksen heard from him that I've done some detecting, she didn't hear that I was the next Miss Jane Marple, I can assure you. Probably he said some thing sarcastic about me being mixed up in some murders. And I think Phyllis Ericksen is enough of an opportunist to hope that I would not just get mixed up in this one, but do some mixing up of my own.''

''So what is she trying to hide? After all, a man that she was apparently devoted to was murdered, so wouldn't she want to discover the killer?''

''I think she may be feeling a little ambivalent about that, since the murderer is most likely a member of her own family.''

''It's going to be a double blow to her,'' Marnie suggested as someone knocked on the door.

''Let's hope it's not another confession,'' Susan muttered, watching the door open to reveal another ranger.

''They want to talk to you.'' Everyone knew to whom she referred. ''I think they're going to retract their confessions.''

''I don't think I should let it be that simple.'' Marnie stood up.

''What are you going to do?''

''I'm not sure. But I don't think I can take this as casually as they might like. After all, two men are dead. If people are going to go around confessing to murder, they shouldn't do it casually. The dummy may have been an ill-conceived joke, but dead men have to be taken seriously.''

Susan thought about that last comment all the way back to the lodge. It wasn't just that murder was more serious than dropping effigies in hot springs, it was such a different type of crime. These murders had appeared impromptu. The shovel that had been used to kill George Ericksen had been handy; Randy had been killed when he just happened to be passing by after a ski lesson. The effigy, however, had required some planning. It had to be made, first off, and that would have taken an hour or more. Added to that, the creator would have had to find clothing that resembled what George Ericksen wore. (Where could anyone find those suspenders? They must have been brought into the park.) And then whoever made it had to ski the mile or so to the pool carrying the thing along. Which seemed almost impossible to Susan, a novice skier. So had the person been a good skier? And weren't the only Ericksens who were good skiers Phyllis and Jon? Or was someone hiding their skiing ability? But it was obvious that the effigy had to have been planned out. And it looked like the murders were impromptu. So were all three events even connected? Or had it just been some sort of strange coincidence that everything was happening in the same family? She was still thinking these things over when she became aware that someone had been calling her name.

"Slow down! I've been yelling to you for the last five minutes."

It was snowing so hard that Susan had a difficult time making out Kathleen, skiing about ten feet from her.

"Were you looking for me?"

"Not really. I need to stop in at the ski shack for some new gaiters. The elastic has begun shredding in one of mine."

"I'll come with you. I haven't been in there yet. Jed and Chad have been in charge of equipping the family. It will be fun to look around." They had arrived at the rack outside the ski shop and paused to take off their skis before going inside.

"I may not be a great skier, but I'm getting pretty good at taking those things off and putting them back on," Susan commented, following Kathleen through the door.

"That's the first step," cheered a burly young man sitting by a wood-burning stove. Susan recognized him as her ski instructor. He asked, "How are you doing on the hills? Still having trouble with your herringbone?"

"Not at all. It's great," she lied. After all, he'd never see her on the trail.

"So what can I do for you? Are you ready for waxed skis?"

"Waxed?"

"You choose the wax you need for the snow conditions. It's easier to ski fast on waxed skis," he explained.

"I need gaiters," Kathleen said, making it unnecessary for Susan to lie again.

The young man sprang to Kathleen's assistance, pulling various-colored gaiters off the wall behind them and elaborating on the difference in materials. Susan wandered about the tiny shop, inspecting goggles and fanny packs, stopping to read the ingredients on packages of gorp.

When Kathleen found her a few minutes later, Susan was standing still in front of a large display of bright red suspenders.

THIRTY-FOUR

"BUT THEY ALL HAD 'YELLOWSTONE' PRINTED ON THEM in white block letters," Kathleen protested.

"Only on one side. The other side is completely red. Or the letters could have been covered—red paint would do it," Susan answered.

"Wouldn't that have washed off in the hot water of the pool?"

"Well, maybe. But we have to see those suspenders—if they could have been bought here, it might change everything!"

Kathleen gave Susan a stern look.

"Okay, I'm exaggerating. But it would mean that the prank was dreamed up after the person got to the park, that it wasn't planned ahead of time, that it was a reaction to what was happening here."

"Probably."

"Okay, probably. So I think we should ask Marnie if we can see the suspenders right away. It would be nice to know at least one thing for sure."

"You think she'll let you see them?"

"She's been very cooperative, so I imagine she will. She even let me talk with Darcy."

"You were going to tell me about that," Kathleen reminded her. They were skiing through the snow back to the Visitor's Center.

"And you were going to tell me what you've been doing this afternoon. But first those suspenders," Susan said, pulling up to the Visitor's Center. She was beginning to feel that she could measure out this vacation in the number of trips between ski racks. Or in falls, she added to herself.

"Are you all right? Do you need some help?"

"Thanks, but I've had a lot of practice getting up," Susan assured her friend. "In fact, it's my specialty," she added, following Kathleen into the warm building.

"So where's Marnie?"

"If you're looking for Ranger Mackay, she's out back, at the warming hut."

Susan and Kathleen thanked their informant and headed back out into the cold.

"This is turning out to be some storm."

"Mrs. Henshaw . . . Susan . . . Is that you?" Jon Ericksen skied up beside them. He was breathing hard. "I thought . . . That is, have you seen my mother?"

"Your mother?" Susan repeated his words.

"Is she missing?" Kathleen asked.

"Yes, we're very worried about her. She's . . . she must be out here somewhere!" He looked around, as though expecting her to pop out from behind a tree.

"Now, wait. When did you last see her, and why do you think she's outside?" Kathleen asked, as always the voice of reason.

"I . . . I didn't see her. Beth and Joyce went to her room to see if she needed anything. They thought that with Darcy locked up—"

"And Jane and Charlotte," Susan reminded him.

"Jane and Charlotte? Why in heaven's name are they locked up?"

Susan explained quickly the most recent events of the afternoon as she knew them. "I don't think anyone believes that they got together and killed your father, but Marnie isn't in any position to pick and choose whose confessions she listens to and whose she doesn't."

"I can see that. It's not her, it's my sisters that I don't understand. Why do they think it will help Darcy if they confuse the issues? What are they trying to do, getting locked up right when we need them the most?"

"Need them for what?"

"To take care of Mother. She should never have been left alone. My father dead, her favorite son confessing to killing him . . . Of course it was too much for her."

"So what happened? You said that Beth and Joyce went to her room. . . ."

"Oh, God, what a nightmare!" Jon stopped to wipe the snow off his mustache. "As I understand it, Beth and Joyce went to Mother's room and found it torn apart—literally in shreds, Beth said. Bottles smashed on the floor, clothing scattered all over, books torn apart. The curtains were even pulled from the windows, and the shower curtain had been slashed. They were shocked, of course. And worried when they discovered that someone—presumably Mother—had written a message on the bathroom mirror in lipstick."

"What did it say?"

"Something about needing to get out . . . I don't remember exactly. I was so upset when they told me about this all," he explained.

"Of course you were. Just go on," Susan urged.

"Well, they both read whatever the message was, and they think she's out here in the storm somewhere. We have to find her, Mrs. Henshaw. No one can live in this weather for very long."

"Did you tell the rangers or anyone at the lodge?" Kathleen asked.

"No, I just got my skis and dashed out. Maybe Beth or Joyce did. Or perhaps Carlton," he added hopefully.

"I don't think you should just assume someone has reported this. The rangers know the area, and they're trained to organize search and rescue," Kathleen said. "You go back and talk with them right away. Susan and I will keep looking for your mother."

"But Beth—and Joyce."

"Where are they?" Kathleen asked.

"They headed up the trail behind Old Faithful. We thought that since Father had been killed there . . ."

"Let's just hope they don't try to ski the entire way. It's getting too dark for a trip that long."

"But shouldn't I keep looking?" Jon insisted. "Or maybe I should head out after Beth. . . ."

"No. You go right over to the Visitor's Center and report this to the ranger on duty at the main desk."

"And then what?" Jon asked.

"Do what the people in charge tell you to do," Kathleen answered logically. "And you'd better leave right now."

"But I think—" Jon began his protest.

"Go now," both women ordered.

He turned and skied away.

"Do you think he's going to tell anybody about this?" Susan asked Kathleen as they watched his back retreat into the distance.

"Who knows? He's terribly upset—as anyone would be."

"I'd like to get a look at Phyllis's room but maybe we had better go over to the warming hut and tell Marnie what is going on. I don't think the Park Service is going to be thrilled to hear that there are people out in this storm. There was a sign in the Visitor's Center requesting that everyone stay well within the Upper Geyser Basin until it's over."

"Let's go find Marnie," Kathleen suggested, wrapping her scarf around her chin and pushing off. "I'll head to the warming hut, and you try the path straight to the Visitor's Center."

Susan followed, bending down to protect her face and eyes from the blinding snow.

The wind speed seemed to be increasing, and frozen trees creaked loudly all around them. A half dozen elk were standing nearby, searching for protection under the low branches and near buildings, more afraid of freezing than of civilization.

"George loved snowstorms." The soft voice seemed to come out of a tall ponderosa pine, bending in the wind. "I fell asleep this afternoon, and when I woke up, I thought for just one moment that the snow crackling against the window was George, trying to get in."

"Phyllis? Is that you?"

It was, but Susan and Kathleen had reasons other than the storm not to recognize her. Her short, curly hair was so covered with snow that she looked as if she were wearing a particularly unattractive sheepskin helmet. A long navy scarf, which Susan recognized as the one George always wore, and had, in fact, been wearing when he was killed, flew out behind her.

"Are you okay?"

"You shouldn't be out here alone." Susan added her concern to Kathleen's. "Why don't we go get something warm to drink?"

"I don't want to be around people. Everyone stares at me."

Susan was stunned by the change in Phyllis in the last few hours. "Why don't we go back to the Visitor's Center? I think we could borrow the office there," she suggested. She took the woman's arm and guided her toward the building. "Your family is looking for you, you know."

"My family? Darcy?" The voice quivered.

"No, Darcy is safe and warm. You don't have to worry about him," Susan said, pulling more tightly on Phyllis's arm. "Jon is looking for you. Beth and Joyce went to your room. . . ." She paused. They didn't know, after all, whether or not Phyllis had trashed her own room, and Susan didn't think this was the time to give the woman another shock. "They didn't find you there, and they were worried. They're out looking for you right now," she ended.

"Jon is a nice son," Phyllis said comfortably. "I have wonderful children."

"Yes, you certainly do," Kathleen agreed. "Why don't I ski ahead and tell the rangers that we're coming in," she suggested to Susan.

"Good idea. Phyllis and I will just take it easy." Now that she had a chance to look more closely, she was shocked by more than just the other woman's hair. Dark circles rimmed eyes set in a face that was almost white. Susan just hoped it wasn't the beginning of frostbite. "Maybe you should pull that scarf up over your face."

Phyllis ignored her.

"We're almost there," Susan said, hoping they were going to make it. Ice crystals were forming on Phyllis's cheeks, and Susan had seen that her nose was becoming a waxy yellow. "Can you move more quickly?"

"Yes. Of course." But she didn't speed up, and Susan was deeply relieved to see the lights from the windows of the Visitor's Center through the snow and trees. "Let's go in the back way, through the auditorium. It should be empty until after dinner, and . . . and you said that you didn't want to see people for a while," Susan added. She wanted to avoid company for as long as possible herself. Phyllis looked terrible. She needed help, possibly immediate medical attention, and Susan wanted a chance to talk with her.

They were in luck and the enormous double doors to the auditorium were unlocked. Susan swung one open and pushed Phyllis before her into the dark room.

"There aren't any lights," Phyllis protested.

"Don't move. I know exactly where the switches are," Susan lied, inching along the wall, feeling for lumps or bumps. "Ah!" She found them and the room filled with light.

Phyllis was still standing by the doorway. The snow was melting off her hair and clothing, and she was blinking.

"I know it's bright. . . ."

"No. It's my nose. I think it's burned or . . . Oh, it's frostbite, isn't it?" Phyllis spoke as though her condition were only of academic interest. She reached up, and Susan grabbed her hand.

"I don't think you're supposed to touch it! Here! Sit down and let me look at you." Susan peered at Phyllis's face.

"Perhaps one of the rangers would know what to do," Phyllis suggested. "It does hurt terribly."

"There must be someone in the main room. You stay here and I'll go get them. I should have thought of this before. Kathleen is probably wondering where we've vanished to."

"Go ahead. I'll be fine here."

"You're sure?" Susan asked, not wanting to leave her alone.

"Yes. Yes, I'm sure. Just try to find someone to help me. This is getting more painful all the time."

Susan hurried to the door at the front of the room, pausing only long enough to look over her shoulder. Phyllis Ericksen sat huddled in a seat at the back of the auditorium, hair soaking wet from melting snow, nose white, and tears covering her scarlet, windburned cheeks.

THIRTY-FIVE

"I DON'T KNOW WHAT WOULD HAVE HAPPENED IF YOU hadn't found her. The frostbite wasn't severe, but it doesn't take much time for a mild case to turn into something that can cause permanent damage."

"We really didn't find her. She found us," Kathleen answered Marnie. "Look, I'd love to stay and hear about everything that has been going on this afternoon, but Bananas needs feeding and—"

"Go ahead. Save a seat for me at dinner, and I'll fill you in," Susan promised as Kathleen stood up. They were together in the still-deserted auditorium; Phyllis was lying down in the office, a ranger trained in first aid by her side.

" 'Bananas'?" Marnie asked Susan when they were alone together.

"That's her son's nickname. He's only a few months old. I think everyone assumes he'll outgrow it in time."

"Let's hope so." Marnie sighed. "You know, it's nice to talk about something ordinary for a change. I really think I'm going to go crazy."

"Any news from outside the park?"

"Yes. There's no sign of the storm letting up. The phone lines are down—they're buried inside the park, of course, but the line to the park is down—so we're communicating with shortwave sets. And in this weather, even that isn't too reliable. The news from outside is that we're on our own." She sighed. "I don't suppose you've solved this puzzle?"

"No, but I think I'm getting close," Susan surprised her by answering. "I need some help, though."

"What?"

"Information from you, for one thing," Susan answered, and proceeded to ask about the suspenders on the effigy.

"Sure. They were Yellowstone suspenders with the white letters covered up with ink—probably Magic Marker. But I don't see how that's going to tell you anything. They're very popular with the tourists, and we sell dozens each week—unless, of course, the guys at the ski shack could tell you which member of the family bought them. . . . Hey, you may be getting somewhere!"

Susan was embarrassed to admit that she hadn't thought of that, so she nodded sagely. "And if they weren't brought into the park, then the prank wasn't planned."

"And you think that would make a difference?"

"It might. I'm trying to work this thing from all angles—who had motive, who had opportunity. . . ."

"And who did? Have motive and opportunity?" Marnie asked.

"Opportunity is tough. Mainly because I think anyone in

the family could have killed him—with the exception of C.J. and Heather. . . .''

''Why not them?''

''They were with my kids all the time—and they're awfully young.''

''We had a murder in the park last summer—and it was committed by a thirteen-year-old girl,'' Marnie said quietly. ''But if you're sure they were with your kids, I guess we can eliminate those two.''

''Yes,'' Susan agreed doubtfully. Now that she thought about it, had they been with Chad and Chrissy the entire time, or had they skied off alone at all? She remembered, uncomfortably, how upset C.J. had been over his grandfather's death. But any sensitive boy would feel that way . . . wouldn't he?

''And the rest of the family?''

''They were all alone at one time or another yesterday morning. It would have been difficult, but any one of them could have done it. Only Jane and Charlotte were inseparable during the entire time—and they claim to have killed him, so I don't think that means much of anything.''

''So we go to motive. . . .''

''That's a little more difficult. George Ericksen was a very unusual man, and I think his personality had a profound effect on the members of his family. Carlton is an alcoholic— and found that he could only stop drinking if he put the Atlantic Ocean between himself and his father. He started to drink again right after he arrived here, so he certainly hasn't outgrown the strain his father placed on him. Jane and Charlotte are very close—everyone who talks about them mentions that they could be twins. And I don't think that's because they look so much alike or because they're nearly the same age. I think it's that they are really extraordinarily close—much closer than most siblings. It might be because they found so much solace in each other as children. Which would mean that they needed each other more than most siblings—so the family was hard on them, too.''

''So what about Jon and Darcy?''

"I wondered about them, too. They don't appear very close, they don't seem to be at all alike. I think Jon had the easiest time of it in the family. Possibly because he is the most like his father. His sister-in-law said that he was trying to be a Renaissance man, which is really a good way of describing his father. And Jon is a scientist, and he'd grown up into something of a straight arrow; he's probably very comfortable in the family. And then there's Darcy. . . ."

"Everybody's favorite suspect," Marnie added, nodding. "But I thought you were convinced he didn't do it."

"I am. He's so vulnerable. To me, he seems more like a victim than a protagonist."

"But victims have been known to strike back."

"I know. That's what's worrying me."

"This all seems a little psychological to me. Have you spoken with Dr. Cockburn about it? He may not be much, but he's the only psychiatrist we have around," she added when Susan gave her a surprised look.

"He's spoken with me about it. I think Phyllis is absolutely desperate over the thought that Darcy might have killed his father, and she hopes Dr. Cockburn can either get him off or set up some sort of insanity plea for him. So she has Dr. Cockburn telling me his theories whenever we meet."

"And you don't think he's right?"

"I think there is more to Dr. Irving Cockburn than meets the eye," Susan answered. She was wondering about the scene she had witnessed in his room. "Have you noticed him spending time with Kathleen's au pair?"

"No, but I've been a little busy to pay much attention to the various relationships among the guests. Besides, if you're talking about the girl I think you are, there isn't a single man here who wouldn't like to spend more than a little time with her."

"They appear to have become close awfully quickly."

"That's Dr. Cockburn. I know, he tried his technique on me."

"What did he do?"

Marnie grimaced. "First he let me know that he was a

single doctor. I was amused at first, but believe me, this man needs all the help he can find when it comes to getting dates. I think if he hadn't made it through medical school, he'd spend every weekend alone. I suppose he ends up dating mainly gold diggers, but I'm not sure he's sensitive enough to care.

"Then he bombarded me with requests for dates. Of course, he's probably fairly restricted here. Except for a ski trip, attending one of the ranger talks, or a meal and a drink, there isn't a wide range of possibilities. And really, most of the single women in the park are staff. There's a group of single teachers here for the week, but usually the tourists are made up of families. This isn't a great place to meet potential mates."

Susan looked at her sharply. She sounded sad. "So Dr. Cockburn asked you to dinner . . . ?"

"And lunch, and breakfast, and maybe a nightcap or a cup of afternoon tea. Everything he could think of, in fact. He even went so far as to ask himself over to the cabin I live in. He actually appeared at my door yesterday. He's becoming quite a pest. I don't suppose you could find a way to convict him of the murders, could you? I'd love to lock him up."

"Do you have any evidence that he had a relationship with any member of the family before coming to the park?" Susan asked, willing to consider any alternatives.

"No," Marnie admitted.

"I would be interested in finding out whether he knew Chloe before this week."

"Who? Oh, the au pair! Wouldn't that be a real coincidence? Dr. Cockburn meeting Chloe before coming here? Or maybe they knew each other before and they planned on being here at the same time. Maybe they both knew George Ericksen someplace else and they had a reason to kill him. . . ."

"What?" Susan asked.

"I don't know. Maybe he cheated Chloe's father in a business deal and ruined him. Or maybe he seduced Chloe, and

Dr. Cockburn is in love with her and wanted revenge. Oh, I don't know, but anything is possible, isn't it?''

"Yes. But even if what you are saying is true and they came here to kill George Ericksen and succeeded, what about the effigy? And what about poor Randy? What reason did they have to kill him?" Susan asked. "It doesn't make sense that the three things could be unrelated. So it almost has to be someone in the family or very closely connected to it. And Chloe and Dr. Cockburn don't fill either of those qualifications.''

"Are you sure?''

"Maybe not," Susan admitted. "But no one in the family mentioned knowing them—although, in fact, I didn't ask directly. I can find out easily enough, though. But it seems unlikely.''

"This whole thing seems a little unlikely to me," Marnie insisted. "Effigies in the pool . . . two deaths . . . three people confessing . . . A woman runs off into the night and nearly freezes to death. . . . What could possibly happen next?''

Susan wished Marnie hadn't asked that. It was tempting the fates.

THIRTY-SIX

WHAT HAPPENED NEXT WAS THAT SOMEONE TRIED TO kill C. J. Ericksen.

The poor kid was found facedown in a snowbank on the trail leading from Snow Lodge to Old Faithful Geyser. He was unconscious, apparently having been hit over the head with a snow shovel identical to the one that killed his grand-father. In C.J.'s case, a fluorescent green ski cap had offered enough protection to keep the blow from being lethal. His mother, who had professed to hate that hat, was overheard proclaiming its miraculous powers at dinner that night.

Kathleen Gordon heard about the attack first, and rushed over to the ranger office to let Marnie and Susan know what had happened.

"I asked if I could see him," Kathleen explained, "but his mother said he needed to rest. She insisted that Marnie shouldn't even be allowed to talk with him until tomorrow morning, and Joyce doesn't really trust me. For all she knows, I could be the person who hit C.J. over the head. But she might let you see him, and I think you should try to—right away. He must know something—something that makes him a danger to the murderer!" Kathleen didn't need to remind Susan about this; she had been thinking the same thing.

"He was alone on the trail?" Susan asked.

"Apparently. It was almost exactly between eruptions, so there weren't a lot of people milling around waiting for the show or leaving afterward. But someone must have worked fast, hitting him and then vanishing."

"Well, we know it wasn't Darcy, Jane, or Char-lotte. . . ."

"Not really. Jane and Charlotte weren't locked up in the warming hut by that time. Darcy refused to retract his con-fession, but the girls did, and I decided to let them go. I know, it was stupid of me," Marnie Mackay said, sitting down between Susan and Kathleen. "I really screwed that one up. But I went over to the warming hut, determined to straighten out this mess. So when the girls said that they had confessed just to keep Darcy from being the only suspect, I believed them."

"It does sound like something that might happen in that family. They've all spent a lot of time protecting Darcy over the years. I don't blame you for thinking the way you did," Susan comforted her. "Besides, we've eliminated Darcy, which is something."

"I suppose we should let him go, too."

"Let's not be hasty," Kathleen suggested.

"Kathleen is right. If nothing else, he's safe where he is," Susan added.

"Why would anyone want to hurt Darcy?" Marnie asked.

"I have no idea. Then again, I have no idea why anyone would want to hurt C.J.—and someone has. . . ." Susan stopped when a new thought occurred to her.

"Susan?" Kathleen nudged her friend when she was silent for more than a minute. "Anything wrong?"

"I was just thinking. . . ." She paused. "You know, C.J. and Chad have been together almost all the time. . . ."

"And you think your son might be in danger, too."

"It's possible." She stood up. "I think I'll go check on him. . . ." She started to exit.

"Wait a second." Marnie stopped her, waving to a young man wearing a ranger's uniform who was standing near the door. "This is Phil Byrd. He'll go with you, and when you find Chad, he'll stay with him until this whole thing is over." The good-looking young man received the message and nodded to Susan. "Chad will be in good hands."

"He sure will, ma'am. I was East Coast lightweight champion my senior year of college."

Susan smiled weakly; first she had to find the boy. "I suppose he might be back in his room. . . ." She hurried toward the ski rack, the ranger following closely.

The snow had continued to fall during the afternoon, and only constant use of the trail between the buildings had kept it open. The illumination from the large floodlights was scattered by the snow falling from the sky and blowing into high drifts. Susan put her face down and headed straight into it, pushing away thoughts of her son, attacked like his friend, freezing in the storm, suffering, perhaps dead. . . .

"Mother, you have to do something about Chad. He's—"

"Chrissy?!" Susan peered through the blizzard into her daughter's face. "You know where he is? Where's Chad?"

"Why are you screaming?" her daughter asked, giving the ranger an embarrassed glance. "Chad is in his room—

he's sitting on the bed with C.J.'s tape deck turned up full blast playing some sort of horrible heavy metal junk. It's been driving Heather and me crazy for the last hour. You would think he'd be a little considerate of Heather at least. After all, her grandfather is dead, her uncle is locked up, and her brother was almost killed—not that that would bother me. . . . Mother?''

''I don't have time to talk to you now, Chrissy. I have to go to Chad. . . .'' Susan's voice was swept away into the wind as she hurried to the lodge.

She found Chad, as his sister had said, sitting in the middle of the bed, listening to a Metallica tape. It wasn't terribly loud.

''Hi. I was wondering where you were,'' she started, making a conscious effort not to mention the dirty clothing covering the floor. ''Why did you leave the door open?''

He turned down the stereo, got up off the bed, and crossed the room to the door, making no effort to avoid walking on his clothing. Susan ground her teeth but said nothing. Chad closed the door then, looked at his mother. ''I wanted to see who was coming to the room before they knocked.''

''And did anyone come? Besides me?'' Susan asked the questions seriously.

''No, but I was afraid they were going to. I have my knife with me, too.'' He slapped the pocket of the jeans he was wearing.

''Your knife?''

''The Swiss army that Dad gave me for Christmas.'' He jumped as someone knocked on the door.

''That's probably Phil Byrd. He's the ranger who is going to take care of you,'' Susan explained. ''Let me answer it.'' She opened the door, and it was, indeed, the ranger.

''I'll just wait out here, ma'am,'' he suggested, and taking the doorknob from her, he closed it again.

''To take care of me?'' Chad sounded more than a little indignant.

Susan decided this was no time to mince words. ''Yes.

Marnie Mackay thinks you may be in danger,'' she explained, hoping he would accept the concern offered.

"I know!" Chad's voice betrayed his attempt at braveness. "I've been thinking and thinking, and I just don't get it."

"Don't get what?" his mother asked, sitting down on the nearest bed.

"What C.J. knew that made him dangerous to somebody!" Chad leapt across the clothing and perched on the desk. "He must know something, or else no one would have hurt him, right? I've heard you talking about this stuff, and that was the only thing I could think of. But I can't figure out what it is. . . ."

"And if you know it, too?"

"Yeah. It would be lousy to get killed because you know something—only you don't really!" He stared at the floor. "I'm not making much sense, am I?"

"I know exactly what you mean," his mother said. "That's why I'm here."

"Why? I already have a guard stationed outside the door."

"I'm not here to watch you, I'm here to talk with you. I was hoping that, together, we could figure out exactly what C.J. knows that made him so dangerous."

"But that's what I've been trying to tell you. I've been thinking and thinking, and I don't have any idea."

"Look, you might not know. You haven't been with C.J. every moment since he got to Yellowstone, have you?"

"No. He spent last night with his family . . . but don't you think it has to be something that happened right before his grandfather died?"

"Why?"

"Well, if he knows who the murderer is—"

"But he may not, Chad." Susan was unable to resist interrupting. "He might know who put the effigy in the pool or who killed Randy—or it might not even be that direct. He might have seen someone buying suspenders at the ski shack. . . ."

"You're kidding me! What does that have to do with anything?"

Susan explained her reference to suspenders before continuing. "There's also the possibility that he heard Randy make plans to meet someone after the ski lesson, or that he saw someone in his family ski up ahead of the group who later didn't admit to doing so—and those are just the obvious things that might incriminate someone. It's probably something completely different. I just wish we could talk with C.J."

"But we can."

"No, his mother wants him to be left alone to rest. The poor kid probably needs it. I don't know how badly he was hurt, but—"

"He's got a bump on his head—it's not even as big as mine when I got clobbered in gym last month—but he's bored to death and dying to talk about this," Chad insisted.

"When did you see him? I thought he was in his mother's room with a guard outside the door."

"He is, but I went to visit him a few minutes ago."

"Chad . . ."

"It's easy. Especially with the deep snow. It actually makes it less slippery."

"Makes what less slippery?"

"The roof. You can get to C.J. by walking on the roof. C.J. and I have been traveling that way ever since we got here. It's fun!"

THIRTY-SEVEN

"Wow. It's really been blowing, hasn't it? The snow's almost filled this corner. It wasn't like that before."

"Before?" Susan repeated, following her son across the roof that jutted out above the first floor. "How often do you do this?" She had just noticed that Chad was wearing his running shoes instead of boots. If she could ignore the floor of his room, she could ignore this, she reminded herself, cringing as he leapt into a drift up to his knees. She did have more important things to worry about.

"C.J. discovered it the first night we were here—it's okay, Mom," he explained, hearing the concern in her voice. "We don't look in windows or anything. It's just a shortcut. The window in the laundry room is sometimes open—it gets pretty hot in there, I guess—so we go through there to the candy machine. Careful," he warned, "these people always have bottles of champagne and stuff out here—they want it cool, I guess."

"I was worried that one of you would fall off," his mother explained, glancing at the fifteen-foot drop.

"Don't worry. The snow gives you traction. And if you fell, you'd land in a nice, soft drift. Here we are." He knocked on a window. The curtains in the room were closed, but Susan was not surprised to see C.J.'s smiling face peer out the gap where the two panels of fabric met.

"What . . . ?" The head disappeared, and with a swish, the curtains were flung to opposite sides of the window to reveal C.J. energetically turning the crank that opened the glass.

"Careful," he warned. "The radiator is hot. My mother thinks boiling me alive will cure me," he added, helping Susan clear the sill and the appliance beneath it.

Chad, experienced, leapt the obstacles with ease.

"I can't tell you how glad I am to see you," C.J. continued. "I'd rather die in a snowdrift than from boredom. Say, you haven't figured this thing out yet, have you?" he asked Susan hopefully.

"I'm afraid not. I was hoping you could help me," Susan explained, sitting on an unoccupied bed.

"Chad insists that I know who the murderer is," C.J. answered, sitting next to her while Chad, once again, perched on the desk provided. "And I've been thinking and thinking, but if I know something, I don't know that I know it. Say, did I say what I thought I said?"

Susan smiled. "I think so. But you don't mind if I ask some questions, do you? Your mother thinks you should be allowed to rest, and she might be right. I don't want you to get sick."

"I'm fine," C.J. insisted. "My mother's just . . ." He stopped, probably remembering that he was speaking with another adult.

"Mothers are like that." Susan agreed with what he didn't say. "So if you start feeling the least bit uncomfortable, you are to let me know immediately."

"Okay."

"I suppose everyone has asked if you can identify the person who hit you."

"Yes, but no. I mean," he elaborated, "that everyone has asked, but that I don't have any idea who it was. I think the person was big, though, great big."

Susan tried not to smile. The poor kid probably couldn't accept that he had been felled by an ordinary mortal. "Male or female?"

"I don't know. I was walking along—"

"Where were you going?"

"To the warming hut. I wanted to see Uncle Darcy. I thought . . . I don't know what I thought. I just wanted to talk to him. I don't think he killed Grandfather, Mrs. Henshaw. I mean, I know he said that he did it, but I don't think he did. . . ."

Susan smiled at him. "I know what you mean. In fact, I agree with you."

"That's what Chad said." C.J. sounded relieved. "And my grandmother says you can help him—I hope so."

"So do I," she said sincerely.

"Well, I didn't even hear anyone nearby," C.J. continued. "I guess I wasn't paying attention to what was going on. I just felt something hit me in the head. And the next thing I knew, my mother was standing beside my bed asking me if

I was warm enough, and I had this stupid, lousy headache. This isn't going to help you, I know—but I've been thinking and thinking, and that's all I can remember.''

"Probably because that's all that happened. There's no way you're going to remember things you never knew."

"Unless he has amnesia," Chad suggested. "We read this story in English class about a man who lost a whole year of his life after an automobile accident. He didn't even remember his name—"

"C.J. remembers his name, Chad," his mother interrupted, worried that Joyce might return and cut short this interview before she had gotten any new information. Her son scowled at her. "I've been wondering about a lot of things," Susan continued. "To save time, could I ask you some questions, and would you answer without asking me why I'm asking?"

"Sure. Fire away."

"Why did you and Heather lie to me about the order in which your family arrived to see your grandfather's body?"

"Mom!" Chad cried out, apparently indignant that she would accuse his friend of duplicity.

"It's okay, Chad. She's right," C.J. admitted, picking at the blanket. He didn't answer immediately, though. Finally he looked up at Susan and sighed. "Heather is going to kill me, but I may as well go ahead and tell you. We were afraid that you would think one of my parents killed Grandfather. That is, Heather was worried about it. I didn't believe it for one minute," he assured her.

"But it was a legitimate worry," Susan said. "After all, I'm afraid that everyone in your family is under suspicion. And it would be natural for you—or Heather—to try to protect the people who are closest to you."

"But my parents aren't . . ." C.J. began, and then stopped. "At least, I don't think my parents would kill anyone. . . ." He shook his head. "But Heather said that it didn't matter what we thought. She wanted to convince everyone else that they were innocent. And she said that all we had to do was make sure you knew that they couldn't possibly have been near when the murder occurred. So she drew up that stupid list and insisted that we find you and tell you. It really was stupid,'' he repeated. ''Why would you or anyone else think that my parents would want to kill Grandfather? My father was thrilled to see Grandfather—the second night we were here, he was drinking, kidding, and joking around. I'd never seen him like that. He certainly wasn't planning to kill anybody.''

Susan realized that the difference in Heather's perception of the situation and her brother's was probably that the girl knew, or had some inkling, of her father's drinking problem. Chad apparently was entirely unconscious of the fact—and she certainly wasn't going to be the person who told him. ''What did Heather think about your mother? Did she worry about protecting her, too?''

''She worried about both of them. She didn't separate them. Say, Mrs. Henshaw, you don't think my parents did this, do you? I mean, I've thought about it,'' he continued earnestly, ''I really have. And I don't see why either of them would want to. And it's not like they're maniacal killers. As far as I can tell, they're the most sane people in this family. I suppose that's because we lived in France for so long.

''I mean,'' he continued, ''Jane and Charlotte don't act their age. They worry about clothing and makeup and boys— or, in their case, men—all the time. They remind me more of teenagers than adults. And, of course, Darcy is gay— which is fine with me, but it isn't exactly average, is it? And Jon . . .'' He stopped for a moment. ''I guess Jon is pretty normal, too.'' He stopped, looking nervously at the door before continuing.

''But what's really wrong with this family is that everyone had to be so damn nice to Grandfather!'' The words almost exploded out of the boy. ''It's been awful! Ever since we got here, someone has been saying we have to do this or that— or even say this or that—just because no one wants to upset Grandfather! The very first words my grandmother said to me, when we arrived at the lodge, were that it would please my grandfather a lot if I learned to ski well.'' His voice grew louder. "Well, I was going to learn to ski! I was looking forward to learning to ski! And then, all of a sudden, I had to do it to please someone else. It ruined everything! I know it doesn't make any sense . . . but it's different to do something for yourself instead of for someone else. You know?"

"I know," Susan agreed.

"And we all had to be so damn good all the time, and I don't know why! It was like there was some sort of awful explosion waiting to happen. We didn't know what would cause it, but we sure knew that it was going to happen because of something we did. . . ."

"Is that what you and your grandfather fought over?" Susan asked gently, seeing the tears in the boy's eyes. Chad was silent, a grim look on his face.

"Yes. I guess I just blew up. He and Darcy had that fight, and Randy was missing, and my mother was looking more and more worried and telling me not to worry about it, that everything was okay, when, of course, it wasn't. She never looks like that unless someone has a fatal disease or something. . . . And then, just as I was getting up from breakfast, my grandfather came over and asked to talk to me. He looked awful. Chad was there, he can tell you."

Chad just nodded at his mother, and C.J. returned to his story.

"I said fine. After all, I liked my grandfather. What reason would I have to not want to talk to him? But . . . but he laid into me about how I was spending too much time with Chad and not enough time with my own family, how this was a reunion of the Ericksens, and I was being inconsiderate and ruining it for my grandmother. . . . For my grandmother," he repeated angrily. "She was always saying that she was happy I had found someone my own age to be with, that it would be boring for me to be around adults all the time!"

"And you got mad." Susan nodded, understanding.

"Yes." C.J. was suddenly silent. "And I said something about it being my own life and I could be with my friends if I wanted to. . . . That was the last time I saw him alive," he added, almost inaudibly. "That was the last thing I said to him."

"I keep telling him that his grandfather would understand," Chad said. "It was just a terrible coincidence that his grandfather had to die right after that."

"You're right." Susan nodded, then she turned to C.J. "Your grandfather's death was a terrible tragedy, but you shouldn't feel guilty about what happened right before it. Think of all the good times you had together."

"That's what my mother said. She was pretty furious when she heard what had happened that morning, but after he died, she said exactly what you said."

Susan was silent for a moment, giving him time to calm down before asking another question. "Do you know if anyone in your family bought suspenders at the ski shack?"

The triviality of the question seemed to reassure C.J., and he answered quickly. "No. I mean, I don't know if anyone did. No one except Grandfather wears—wore—suspenders, though."

"Did you see Randy after the ski lesson we all took the second day we were here?"

C.J. thought for a moment. "No, I followed Chad to that practice trail and spent awhile going around it. I saw Randy leave the lesson, but I didn't see him after that. He was killed that day, wasn't he?"

"Hmmm. Yes." Susan hurried on to her next question. She really did not like children being involved with murder. "Did you see anything that might lead you to guess who made the dummy and put it in the pool? Any extra clothing around? Anyone carrying anything that could be made into a body? Remember, this was the same day as the lesson— that afternoon."

C.J. thought about his answer longer than he had the others. "No," he finally answered. "The only place I've seen piles of clothing is in the laundry room. There are always huge piles there—besides on the floor of our room, of course," he added, with a wicked grin at Chad.

Susan was glad the boy was cheering up. She stood, anxious to follow up on the clue he had just unwittingly offered her.

THIRTY-EIGHT

"ARE YOU WONDERING ABOUT THEM, TOO? I KEEP thinking I'll come in here and the whole mound will have disappeared."

Susan stared at the pile of sweaters she had folded the day before yesterday. A woman she had noticed around the lodge, distinct in having a half dozen children under age ten following her around, was speaking. "I've thought of mentioning it to one of the rangers. . . . In fact, I did say something to one of the kids who works at the front desk, but he just answered that people were always leaving laundry behind when they leave the lodge. I suppose the staff divide up the goodies among themselves. . . . And those are beautiful sweaters, aren't they? Especially that Fair Isles pattern on top. I knit myself, so I know what a difficult pattern that is. . . . My goodness, I didn't know they were yours," she added as Susan, decision made, swept up the garments into her arms.

"My son's," Susan called back over her shoulder, leaving the room. "I kept thinking he was going to get them himself. . . ." She left the statement unfinished. Another mother would understand perfectly.

Returning to her own room, she dumped the sweaters on her bed and reached for her ski equipment. There was only one thing to do.

And she did it. Not without the help of a stubborn ranger,

however. Without Marnie Mackay's permission, he explained, blocking the open doorway, no one was to speak to or see Darcy Ericksen. Susan, too anxious for a quick answer to search for official permission, talked the young man into showing Darcy the Fair Isles sweater that had been so admired in the laundry room. The answer came back almost immediately. The sweater had, indeed, belonged to Randy. In fact, it had been a Christmas present from Darcy to his murdered lover.

"And he's very upset over seeing it again." The ranger looked sternly at Susan as if suspecting her of intentionally hurting the young man.

"Please tell him that I'm sorry, but that it just might be getting us a little closer to finding out who murdered Randy. And tell him . . ." Susan paused, searching her mind for a suitable message. "Tell him that I'm thinking of him and I am doing everything I can to help him."

She thrust the sweater into the puzzled ranger's hands. "It's difficult for me to ski while carrying anything, so you take this." She hurried off. If she was lucky, the ski shack might still be open.

It was almost impossible to see through the continuing storm. Susan skied slowly from lamppost to lamppost, hoping she was heading in the right direction. The ski shack was near the lodge, and luckily, the beams of light led her directly to it. She freed herself of her skis and hurried to the entrance. Light streamed from the building's tiny windows, but the door was locked. Susan banged on the heavy wood door. The wind was shrieking around her. Maybe no one would hear. Maybe no one was in there. . . .

"Hey! We're closed. Come back tomorrow!" A man peered through the door into the blizzard. "Hey, you're Mrs. Henshaw, aren't you? I remember you from your lesson. What's wrong?" He opened the door all the way. "Come on in, but hurry. The snow is blowing straight inside."

Susan scurried up the steps and into the bright room. Three young men were there, sitting near the warmth of the wood stove. A couple of mugs and an open thermos mixed the scent of strong coffee with that of smoldering pine.

"Would you like a cup?" one of the young men offered. Another scooted over on the bench where he sat, making room for her.

"There's still a group out on the trail to Lone Star Geyser. We're waiting around to see if they need rescuing," came a voice from behind the store's counter. Susan was surprised to see Dillon joining the group, an empty mug in his hand.

"But you're not a ranger," she said.

"When there's an emergency, we all work together. And if this storm, two murders, and six tourists skiing along the Fire Hole River after dark isn't an emergency . . ." He left the sentence unfinished. "But why are you here?"

"I need to find out if someone who works here sold a pair of suspenders to a member of the Ericksen family. You know . . . the red ones with 'Yellowstone' written on them," she added when Dillon looked blank.

"No, we think they must have been snatched," one of the young men she hadn't met answered.

Now it was Susan's turn to look blank.

"We talked about it—you're wondering about the suspenders on the dummy, aren't you?"

Susan nodded.

"Well, Dillon noticed that they were the kind we sell here right away. . . ."

Now it was Dillon's turn to nod.

"And we all talked about it, and no one—that is, no one who works here—remembers selling suspenders like that to anyone in the family. We figure that leaves three possibilities. . . ."

"Which are?" Susan asked.

"Well, ma'am, they could have been brought into the park by someone who was here before, they could have been bought by someone that someone in the Ericksen family asked to purchase them, or they could have been stolen."

"Stolen?"

"We don't have a lot of theft up here, but we do have some."

"Is there an inventory kept of the merchandise in the store?" Susan asked.

"Not for things like that. For skis and expensive parkas, sure, but things like those suspenders are counted under miscellaneous."

"So there's no way to track down where that particular pair of suspenders came from," Susan concluded.

"No way at all," Dillon agreed, shrugging. "Anything else we can do for you?"

"No, thanks," Susan answered, as someone knocked on the door.

"Maybe that's news of our lost tourists." Dillon leapt up and opened it.

Marnie Mackay entered the room, shaking snow on them all as she pulled off her ski cap.

"Disgusting night," she commented cheerfully. "You'll be glad to hear that our happy wanderers have returned—and not a frostbitten toe, nose, or earlobe among them."

"Then we can switch to this," Dillon announced, pulling a bottle of Jim Beam from behind the counter.

"Don't even think about it. The storm shows no sign of letting up, and I need everyone to be on their toes. Besides, I've put you down for the midnight-to-six-A.M. shift—guard duty. You did volunteer, you know."

"Only because he thought you were going to be there with him," one of the other young men suggested.

"I am. As well as two other rangers." Marnie smiled. "Too bad it's too cold to play strip poker."

"I always thought the Visitor's Center was a little warm myself," Dillon insisted, causing loud laughter.

Marnie grinned and sat down next to Susan. "He seems a little more cheerful for some reason," she said. They both knew who she was speaking about. "I heard about the sweater. I suppose it means something?"

"It means that someone wanted us all to think Randy had left the park when he was, in fact, still here. At least, I think that's what it means. You see, Randy and Darcy left New York City the day before my family did. They flew straight to Wyoming, spent the night in Jackson Hole, and took the morning snowcoach here.''

''So?''

''So there was no reason for him to wash and dry all his sweaters less than twenty-four hours later,'' Susan ended.

''Meaning?'' Dillon looked mystified.

''Well, I'm not completely sure, but I think it means that the person who killed Randy wanted it to look like he had packed up and left Snow Lodge. So all his clothing was taken from the room he shared with Darcy and put in the one place where we're all accustomed to seeing piles of clothing—the laundry room. When I was there in the middle of the night''— the young men looked a little startled by this description of her nocturnal activities—''the clothing had been run through the dryer. I took them out and folded them myself the next day—I'm a little compulsive about housework, I guess,'' she added, sheepishly.

''And, in fact, Darcy did think that Randy had left the park, didn't he?'' Marnie said.

''But what difference did it make?'' Dillon asked.

''What would you have done if Randy disappeared and you hadn't thought that he had left the park?'' Susan asked.

''Just what we were going to do tonight,'' the ski instructor answered. ''We would have conducted a search.''

''And you might have found the body,'' Susan suggested. ''And whoever killed him didn't want that to happen.''

''But why?'' Marnie asked. ''We've found the body now, but that hasn't really led us any closer to the killer, has it?''

''I think it has,'' Susan said, enjoying the moment. ''You see, you found the body under the sign that says ice cream— over near the track that we all practiced our skiing on after our lesson, right?''

Marnie nodded.

''Well, I skied into that . . . that body,'' she explained, a little less confidently. ''And George Ericksen was there. And that must have been right after Randy was killed.''

''I see . . .'' Marnie began.

''I don't,'' their ski instructor disagreed. ''You're saying that he was killed near the parking lot—that's what's underneath all that snow—and right after the ski lesson, aren't you?''

"Yes. Exactly," Susan agreed. It was all coming together.

"But that's not possible," the young man disagreed. "You see, I was with Randy after the lesson. We met in the bar over at the lodge. We had a cup of coffee together."

THIRTY-NINE

"I DON'T MEAN TO BURST YOUR BUBBLE, BUT HE WAS very much alive when I talked to him. He had some sort of surprise that he was planning for his lover—the guy that you're holding for murdering his grandfather—and he was happy as a clam," the ski instructor explained.

"But where . . . ? What . . . ?" Susan was so surprised by this revelation that she didn't even know what to ask.

"I guess he was killed pretty soon after he left the lodge, though," the young man continued. "That's what the doctor who examined him said, isn't it? That he was killed before the old man?"

"True," Marnie agreed. "What time did he leave you?"

"Well, let's see. The lesson usually runs from nine till eleven or so, and I went straight to the dining room. . . . We only had a cup of coffee apiece—he said he had to do something. . . ."

"What was that?" Susan asked. "You mentioned a surprise."

"That was when we were having coffee. He said something about having big plans, plans that would really make

Darcy happy. But I don't know if that's what he was going to do after he left the lodge. I don't know what he was going to do then. We paid the bill and got up from the table, and he said something vague, like 'Well, I have things to do,' or 'I better get going,' or maybe he said something about meeting someone—that's all I remember.''

''But he didn't say who he was going to meet or what they were going to do?'' Susan persisted.

''No. And it might have just been one of those vague, polite things that people say when they split up. You know?''

Susan nodded. ''Do you have any idea where he went after he left the dining room?''

''None. I didn't even see him go through the door. I went out the back way, through the kitchen. The girl I'm living with was back there making up sandwiches for the lunch crowd. . . .''

''Did you see him again?''

''Not that day. Not that I remember. In fact, I don't think I've seen him since that time in the restaurant.''

Susan was silent, thinking of all the possible places where Randy might have gone. And wondering if he had gone to one of them with the person who was to be his murderer.

Dillon spoke up. ''You know, I may have seen Randy after that—after you had coffee.''

''Where? Was he alone?'' Susan jumped on the information.

''Now wait, I'm not sure about the timing of all this. I don't want to confuse everything here. And I don't want to get anyone in trouble. Especially an innocent person.''

''Don't worry. Just tell me!'' Susan insisted.

''Well, I think this must have been right after Randy left you.'' He nodded to the other man. ''I was scheduled to drive the afternoon snow bus out of the park, and the bus was parked in front of the lodge. I was standing on top, trying to readjust some of the carrier cords that had loosened up the day before, when I noticed that Mrs. Ericksen was standing on the front steps, watching me.''

"Did she say anything to you? Or did you say anything to her?" Susan asked.

"Nope. But I'm sure it was her. She'd been around the lodge for a few days, and with her husband, she sort of stands out in a group, you know. Well, I kept working and I noticed that she was looking at her watch every few minutes—not really nervous, but sort of impatient like. And then Randy came out the door, and the two of them put on their skis and took off together."

"Did they say anything?"

"Yes, but I had the motor of the coach on—trying to warm her up—so I couldn't hear. . . ."

"Did she smile or seem happy to see him?"

Dillon paused for a moment. "If I had to answer that question, I'd say she seemed in a hurry to get going, but that's just an impression I got, and it may have been nothing. I was working and not paying that much attention, after all. . . ."

"In what direction?"

"Toward Old Faithful," Dillon answered, correctly interpreting her question.

"Fast?" The ski instructor spoke up.

"Sure were, come to think of it. That old lad— Mrs. Ericksen is a real quick skier, and he kept right up with her."

The instructor asked another question. "Not much like a novice skier, was he?"

"Are you saying . . . ?" Susan was startled.

"Exactly what you think I'm saying. That ski lesson was not Randy's first time on skis—not by a long shot."

"You're sure?" This from Marnie.

"Absolutely. I noticed it right away during the lesson. He had no trouble standing, skiing, or anything. In fact, I think at first he had some trouble falling down. You know, pretending to fall down. But after a while he just stopped trying. Everyone falls so much and feels so awkward their first time out that there isn't a lot of noticing what anyone else is doing."

"But—"

"Although actually, come to think of it, Darcy did see how well his friend was doing. He made some sort of comment about it, and Randy just laughed. But he did give me a guilty look over his shoulder. I think he knew that I knew he was faking it."

"And he seemed guilty?"

"Not really. When I said a guilty look, I meant that kind of . . . well, casually. Like he was playing a joke on someone, not trying to deceive for any serious reason. You know?"

"I know what you mean," Susan agreed.

"You think it's significant?"

"Who knows? Is there any way for you to guess whether or not Phyllis was surprised by Randy's ability?"

"Nope." Dillon shook his head. "But they sure did seem in a hurry to be off. . . ."

"Maybe they were anxious to see an eruption." Marnie offered a simple explanation.

"Nope. That is, not unless they got their times wrong. Old Faithful had erupted about fifteen minutes before that. The crowds were coming back from it just as I drove up."

"Susan?" Marnie prompted her.

"Did you see either of them again?" Susan asked slowly. She had been wondering whether the eruption Dillon mentioned was the same one George Ericksen had spoken of. If so, maybe she could begin to find some sort of time frame for the events that day. . . .

"Not together." Dillon was answering her question. "I didn't get back to the park until the next morning, of course. And I think I saw Mrs. Ericksen sometime that day. But I didn't see Randy again . . . at least not alive, that is."

"Dillon was with the group that found Randy's body," Marnie explained to Susan.

"You know, I don't know how he died," Susan said slowly.

"Apparently he was hit over the head with something . . . maybe one of those shovels again or maybe not. There hasn't been a full autopsy, remember," Marnie cautioned. "And the blow may not have killed him. He may have been knocked out, then buried in the snow and left to die. It wouldn't have taken long. It sounds gruesome, but it's really a pretty elegant murder.''

It wasn't the word Susan would have chosen, but she could understand what Marnie meant. ''And the body was directly under the sign that says something about ice cream?''

Dillon laughed. ''It just says 'ice cream.' That building is an ice cream shop in the summertime. There are long lines leading to it all day, every day. With the first snow in September, it becomes a lot less popular, and it's closed until Memorial Day. And yes, that's where we found the body. It was under a rather large pile of snow—part drift and part pile made when the walkway near there was cleared of snow.''

''You just look under every snow pile to see what's there?'' Susan sounded disbelieving.

''Of course not.''

''So why that one?''

Dillon paused. ''I've been wondering that myself. I'm not exactly sure why. I'd been noticing that pile for a few days. . . .''

''Why?'' Susan prodded.

''It changed shape. I know it sounds strange, and I'm looking back with some hindsight, but I think it had been changing shape for more than a few days. . . .''

''Wind sweeps around that corner, and with this storm coming in, the wind was increasing. That could cause the change in shape,'' Marnie suggested.

''I know, but it wasn't that type of shape change. It was more like someone had been digging in it. . . .''

''More than once?'' Susan asked.

''That's what's so strange. I think—and, please believe that I wasn't paying any special attention to this mound of snow at the time; I never thought there was going to be a murdered man found there—that the pile had changed the day that I watched Randy and Mrs. Ericksen go off together. And since I never left the snowcoach after seeing the two of them, I must have seen it that morning. . . .''

"When I skied into it!" Susan exclaimed, going on to explain what had happened to her after the ski lesson.

"If only we knew whether the eruption George Ericksen referred to was the same one that happened before Randy and Phyllis Ericksen went off together," Marnie said. "You didn't happen to look at your watch, did you, Dillon?"

"No."

"Too bad . . ."

"But I did see the ski lesson going on when I passed by the snow pile. . . ."

"You're sure?"

"Yes. I noticed the bright parkas that your daughter and her friend wear," Dillon said, tactfully not referring to how he had chuckled watching Susan ski off the trail and into an innocent ponderosa pine.

"And the pile had been disturbed at that time?"

"Definitely. That's when I noticed it, in fact."

"Recently?" Marnie asked.

"It was rough, like someone had just dug in it, yes."

"You're sure?" Susan asked.

"Yes. It's been a windy week; the surface of the mound wouldn't have stayed rough for more than a few hours, if that. It's a pretty exposed corner," Dillon answered. "And it didn't just look like someone had dug in it, or buried something in it, it looked like it had been smoothed over—so that no one would notice anything."

"And that was before I crashed into it," Susan muttered.

"And you felt something underneath the snow?"

"Yes. I thought . . . well, after I found out about Randy's death and where he was found, I thought that I had run into him."

"It sounds like that isn't possible, doesn't it?"

"Yes. I can't tell you how relieved I am. I thought I must have run into him right after he was killed. I had been thinking that I should have done something. You see," she explained to the group around the stove, "whatever I ran into was soft—not frozen."

FORTY

Susan needed time to sort things out. And some help. And dinner. Marnie Mackay provided all three.

"Don't think this is usual for us," the ranger explained to Susan and Kathleen as the three women sat around the desk in the ranger's office at the Visitor's Center. "In all the time I've been here, I've never known the lodge kitchen to make and deliver meals. But I guess nothing is normal around here these days," she added a little sadly, looking down at the three bowls of beef carbonnade, salads, and sourdough bread and butter, as well as plates, napkins, cutlery, and a large pot of coffee that had just been brought to them by a representative of the kitchen staff.

"How is Darcy getting his meals?" Kathleen asked, picking up a cherry tomato and popping it in her mouth.

"As I understand it, his mother is ordering from the menu, then one of his brothers picks the food up and drops it off with his guard. The rangers I've talked with say he isn't eating, though, just drinking a little coffee and fruit juice. We may as well dig in," she suggested, passing around cups and saucers.

"So what do you have?" Kathleen asked, filling alternate bowls with salad and stew.

"I suppose," Susan said slowly, accepting her meal, "we have a lot of information. It's just not in any order and doesn't make much sense. Although I was glad to hear that Randy wasn't under that snow pile when I ran into it."

"What?"

Susan explained their recent discoveries to Kathleen while Marnie started her meal.

"So you probably ran into the effigy," Kathleen said at the end of Susan's recital as she picked up her fork.

The fork hit the table. "What?"

"The effigy . . . the dummy . . . the thing that was thrown into the water . . ." Kathleen explained, looking at Susan curiously. "Isn't that what you're saying?"

"I didn't think so. . . ."

"Was it body-shaped?" Marnie asked, leaning across the desk. "You thought it was Randy, remember. . . ."

"Wait a minute. Let me think." She broke a roll and buttered it before speaking. "It could have been the effigy. Definitely. I may have even lifted it off the ground with my skis, and you know," she added, gaining confidence as the memory returned, "George Ericksen did say that it was just a pile of clothing that someone had left there. . . ."

"Interesting that he was on the spot, isn't it?" Kathleen murmured, her mouth full of food.

"Do you think that's significant?" Marnie asked.

"I think it's interesting," Kathleen repeated. "Did he seem at all anxious to keep you away from the pile of clothing?"

"You could say that, but you could also say that he was trying to be helpful."

"In what way?"

"Well, he said that I was trying to get up wrong and that I should take off my skis first. And he even helped me snap the bindings, and he moved the skis for me. . . ."

"Moved them?" Marnie asked.

"You know, pulled them out of the pile of snow and put them down on the ground going the other direction so I could . . . He could have been keeping me from dislodging the stuff in the pile, come to think of it." She was silent for a moment.

They all were. An observer would have thought that they were only intent upon their meal. Kathleen spoke first.

"Is Dr. Cockburn the only doctor to see either body?"

"Yes. He's the only doctor in the park right now, as far as we know," Marnie answered. "Otherwise we would have chosen anyone else."

"Because he's a psychiatrist?"

"Because he's a pest. Always bothering me or one of the other rangers with his theories about who did what and why."

"But he started doing that before the first death," Susan reminded her. "He started doing that right after the effigy was found. I remember, we were in the main room next door when he came in and started offering his opinions about the situation."

"So he probably would have been obnoxious whether or not we asked him for help," Marnie said. "But we really had no choice. We knew George Ericksen was dead, anyone seeing the body knew that George Ericksen was dead, but we had to have verification by a medical doctor. It's the rule. It may be the law in Wyoming, for all I know. And then, when we found Randy, we had to ask his help again."

"So did Phyllis Ericksen," Susan muttered, putting down her fork.

"What?" Kathleen looked up sharply.

"Phyllis Ericksen asked him for help, too."

"But he got involved before that. She asked for his help after her husband was killed—not when the dummy was found," Kathleen reminded her.

"Do you think it means something?" Marnie asked.

"It may, but it may not. Dr. Cockburn seems to be the type of person who needs a lot of attention—getting involved in each crisis around here may be his way of doing just that. And he might honestly want to help people who are in trouble, remember," Susan added, sounding as if she doubted her own words.

Neither of the other women bothered to argue with her.

"Interesting that George Ericksen described the effigy as a pile of clothing—assuming it was the effigy." Kathleen made the comment as calmly as though they were speaking about the weather.

"You think he hid it?"

"How could he have?" Susan asked Marnie. "No, that's not what I mean. What I mean is why would he have?"

"Let's think about that," Kathleen insisted. "Do we have any real idea who was responsible for the effigy? You checked about the suspenders, didn't you? And you still don't know who bought them. . . ."

"Or if they were brought into the park, right," Susan answered.

"So we really can't rule out George Ericksen as the person who built it, can we?"

"Well, I would have thought that how angry he was when he saw it was indication enough that he didn't do it," Marnie suggested.

"If he did it and didn't want anyone to know, that's exactly how he would have acted," Susan said.

"The key phrase is 'suspect everybody,' " Kathleen elaborated.

"But why would he do it?" Marnie protested.

"Why would anybody do it?" Kathleen persisted.

"Senseless mischief," Marnie answered.

"I don't think so," Susan said. "It's probably time we sorted through the possible motives."

"How can anyone know what the motives are without knowing who did it?" Marnie asked. "I mean, what I've been thinking is things like, if Darcy did it, he did it because he wanted his father to look foolish, he wanted revenge. . . ."

"Okay," Susan agreed. "Now try just thinking of motives."

"Like revenge?" Marnie said.

"Sure. Or to embarrass George Ericksen," Kathleen chimed in.

"Which could also be called revenge," Marnie suggested.

"True. I suppose they're just variations on a theme, aren't they?"

"Because they all revolve around George Ericksen . . ." Susan started. "But there might be some other possibilities. Like shocking one of the people who saw the effigy."

"Good point," Kathleen said. "But was it possible to know who was going to be in the group that first got to the pool? There wasn't a sign-up sheet for the walk, was there?"

"No, we request that people sign up ahead of time in the summer, but there just aren't that many tourists around in the winter. We can always accommodate whoever wants to go on one of the tours," Marnie answered. "And I can't guarantee that no one would get to the pool before the afternoon tour group, but it would be pretty unusual. That trail isn't used much by anyone except for the rangers. In the first place, most people miss the turn to the last group of geysers that are before the pool, if they even want to go there—the more popular route is to Morning Glory Pool. Morning Glory is a little like Old Faithful. Most people don't feel like they've seen Yellowstone until they've been there. In fact, we choose the route that we do because it's not often taken. In the first place, people get to see things that they won't if they just ski off on their own, and because it's less popular, it's a more natural trail to travel. It's quieter, and more peaceful, and we're more likely to get the opportunity to see some wildlife."

"Who would know that?"

"Who would know that they could put the effigy in the pool and that the tour would probably be the first group to see it?" Susan elaborated on Kathleen's question.

"Well, no one could be sure of that," Marnie answered. "Even the rangers who tour the entire upper geyser basin daily would have no idea who was going to be where and when. On the other hand, anyone could ask one of the rangers or one of the guys at the ski shack how often any trail was likely to be used. We're here to pass out information; we don't ask if it's going to be used for innocent purposes or not."

"But it would have to be a pretty good skier to carry the effigy to the pool, wouldn't it?" Susan asked, approaching the problem from a different angle. "I mean, I have trouble hanging on to those damn poles."

"That's true. It could have been stuffed in a large backpack, but it isn't easy to carry one of those things unless you know what you're doing. It throws off your balance.''

"So assuming it was one of the Ericksen family who did it, it must have been either Jon or Phyllis or George," Kathleen suggested.

"Or Jon's girlfriend," Marnie added.

"Or Randy," Susan said. "And I'm beginning to think it was Randy. And that maybe he was helped by someone else. I just don't know if that someone else was Phyllis or George."

FORTY-ONE

"OF COURSE, IF GEORGE HELPED RANDY, THAT WOULD explain why he was standing so near the dummy. But Randy did go off with Phyllis. . . ."

Marnie could stand it no more. "What are you talking about?" she asked, forgetting her professional manners. "In the first place, why Randy?"

"Because he said he was going to do something that afternoon," Kathleen suggested.

"More than that. Look at the facts first: Not only did he tell the ski teacher that he was excited about something he was going to do, but he had lied about his skiing skills. Now, why would he do that? There is absolutely no evidence that Randy was in any way mean or hurtful. In fact, everyone comments on how nice a person he was. Also, he apparently had a very close relationship with Darcy, and was sincerely in love with him. So why was he lying to him? Why was he hiding his skiing ability? Not to do anything that would hurt him; that doesn't make any sense. . . ."

"But why—" Marnie began.

"Wait a minute. Let me explain," Susan insisted. "The other part of this has to do with Randy's background. Darcy told me that Randy was an orphan, brought up by an elderly aunt. He had lived a sheltered life, in boys' boarding schools and summer camps, and unlike Darcy, he didn't acknowledge his homosexuality in public until after he had completed college. So he grew up with no real family life, and by choosing to keep his sexual preference a secret, he separated himself from the gay community, while not fitting in with the rest of the world.

"Naturally, Darcy was terribly upset about Randy's death. And part of what made it so painful is that Randy had been looking forward to this family reunion so much—Randy wanted to be part of a family, at least for a little while."

"That is sad," Kathleen agreed, thinking of her husband and child.

"And significant," Susan continued. "Because, in fact, Randy didn't know very much about families; he'd never been part of one." She paused to let that sink in. "He didn't know how families act. Anyone who's been part of any real family knows that holidays and reunions can be stressful—and that would be especially true for a family where individuals aren't expected to deviate from the norm. And this family had a lot more problems than most. There's evidence of that: Randy wasn't the only outsider here.

"Both Beth and Joyce knew what it was like looking in at the Ericksens, so to speak. And both of them had, at first, glowing images of the family. Beth was surprised by the unhappiness at this reunion before the murders. And she was surprised because Jon had spoken of his family in idealistic terms, talking about summer homes, family celebrations, vacations. But even Jon, who appears to be living the most trouble-free life of all his brothers and sisters, was quiet the night before arriving at the park; apparently even he knew that a family reunion can be a trying time.

"And when Joyce talks about her introduction to the Ericksen clan, she remembers an enchanted image of charming people living in the middle of a flowering orchard. She adds that the reason the image sounds like something from a fairy tale is that it is fiction. The Ericksens presented a fabulous image to the world, but underneath the truth was something different. And Randy didn't know that.''

"So not seeing the reality, he believed the image."

"Exactly," Susan agreed with Kathleen. "And since he didn't see what was going on, he didn't know how to act."

"So he made a dummy and threw it into a thermal feature out of social ignorance?" Marnie was still to be convinced.

"No, I think he did it because someone told him that it would be a good joke—the kind of thing that the Ericksen family would get a good laugh over."

"Someone in the family," Marnie said, sounding less doubtful. "But who?"

"Well, circumstances would indicate that it was either Phyllis or George.

"Phyllis because she met him after lunch—apparently had an appointment to meet him. So if he was going to do something then, she most likely knew about it.

"And George because it looks to me like he was guarding the dummy—making sure that no one found or disturbed it . . .''

"You're right, of course. I don't know how you found out about it, but you're right." Phyllis Ericksen stood in the doorway. Except for a very red nose, she appeared to be back to normal.

"Come in. Please come in and sit down," Marnie said, jumping up and vacating her seat.

Phyllis looked around at the three women before speaking. "I will, if you don't mind. I . . . I heard what you were saying. . . . I was in the hall and I overheard voices. When I recognized who was speaking, I couldn't resist eavesdropping. I thought it might have to do with Darcy. . . . I would do anything to save him!" She raised her voice. "Anything!"

"But we weren't talking about Darcy," Kathleen reminded the older woman.

"I know. So there's no excuse, is there? But what I heard—about the dummy—I thought I should explain. Maybe, if you understand that, you'll understand everything."

"Why don't you explain?" Susan suggested as Phyllis sat down and Marnie leaned back against the wall, her arms crossed.

"It . . . it sounds insane."

"A lot of insane things seem to be happening," Kathleen suggested. "Why don't you just tell us what happened and not worry about what it sounds like?"

"Yes. You're right, of course." She stopped for a moment. "When I was standing in the hall, I heard Susan say that someone must have convinced Randy that throwing the dummy in the water would be a joke. She's right, of course. What else could it have been? Randy was a perfectly nice, ordinary person. He would never have imagined doing anything malicious. And the person who convinced Randy that it was all a joke was George. You see, Randy didn't have a chance. Why would he doubt what my husband was saying?"

"Maybe if you started from the beginning," Marnie suggested.

"And if you'd explain how you know about it," Susan added.

"I know about it because George told me about it. He told me about everything. Sometimes it was a burden. A very large burden. You see, my husband never accepted the fact that Darcy is gay. Darcy told us about it almost four years ago, but the time made no difference to George. He was simply determined not to accept it."

"You felt differently?" Kathleen asked gently.

"I saw that if we didn't accept our son the way he was, we would lose him. George didn't see it like that. And he avoided Darcy's lovers. I don't fly, but in the past three years I've traveled to the East Coast numerous times to visit Darcy in college and in the places he found summer employment. And I've met more than a few of the men he's been involved with. . . ." She stopped.

"So you got accustomed to meeting your son's lovers," Marnie suggested.

"And you knew that Randy was different," Susan said.

"Yes, I knew that Darcy's feelings for Randy were deeper than those he'd had for others in the past. And my approach to this was different from my husband's. I tried to help them. I found a job for Randy—a better job than the one he had at that advertising agency in the city. It didn't work out for him, but at least I tried. And I helped them decorate the apartment they were living in. Neither of them had the time or the money to do it, so I just pitched right in, taking dozens of taxies around the city, visiting hundreds of stores. . . . But I couldn't even talk to George about that. When I got home from one of my visits to my son, I couldn't even speak about most of the things I had done, because George couldn't stand hearing about that part of Darcy's life.

"That's one of the things that convinced me to arrange this reunion. I thought it was time that George accepted Darcy's life-style. And I thought that Randy was someone that George could come to accept. And I thought it might be working! At first, George was disapproving. We had everyone in for cocktails, and he certainly was barely polite to Randy. But then, after dinner, I thought that maybe, just maybe, he was getting accustomed to him. We had a talk about Randy before going to that interesting speech you gave at the Visitor's Center that night." She smiled at Marnie. "And George promised that he was going to try to be better, that he was going to try to get along with Randy. He told me that he had a plan . . . but he wouldn't tell me what it was. I was tired that night and I went back to the lodge, planning to go to bed early. But the best-laid plans . . ." She shrugged.

"You came and spoke with us in the bar," Susan prompted, surprised at the look on Phyllis's face. Apparently she had forgotten that part of the evening.

"Yes, I wasn't thinking about that. What I was thinking about was what I found on the bed when I finally made it to my room. At first, of course, I thought it was George lying there. That dummy certainly looked more than a little bit like him. Then I realized that it was a stuffed image, a dummy. I was surprised, but I knew that George was the only person who had a key to the room. I just settled down and waited for him to come in and explain it.''

"And he did?" Marnie asked.

"Yes. Oh, he was very casual about it. He said that Randy was going to put it into a hot spring or something the next day. He said that it was a joke.

"Well, you can imagine how surprised I was. I didn't even know that the two of them were speaking, and I certainly didn't think that they would be planning some sort of fey practical joke together. I could hardly believe it. But George was tired and didn't want to explain any more than the bare facts, so I had to be content with what I knew. That was frequently true in my life—I was accustomed to being left in the dark. But he had told me enough. Lying in bed that night, I decided to meet Randy before he picked up the dummy. I thought I could talk him out of it. But the poor boy was so thrilled that George liked him and that they were doing this together. . . . I couldn't convince him to give up the plan.''

"Why didn't you try to talk your husband out of it?" Kathleen asked.

"George never listened to me. I knew it was useless. And I felt so helpless over it all. Poor Randy had no way of knowing that George would deny any complicity in the matter. I suspected as much, but I didn't know what I could do. So I took the coward's way out, I'm afraid, and I didn't do anything. It was truly mean of George to manipulate Randy like that, but I'm afraid my husband wasn't always very nice.

"And that's really all there is to the story," she ended, looking around the tiny room.

"Well, it certainly clears up a few things." Marnie spoke up first.

"Yes," Kathleen agreed.

"There are some other things you might be able to help us with," Susan persisted, unwilling to end this conversation until she had heard all there was to hear.

"Of course. Anything I can do, you know that."

"I've been wondering if you or any members of your family knew either Dr. Irving Cockburn or Chloe Desparde before coming to Yellowstone."

"I don't even know anyone named Chloe Desparde," Phyllis insisted.

"I don't think we have to worry about Chloe anymore," Kathleen announced, looking at Susan. "I'll tell you about her later."

"I . . ." Susan didn't finish her sentence.

"However, you do know who Dr. Cockburn is," Marnie said, giving Kathleen a puzzled look.

"But I did not know him before coming here. He has been very helpful to our family, I must admit. Although perhaps he is not exactly the person we would have wished in these circumstances—I'm sure he has helped out to the best of his somewhat limited abilities. He is, of course, a psychiatrist, not an internist or something more practical in this situation."

"But you asked him to speak to me—as a psychiatrist," Susan reminded her.

"Yes, but to be frank, that was more to get him off my back than anything else. He is a perfect bore, isn't he?" Phyllis sat back in the chair.

"You weren't trying to set up some sort of psychiatric defense for Darcy?"

Phyllis seemed startled by Susan's question. "I . . . It's true that I think that's probably a good idea. Especially if he persists in confessing to these terrible murders . . ."

"He has not confessed to killing Randy," Marnie corrected her.

"No . . . and I do not believe that he killed anybody," Phyllis added more determinedly. "I believe absolutely in my son's innocence. Absolutely. And I think that I should get back to him. Now that he has spent so much time alone, he may have reconsidered this ill-conceived confession."

"I thought he refused to see you," Susan said as Phyllis stood up, covering her fluffy curls with a wool hat.

"He's terribly hurt and ashamed. I understand that," she

said, her hand on the doorknob. "You have been good to try to help our family, Mrs. Henshaw, but I think it is probably time for your investigation to end."

"I don't think you're winning friends and influencing people," Marnie commented as the door closed behind Phyllis Ericksen.

"True." Susan shook her head and turned her attention to Kathleen. "So what's the story about Chloe?"

"It's a stupid story. And I don't think it has anything to do with the murders."

"So?"

"Chloe wants someone to sponsor her so she can stay in this country—it seems that her contact at the embassy can't help her with this one. And being a beautiful young girl, she decided that the male half of the population might be more likely to feel that the country would be a better place if she stayed here."

"That's all?" Susan asked.

Kathleen nodded. "That's it. At least it explains why she's been flirting with every man in sight. I was beginning to think we were leaving Bananas with a nymphomaniac. Actually, it may explain why she's been such a wonderful employee.

"I have to admit," Kathleen continued, "that Jerry thought there was something a little strange about her from the first. Her flirting made him uncomfortable."

"Well, at least we have two things settled," Susan said. "We know what Chloe has been up to, and we know that Randy put the effigy in the pool. It's nice to have a few answers."

"We also have a lot of questions," Marnie reminded her. "Anyone want dessert?"

FORTY-TWO

"You seem to know where you're going," Kathleen said, following Susan outside.

"If I can find it in this storm, I'm heading to the warming hut. I need to talk with Darcy. He holds the key to all of this. I think he's the only person who knows exactly what has been going on all along. I should have seen it, too, but I was so wrapped up in peripherals, so distracted. . . ."

"What? Slow down, I can't hear you!" Kathleen skied after her friend.

"Even if he agrees to see me, he may not allow you in. Would you go back to the lodge and check on Chad? There was a ranger left outside his doorway, but he may not be in his room. He's probably with C.J., and C.J. is in his parents' room. . . ."

"Don't worry. I'll find him. But first I'm going to make sure you find the warming hut—"

"No problem. Here we are."

"—and that someone can help me find my way back to the lodge," Kathleen continued.

"I can do that, ma'am. I'm going that way myself," offered the ranger who opened the door to them. "In a way, you've saved me a trip. I was just going to find you." He nodded at Susan. "And then I would have had to escort you back here from wherever you were. As it is, I can head back to my room after dropping you off. I'll be able to get to bed much earlier than I expected."

"Why were you coming to look for me?"

229

"He wants to see you." The ranger pointed over his shoulder into the hut. "He's been asking for you for the last half hour or so, but I couldn't leave to find you until I had been relieved. There's another guard in there with him now."

"So why don't you two ski back while I talk with Darcy?" Susan suggested, entering the shack. A second later she was back outside. "Maybe you could get the entire family together in one place? I think it may be time for a talk when I'm done here."

"Great. And even if you don't come up with some answers, it would be nice to get everyone in one place where I can keep an eye on them," Kathleen agreed.

"Good thought." Susan said, reentering the hut.

"You came."

"I understand you want to talk to me. I wanted to talk to you, too," Susan explained.

Darcy was sitting in front of the stove, where she had interviewed him before. But something was different, something more than the presence of a ranger. The young man looked less distraught, more in control of himself.

"They tell me you're not eating very much."

"I had some stew for dinner," he answered, almost smiling. "It's not as though I'm burning a lot of calories sitting here. . . ."

"But at least he has something to do now." The ranger spoke up.

Susan looked at the two men curiously.

"Someone sent over my sketchbook and charcoal," Darcy explained. "I've been doing some drawings. At least it passes the time." He nodded depreciatingly at the notebook on the bench beside him.

"I know a lot of artists don't like to show their work before it's finished . . ." Susan began.

"Go ahead. It doesn't bother me at all." He even handed it to her.

Susan spent some time looking carefully at the work before speaking. "I don't know why I'm surprised that you're so good. Everyone has said so. I especially like your drawings of the park, of the geysers and the ice-covered trees. It's amazing the sparkle you manage to get out of black and white." She purposely didn't mention the last sketches he had done—of Randy.

"Thanks. I have a pretty good view of Old Faithful," he added, motioning toward the small window at the rear of the hut.

Susan returned the notebook to its place at Darcy's side. "I hope you're going to lose that view before long. I have some questions to ask you. Some things are starting to make sense, but I need more information. Information that only you can give me."

"Of course. Anything."

"Did you know that Randy dumped the effigy into the hot spring?"

"Yes. He told me about it. Right before the ski lesson, in fact. I was amazed. But we never had a chance to talk about it. Carlton and Joyce appeared, and your family. . . . Well, we just weren't alone after that. But he seemed to think it was some wonderful joke that he was going to play," Darcy admitted. "But I can't for the life of me imagine why. Randy was a warm and wonderful person. Why would he do something that would upset my father so much?"

"What would you say if I told you that the whole thing was planned by your father?"

"Impossible. Absolutely impossible. Why would he do that?"

"As a joke?" Susan suggested.

"No way. My father was one of the straightest people I've ever known. I doubt if he ever played a practical joke in his life. And this one wasn't even funny. And it risked damaging the environment. My father would never have done it."

"But think for just one minute about Randy, not your father. What if your fa—someone came to Randy and said that pulling a prank like this would please the family, make him more accepted. Is it possible that Randy would have believe that?"

"I don't know. Maybe. Randy could be a little naïve

sometimes. I suppose it's possible. But Randy really would never have done it if he thought it was going to hurt anyone. And I truly cannot imagine why my father would suggest such a thing to him.'' Darcy stared off into space. ''You must have gotten your information wrong.''

''Well, maybe.'' Susan wasn't going to spend the time arguing. She had more questions to ask. ''Could you tell me about the job that your mother found for Randy?''

''I . . . sure.'' In the moment that he had paused, Susan thought that Darcy had decided to trust her—and her judgment. ''Randy had a job at an advertising agency. It's a lousy job. He was a pretty talented artist, but he was just doing hack work for the agency—churning out storyboards and quick sketches for in-house presentations. My mother came to visit us once in a while, and on one of her trips East, she happened to be there when Randy was complaining about his work. About two weeks after she left, Randy got a call from a different ad agency. They said they were looking for someone to do design work and that they were interested in seeing his portfolio. Well, Randy sent in his work, and word came back that they were interested in meeting him. Randy was so happy,'' he added wistfully. ''And then he was offered the job.''

''We really agonized over that one, I can tell you. The agency was a small one, but they had some great accounts and they were very involved in gay issues—did freebie work for various causes and groups fighting to get funding for AIDS vaccine research. And the job was exactly what Randy wanted. He was a knockout designer, and the job he had certainly didn't play to his strengths. But finally he decided to stay put. . . .''

''But why?''

''Well, I was pretty much committed to spending the rest of the year in New York, and we didn't say it aloud, but I think that both of us knew that our relationship wouldn't survive a separation so soon. . . .''

''What?''

''Oh, didn't you know? The job was in the San Francisco

office of the agency. I thought you knew that. Mother was terribly upset. She had arranged the whole thing. The head of the agency was an old college friend. She had called on him and shown him Randy's work, and that started the ball rolling, but no one told her that the job wasn't in New York, and naturally she assumed that it was. . . ."

"Naturally," Susan said dryly.

"You know, my mother is having a difficult time these days. . . ." Darcy started to excuse her.

Susan wasn't having any of it. She was tired of this son's sympathy for his mother, thinking it more than a little displaced, but it wasn't her job to sit in judgment here. "She did seem a little unhappy one of the first times I spoke with her," she admitted grudgingly.

"She did? What about?"

"Oh, you going off to Europe. I think she was going to miss you. . . ." she suggested, thinking quickly.

Darcy laughed wryly. "I don't think you're right about that one. If she was sad, it wasn't about that. She was planning on spending a lot of time with me. She had her reservations on the ship to Hamburg the day after I decided to go."

"Oh." Susan was so surprised that she almost forgot to ask her last question. "When . . ." She paused for a minute. "This is going to sound stupid, but when did you start nursery school?"

"When did I what?" He looked at her wonderingly.

"How old were you when you started nursery school?"

He shrugged. "I went for one year before I went to kindergarten. I went to kindergarten at the normal time. . . . I guess I was five."

"So you were four."

"Yes, I guess so."

Susan turned to the ranger siting in the corner. "Is there any way that you can reach Marnie Mackay? I'd like to talk with her right away."

"No problem, ma'am." He looked at his watch. "She'll be here any minute. We were planning to move the pris—

him to the Visitor's Center after the talk tonight. And that should be ending about now."

"Maybe, since we have a little extra time, you could tell me how you knew that my father didn't kill Randy?"

Susan sighed, remembering the words on the note she had written the first time she wanted to see him. Of course, things were different now. Because now she knew who the murderer was.

FORTY-THREE

"THEY'RE ALL TOGETHER. IT'S THROUGH THERE." MARnie pointed Susan and Darcy toward a door off the lobby that Susan hadn't noticed before. "That's where the hotel laundry is done. It's private and we won't disturb the other guests."

"Why don't you go on in," Susan suggested to Darcy. "That is, if you don't mind," she added to the ranger.

"Not a bit. Go ahead. It will do your family good to see you, I'm sure. . . . And you can tell me what's going on," she ended in a whisper to Susan as the young man left. "Do you know who the murderer is?"

"I'm fairly sure that I do, but—"

"Okay. I'll trust your judgment. I just want to get this over with."

"So do I," Susan agreed, remembering the peaceful vacation she had envisioned back in Connecticut while she followed Marnie into a large white room. The Ericksen family was sitting around a big Formica table; huge industrial washers and dryers lined the walls. In one corner, Dillon leaned against a tall pile of folded towels that was in great danger of toppling out of the hamper and onto the floor.

Susan glanced around quickly. With the exception of C.J. and Heather, the entire family was present. Susan walked across the floor and sat down in the last empty chair. Kathleen smiled at her across the table; her son slept peacefully in her arms. Marnie joined Dillon, taking a moment to prop up the laundry. Everyone was here. It was time to begin.

"I suppose it's appropriate that we're ending this in a laundry room since, in some ways, I first thought that things were not what they seemed while standing in the middle of a laundry room," Susan began.

"Randy's clothing?" Darcy asked, catching on.

"Exactly. I went into the laundry room the night your father was murdered, and there was a pile of laundry in one of the dryers. Since most of the guests in the lodge were asleep at that time, I thought it was rather unusual. Later it turned out to be pretty significant." From the looks on the faces of Jane and Charlotte, she guessed that she was rapidly losing the interest of her audience. Only Kathleen seemed completely attentive. The Ericksen family was stirring restlessly. Dillon looked bored. Marnie was moving sheets again. Bananas burped in his sleep. No one seemed terribly interested in what a housewife had to say about laundry.

Susan persisted. "The laundry was put there by someone who didn't want us to know that Randy was dead, who wanted us to think he had packed up his belongings and left the park. But I'm not beginning at the beginning." She took a deep breath.

"The problem," she began again, "is always finding out the truth. When someone is killed, of course the killer immediately starts telling lies—he or she is trying desperately to hide, to protect himself or herself. And sometimes other people lie—to protect the murderer, to keep their own involvement in the murder a secret, to protect secrets that have nothing to do with the murder, but that might surface in any murder investigation."

"And you think that's what happened here?" Jane asked, barely able to keep the boredom out of her voice.

"No, I don't. I don't think there are many people lying here—just the murderer. But the rest of you don't know the truth. You don't know the truth about the murders, you don't know the truth about your family, and I suppose you don't know the truth about yourselves.

"You see . . ." Susan went on more forcefully. She had her audience's attention now; from the expressions on their faces, she judged that the entire family was mad at her. "Every family has its myths. I think your family has more than most. Or maybe you just believe them more. . . ."

"When I asked you to help my family, I never thought you were going to end up insulting us," Phyllis spoke up.

"No, you thought you were going to be able to hide behind my ineptness as I tried to discover what exactly was going on. Believe me, I know exactly who has been insulted here." Susan's eyes flashed. She had been waiting for this confrontation. . . .

"We may not want the truth . . . but I think, now, that we need it," Carlton said quietly. Joyce, sitting next to him, took his hand in hers, smiling encouragingly into his eyes.

"I hope you feel like that when I'm done." Susan licked her lips and continued.

"One of the things that interested me from the beginning was how outsiders—in this case, Joyce and Beth—saw the family. Beth told me early that the Ericksen family was 'almost too good to be true'—and, of course, that turned out to be an understatement. The family living in the midst of flowering trees turned out to be nothing like its superficial image." She shrugged. "And maybe no family is. But this family is different. In the first place, it's made up of small groups. The obvious one is Jane and Charlotte, of course. Everyone comments on it, and they even talk about it, admitting to dating the same person as well as taking annual vacations together and staying closely in touch, although they live on opposite sides of the continent. And then there's Jon and Carlton. Although separated by almost fifteen years, they're both scientists, both accepted by the family as similar people. Carlton's old hobbies were inherited by Jon, and Jon carries on the tradition passed from George to Carlton to himself, of scholarship in a scientific field.

"Then, of course, there's the obvious pairing—that of George and Phyllis, husband and wife."

"You certainly don't consider that particularly abnormal."

"No, Phyllis, I don't. And I don't necessarily consider the closeness between a mother and her youngest son abnormal. But in this case I do. . . ."

"You must have been listening to that stupid Irving Cockburn. His understanding of the theories of Freud is highly limited, to say the least."

"I wouldn't disagree with you there. And I did not appreciate you giving him leave to get involved with this. The man is a pest," Susan added. "But that's not what we're talking about now. Now we're talking about a mother who intentionally keeps her son from being close to anyone else. . . ."

"Now, that is ridiculous. . . ."

"Who keeps him tied to her through lies and deceptions."

"That's insulting—"

"You're talking about the job for Randy." Darcy spoke up, interrupting his mother. "I wonder about that. It seemed so strange that she wouldn't know that the job was on the West Coast."

"I swear to you—"

"I don't know if your mother actually did know that. I do suspect that she was aware of the environment at that particular agency and that Randy was more likely to meet someone else. I don't think your mother liked Randy; she probably thought—"

"He wasn't good enough for you," Phyllis finished as Susan was going to, glaring at her.

"Of course not; you wanted to keep him to yourself, didn't you? The way you always kept him to yourself—even when that meant keeping him from a relationship with his own father. A mother who told her son that his father had never wanted him to be born. A mother who insisted that the child was wrenched from her at a young age—when, in fact, he was only sent to nursery school at the normal age that many middle-class children go. A mother who was always there between father and son, interpreting the behavior of the man to the child in a manner that would convince the boy that he was being rejected. A really evil thing to do.'' She shouldn't have said it, but she was tired of the havoc this woman constantly wrought, the way she went through her own family like a destructive whirlwind.

Phyllis Ericksen flung herself up so quickly that the metal chair she was sitting on flipped over, banging against a washing machine. Bananas awoke with a jerk, screaming as only a startled baby can. Dillon knocked over the pile of sheets as Phyllis rushed out the door.

''It's okay. There are rangers stationed out there who will stop her,'' Marnie said, running to the door to prevent anyone from following her.

''Maybe I should leave. . . .'' Beth offered.

''Please don't.'' Jon reached out to her. ''I'd like you to stay here with me. I need you.''

Beth sat down immediately. ''You didn't . . . ?'' She couldn't force herself to ask the question.

''No, he didn't kill anyone; the only murderer is Phyllis Ericksen,'' Susan said.

''Mother? That's impossible!'' Charlotte spoke up for the first time. ''My mother would never kill anybody—would she?'' she asked, turning to her sister.

''I . . . I don't know. It . . .'' Jane couldn't seem to think straight.

''Why don't we listen to what Susan has to say.'' Carlton repeated his suggestion.

''Your mother has been lying since . . . well, for a long time,'' Susan began. ''She desperately wanted to get Randy away from Darcy. Randy, in her mind, was simply not good enough for Darcy. When I asked her about Randy, she said that he was a 'perfectly nice, ordinary person'—and the key is ordinary. I don't think your mother ever wanted what is ordinary for you," Susan said to Darcy.

"No, she always wanted me to be special. All my life she's told me how unique I am, how creative, how sensitive, how perfect. I've often felt like some sort of freak flower that she raised in a hothouse and is afraid to let loose in the world—like I'll wilt or something. . . . I'm sorry. Go on."

"When your mother visited you in New York, she tried to stay involved in your life, decorating your apartment, finding Randy a new job. I don't know if she was aware that that job was in California, but she did know the agency had no problem with employing homosexuals—maybe she just thought Randy would meet someone else. When he didn't take that job, I think she decided that this reunion was in order. I think the entire purpose of this reunion was to break up you and Randy. She just didn't want you to have a serious relationship with anyone; she wanted to keep you for herself. So she played a lot of games with other people's lives. You see, your father didn't convince Randy to play that stupid joke with the dummy—your mother did. Think of it," she continued, having finally gotten everyone's attention. "Your father hated practical jokes of any kind, and he had a tremendous respect for the environment. He would never have encouraged something like that. And remember, Randy wasn't considered to be the perpetrator of that prank because no one knew that he could ski—no one except Phyllis, who had known him before this trip. My guess is that the subject came up in New York, and Phyllis began to plot. Randy probably wasn't very hard to convince to do something like that, he—"

"He wanted so much to be accepted, to be part of a family." Darcy spoke in a strangled whisper. "I can see it happening like that."

"And then, when she overheard us talking in the Visitor's Center, she interrupted and announced that she knew George had instigated the whole thing. She told those lies about your father to protect herself. . . ."

"You're saying that she killed Randy, aren't you?" Charlotte said.

"And Father found out somehow, so she killed him," Jane finished.

FORTY-FOUR

"It's true." Susan looked around the room. "Do you all really want to hear this?"

"I guess we need to." Carlton appeared to have become head of the family, speaking for the rest of them.

"We'll take anything you say about us with a grain of salt," Jane added sarcastically.

Susan chose to ignore her. "The first thing that struck me about your family is that you all actually came to this reunion. Five adults with lives of their own dropped everything and came at the bidding of their parents—despite the fact that some of you (here she looked at Jane and Charlotte) were complaining almost as soon as you got to the park. If you didn't want to come, why were you all here? It became apparent that your parents had a tremendous hold over you all. When Joyce spoke with me on the snowcoach ride into the park, she referred to everyone, from Carlton down to Darcy, as 'the kids.' And I suppose, in some ways, particularly when it came to your parents, there was a fair amount of immaturity in the family. And, like Dr. Cockburn, I'm afraid I tend to blame it on your mother.

"You know, everyone says that, as a child, Darcy was too attached to his mother, too dependent on her. But no one seems to blame Phyllis for that. It's as though the family expected that the child would be wise enough to do the right thing, but not the mother. There's no information that she did anything except encourage an unhealthy closeness between the two of them. To the extent that she told Darcy that his father had never wanted him to be born—just about the cruelest thing she could ever do to her son. And the relationship between Darcy and his father was the stuff bad movies are made of. The image of the little boy refusing to play soccer because his father cheered him on is more than a little strange, to say the least. Who thought it was appropriate for a child to decide these things for himself? Who allowed this to happen? Phyllis. And maybe, in some ways, the rest of the family.

"I think that poor Darcy, sitting in the warming hut, having confessed to a murder that he hadn't committed, is sort of a symbol of everything here. For years this family's failures and weaknesses fell down to Darcy, a boy who was described as looking like an angel. Everyone protected him; everyone thought of him as vulnerable. But when tragedy struck, Darcy volunteered to sacrifice himself for the rest of you. He's stronger than you think—he's probably stronger than he thinks." Susan smiled at him and then continued.

"So, you see, things were really set up for this trip. Phyllis was in control of the situation without anyone knowing it. She had already manipulated Randy into doing something that was bound to outrage George. And she was on hand at all times to give everyone the idea that George was in control of everyone in the family. She told me that she had quit skiing when her husband was hurt, giving me the initial impression of a rather sweet, subservient wife. But, in fact, the opposite was true. I think, and this is only a guess, that she was forever pushing to add to the tension that was increasing almost hourly from the minute everyone arrived here. You all said that Phyllis wanted the family together—to ski together, to eat dinner together, to attend evening shows together. Carlton told me he thought that the trip would be bearable because there was plenty to do here—that the family wouldn't be forced to be together constantly. And I think he had a point. But the evidence is that Phyllis was constantly gathering the family together—and that was putting extra pressure on what was already a situation of great stress to everyone here.

"Carlton was drinking for the first time in many years. Joyce was worried about him and, probably, the effect this was having on her children. Jane, Charlotte, and Darcy were meeting late at night for anguished conferences. And Jon was pulling away from Beth, leaving her wondering about the seriousness of their relationship. And so the murders occurred in what was already a terribly tense situation. The resulting pandemonium was no surprise. And no one asked the logical question. Why was your father waiting behind Old Faithful?"

"Waiting? He had skied . . ." Jane looked from Susan to her sister as what was being said struck her. "He wasn't wearing skis!"

"No. He walked around the geyser; he didn't ski there like everyone else. He wasn't trying to get exercise, he had a purpose."

"He was meeting someone," Charlotte whispered.

"He wasn't meeting one of us," Jon said. "We were all with someone else."

"He was meeting Mother. She was alone, skiing faster than anyone else," Darcy said, starting to cry. "And she was meeting him to kill him."

"Grandmother killed Grandfather?" The adolescent voice broke in the middle of the sentence.

"C.J.!" Joyce cried out, seeing the horrified face of her son. He had apparently entered the room without anyone noticing.

"I saw her. She just talked to me," the boy continued, staring straight ahead at the center of the table. "There were some rangers with her, but she told them that she had an emergency—that she had to help someone in the family. They let her come over to me. She said . . . she said she loved me. . . ." He raised his head to face his parents. "She said good-bye, and then she just walked out into the snow. . . ."

Marnie rushed out the door, Dillon close behind, slowing down only to pat C.J. on the shoulder as he passed. Joyce and Carlton hurried to their son's side. The rest of the family sat still, stunned by what had just happened.

"She couldn't stand being arrested and . . . and everything," Jane said.

Susan and Kathleen exchanged looks. "Then this might be for the best," Kathleen suggested, running her lips across the head of her again-sleeping baby. "I think I'd better put Ban into bed." She turned to Darcy. "Maybe you want company skiing back to your building?"

"We'll join you." Jane got up quickly. She paused to look back at Susan. "Unless you'd like to tell us some more insulting things about our family?"

Susan didn't even bother to reply, turning and pulling on the cord that controlled the curtain that hung over the window behind her. She stared out into the blizzard. She heard the door close, and sighed. She could use some time alone. Time to think about the Ericksens. Time to think about Phyllis . . .

"Why didn't you tell us the complete truth?"

Susan spun around at the voice.

"I'm sorry."

"We didn't mean to scare you." Beth elaborated on Jon's apology.

"We just wondered if you thought that Mother was going to confess or if she really was going to let Darcy be convicted of the murders."

"I'm afraid the latter," Susan answered slowly.

"But why?" Beth asked. "Why do you think that?" Jon was silent, staring at the floor.

"After George was killed, Phyllis clung to Darcy. Everyone mentioned it. I think she assumed that it was the last time they were going to be able to spend together. But it was something that happened earlier that is the most convincing.

"When Phyllis first talked to me about Darcy, she told me that he was going to spend next year in Europe," Susan started. "She definitely sounded sad about it. I thought it was a natural reaction—that she was very close to him and she would miss him. But Darcy told me that she had made reservations to join him as soon as she heard that he was going. So that wasn't the reason she was sad.'' Susan stared into two puzzled faces. She was going to have to explain further. ''You see, she knew that he was going to be disappointed, that he wasn't going to go. . . .''

''For God's sake, why not?'' Jon asked, the strain of the day showing.

''Because she planned all along to let him take the fall for this, didn't she?'' Beth asked, horrified. ''She was going to let him be convicted of the murder.''

''I think so.'' Susan nodded. ''She was getting desperate. She trashed her room as though she was a crazy person—as though she was out of control. I think the pain of what she had to do to survive finally got to her. She may have started to crack when she tried to kill C.J. You see, she did to C.J. what she had been doing to Darcy for years: She told him that she approved of what he was doing, and then she sent his grandfather to tell him something else. But C.J. hadn't grown up in a family where this happened all the time; he would have protested eventually, and then the whole thing would be out in the open. She had to kill him. We're just lucky that she didn't hit him hard enough—or that teenage boys have more lives than a cat.

''I just hope Darcy never realizes exactly what happened. . . .''

''You're right,'' Jon stated. ''We'll never tell anyone, will we?'' He put his arm around Beth, pulling her close to him.

''No. Never.'' The girl smiled up at him.

Susan turned back to the window. ''I think that's Marnie out there. And she's alone.''

''Mother couldn't live without her family, and none of us could really be her family again after this,'' Jon said quietly.

Beth tightened her grip around his waist. ''If she killed herself . . .''

He nodded at what she didn't say. ''It's for the best.''

They went to get the news about Phyllis Ericksen together.

FORTY-FIVE

"WHERE IS MOTHER?"

"I told you that I don't know!" Chad yelled to Chrissy, squinting into the sunlight. During the night, the storm had ended, and hotel guests had stirred in their sleep, not knowing that they were disturbed by the calm following the violent winds. And this morning the sun gleamed off waves of fresh snow. Everyone found being outside irresistible, and everyone was smiling. Except Chad. "Why do you keep asking me the same question?" he asked, skiing up to his sister. "If I knew where she is, I'd tell you!"

"Well, I've been looking and looking and I can't find her. The Ericksens are leaving the park. . . ."

"You told me that," he reminded her. "And I know they want to say good-bye to her, but I don't know where she is!"

"Well, this vacation certainly hasn't improved your disposition," Chrissy said with sisterly sarcasm, turning and skiing off quickly.

"Or your skiing ability!" he called out as she fell.

She chose to ignore him.

"Are you plaguing your sister again?" Chad's father appeared behind him.

"She keeps asking me where Mom is," he explained.

"Your mother's over at Old Faithful. Why is Chrissy looking for her?"

"C.J.'s parents are leaving. They didn't want to leave the park without talking to her."

"That's okay. Jon found her awhile ago, and she went

back to the lodge for a few minutes. She wanted to talk with them, too." He pushed off on his skis, Chad at his side. "C.J. and Heather seem to be taking this pretty well, I thought," he added. "I mean, it's awful to find out that your grandmother is a murderer, and then when she went and killed herself last night . . . Well, that's a lot for kids to deal with," he said, wondering about his own children's reaction to this tragedy.

"You know, they weren't really all that close to their grandparents—having spent so much of their lives in Europe and all," Chad explained. "I guess that turned out to be best," he added, thinking of the expression he had seen on Darcy's face.

"I guess you're right. It's been a pretty strange vacation, hasn't it?"

"Yeah. Say, Dad, do you think C.J. and I could get together again sometime? Like maybe I could go along with you on one of your business trips to L.A.? He says it's really cool out there."

"It's an idea." Jed smiled at his son, pleased at the boy's resilience.

"Hey! There's Mom!" the boy cried out, pointing to the lone figure standing and watching Old Faithful puff steam into the air.

"Sure. You find her just as I do. Big help you are." Chrissy appeared on a trail that joined the one the males in the family were traveling.

Susan heard voices, and turned and waved. "Come on and wait with me!" she called out, dangling her watch in one hand. "Nine more minutes till it erupts. Believe me," she added as the rest of her family joined her, "I'm not going to miss this one!"

ABOUT THE AUTHOR

Valerie Wolzien lives in Tenafly, New Jersey. She is also the author of *Murder at the PTA Luncheon, The Fortieth Birthday Body,* and *We Wish You a Merry Murder.*

The Mysterious Mind of Valerie Wolzien...